just girls

by

rachel gold

Bella
BOOKS

2014

Bella Books, Inc.
P.O. Box 10543
Tallahassee, FL 32302

Printed in the United States of America on acid-free paper.

First Bella Books Edition 2014

Editor: Katherine V. Forrest
Cover design: Kristin Smith
Front cover photo copyright: Aleshyn Andrei
Back cover photo copyright: Nejron Photo

ISBN: 978-1-59493-419-3

About the Author

Raised on world mythology, fantasy novels, comic books and magic, Rachel is well suited for her careers in marketing and writing. She also spent a decade as a reporter in the LGBT community where she learned many of her most important lessons about being a woman from the transgender community. When she's not working on her novels, you can find Rachel online checking out the latest games.

For more information, or for resources about any of the issues in this book, please visit www.rachelgold.com.

Other Books by Rachel Gold

Being Emily

Dedication

For Kate Bornstein
Who taught me how to be a girl

Acknowledgments

It takes a lot of people to write a book and I'm grateful to everyone who gave me encouragement, support, information and help!

As always, a big thank you to my alpha reader Alia Whipple, whose crucial job it is to say, "That's great, keep going."

Thanks to Autumn Nicole Bradley who not only beta read but also pointed me in the direction of Julia Serano whose ideas about femininity were a great fit for the story I had in mind.

Thanks to Stephanie Burt for both loving the story and tearing it apart in the middle where it needed it. She gets the award for being the apex reader on this project.

Thanks to Sharyn November for early encouragement and saying basically: "Write that one; that's the book I want to read."

Many thanks to my amazing team of beta readers: Kim Nguyen, Li Zhu, Jeni and Ally Mullins, Wendy Nemitz, Sara Bracewell, Melissa Trost, Dawn Wagenaar, Lisa Hager, Nathalie Isis Crowley, and Emma Todd.

Thanks to Kirstin Cronn-Mills for being a great ally with me and a friend, and for letting me borrow Gabe and Paige for a cameo in this book.

Thanks to Katherine V. Forrest for being a smart, funny and insightful editor—and to everyone at Bella Books for continuing to publish and celebrate trans YA novels.

Thanks to my family—human, animal and magical—for all their support and for bearing with me through many rewrites and edits, especially the ones that made me grouchy.

And a big thank you to everyone who read *Being Emily* and gave me feedback, told me they loved it or shared the impact it had on their lives.

You might already know what cisgender and genderqueer mean, but just in case:

"Trans": like transgender and transsexual, comes from Latin "on the *other* side of"

"Cis": is Latin for "on the *same* side of"

Cisgender: When you were born, if the doctor looked at you and said "It's a girl!" and later as you grew up you thought "Hey, I'm a girl."

Transgender: If the doc said "It's a boy!" and later you realized "Hey, I'm a girl" (or vice versa).

Genderqueer: People who don't feel like they fit neatly into "boy" or "girl." Some even use pronouns that aren't he or she—like instead of he/him/himself or she/her/herself you might use:
Ze, zir, zirself
Per, pers, perself
Yo, yos, yoself.
Oh, and LGBTQIA stands for lesbian, gay, bisexual, transgender, queer, intersex, asexual & allies.

Much love,
Tucker

CHAPTER ONE

Ella

I had to be the only girl on campus upset about having a suite to herself as a first-year student. I put one hand on the empty bed in the single room that shared a bathroom with mine. The room was untouched. Of the 10,000 students here, about 1,000 were new undergrads and slightly more than half of those were women and here I was, one in 500 in more ways than one. If admissions hadn't mistyped my social security number, if I lived in a state where I could get my birth certificate changed, if I hadn't had to show them the only part of my life that still said, "M," there would be someone in this room adjoining mine.

The whole suite smelled of lemon-pine cleanser and cherry licorice over fresh paper; I went into my room and opened the window to see if it really opened. It slid open smoothly and I could peer out and see the lawn below. I'd never be able to complain about my accommodations now.

My residence hall was on a corner of the main quad but turned out toward the street a little so that you had to walk a half block from the front door to be on the quad proper.

The entrance was close to the street where my dad had parked illegally, like a hundred other parents, so we could all carry my many boxes up from his truck.

The dorm room door swung open and hit the far wall with a crack and Dad staggered in carrying two boxes, followed by Mom who had my small suitcase in her hand.

"He insisted," she said.

"You have to start it off right," he said. He put the boxes on the desk and handed me a plush Galapagos tortoise from the top of the higher box. I set it on the bed by the pillow.

He winked and headed for the door. "No parking zone," he said. That was true, but he also had a hard time being still when he was excited or agitated. He ran marathons and played racquet sports that I could never keep clear in my mind: what was the difference between racquetball and squash anyway? The most he'd been able to teach me was ping-pong. I liked yoga and long walks—the slower stuff where you weren't in danger of having some mean projectile ricochet off a wall and smack you in the eye.

Mom wandered into the bathroom. "This is nice," she called distractedly. I heard her open the door into the empty single room and grow silent.

"It's okay," I told her. "I can set up a lab in there if I get bored."

"I wondered what they were going to do," she said from the other room. "Maybe she's just late."

"*We're* already late," I pointed out.

I had wanted to move in after my roommate was already settled so that I could tell what kind of person she was by her décor. Well, the décor certainly said a lot about something.

A girl stuck her head in from the side of the open doorway. Her looks put the "non" in nondescript: light brown hair, lighter tan complexion, and brown eyes.

"Hi, I'm Hayley, your RA, just checking to make sure you're settling in."

"Ella Ramsey," I said.

I looked over my shoulder toward the bathroom to see if my mom had heard Hayley come in, but she was still in the other room. I didn't know if you used first names when introducing parents to your RA She didn't look more than a year older than me, so I thought it would be awkward to do the whole "Julia and Greg" thing—it's not like I wanted her to call them that anyway.

"My mom's in the other room," I told her. "Do you know why it's empty?" I figured I should get that out of the way as soon as possible.

"I never got a name for that room," Hayley said brightly. "I called over to admissions and they said it was some kind of paperwork mix-up. I'm sure they'll put someone in after a few weeks. That happened last year with overflow from the crowded dorms. We're lucky, they just renovated this one two years ago."

I mirrored the smile of her bland cheerfulness.

"El, what are these for?" my mom asked from behind me and then added a surprised, "Oh!" when she saw Hayley.

I turned around to see that Mom was standing in the bathroom doorway holding a box of tampons. At least my back was to Hayley as all the blood in my body made a burning rush for my cheeks.

"Mom, this is my RA, Hayley, and um, this is my mom," I said, moving sideways away from both of them.

Mom looked around, shifted the box of tampons to her left hand and gamely held out her right for Hayley to shake. My heartbeat pounded in my ears. That wasn't helping my ability to come up with the right answer to my mom's question. Seriously, whose mom didn't know what tampons were for? Had Hayley already figured out that the issue wasn't the tampons—that it was me?

"Excuse me," Dad called cheerfully from the hall and Hayley moved further into my room. Dad carried two boxes to the foot of the bed and set them down, then stretched his arms up until his back cracked.

"Just a few more loads," he said. "Are you sure you brought enough?" Then he saw Mom's awkward stance with the tampons and gave her a confused look.

"They're Ella's," she said.

"Oh?" he turned his puzzled face toward me.

"Aren't you in a no parking zone?" I asked Dad.

"I'll help," Mom said too eagerly and they both hurried out of the room, Mom still carrying the perplexing tampon box.

"Your mom doesn't know what tampons are for?" Hayley asked when they were well gone.

"She's an anthropologist," I said, as if that answered everything.

Hayley's eyebrows pinched together.

"She's into all that crazy natural stuff, like menstrual sponges," I told her. That was total bull. Mom used tampons like everyone else I knew. But nothing worked quite like the phrase "menstrual sponges" to shut down a conversation.

"Oh ew, nasty," Hayley said.

"I know, right?"

I felt like a jerk for taking the easy way out, but I hardly knew this girl. Explaining that my mom was surprised to find tampons on the top of my bathroom-supplies box because I don't get a period was a lot more complicated to get into with strangers. Hayley seemed like the chatty type who would want to know why not, and then I'd have to talk about being born a girl without some of the girl parts, like the period-getting parts and the I'm-putting-female-on-your-birth-certificate parts, and for all I knew she'd share that information with the other girls on the floor. Not how I wanted to start college. Not at all.

"Um, well, I'm down at the end of the hall if you need anything," Hayley said and hurried out of the room before I could bring up anything else from the menstrual-practices-from-around-the-world handbook.

I went into the bathroom and quickly looked at the top of the open box to make sure there wasn't anything else visible that was shockingly normal. Mom came in while I was hanging up my towels and put her arm around me in apology. I leaned into her and rested my cheek on her shoulder. I might have a smidge more growth left in me, but I'll probably always be the shortest member of my family. Amy got Dad's lanky height and I got Mom's delicate bone structure. I totally lucked out in that deal because Amy hates heels and I can wear them without towering over all the guys around me. I got Mom's blond hair too and Dad's green eyes, so really it was like the genetic dice were loaded in my favor for almost everything.

"What did you tell her?" she asked.

"That you use a menstrual sponge," I said.

Mom laughed. "I'm sorry," she said.

"I just got them so my roommate wouldn't wonder, you know, why I didn't have any. But I figured in a pinch I could use them to make tiny Molotov cocktails."

"I don't think you'd get enough oxygen in the mouth of the bottle for that to work, the cotton is bundled too tightly," Dad said from the other side of the open doorway to my room. He was smiling, but his eyes had tight lines around them.

"I guess I'm not starting a revolution this year," I told him and sighed. "You want to come look around the building with me? It's supposed to be sustainable, but they don't have solar panels or wastewater processing or anything."

"Frauds!" Dad exclaimed and tilted into motion again. Mom followed him.

I looked into the empty room again. The bed was just a mattress on a frame and the desk and dresser were completely bare. It wasn't a paperwork mix-up. Because I was born in Ohio, I couldn't change the sex listed on my birth certificate. I was mentally, emotionally, physically and hormonally female, but anyone who looked at my birth certificate would see, "M" for "male." At least my driver's license accurately described me as female.

The birth certificate thing wouldn't have been an issue except that my social security number got messed up in the system and the university admin office called over the summer and told me I had to bring my birth certificate to get it corrected. That caused more questions than it resolved.

I joined Mom and Dad in the hall, locked my room, and picked a direction for wandering. We discovered the common room together, and the little gym facility, and the laundry room in the basement with the soda machine and a crazy recycling sorting and compost waste station. Crazy because for years in Columbus we'd had single-sort recycling and I was pretty sure even worms didn't want to eat half of the crap that students would dump into the compost bins—not that I'm dissing the worms.

Then they wanted to stand around on the curb doing the tearful parent goodbye, even though I was probably going to hop the bus home by the weekend. I understood it was part of the ritual. Amy said that when they dropped her off, Mom alternated between crying and listing the various coming-of-age rituals of a number of South American indigenous peoples. At least I didn't get that.

Mom cried and I cried and Dad cleared his throat a bunch and then we all hugged and suddenly I found myself standing on the side of a street all by myself for the first time in my life. The only person I knew for about a hundred miles in any direction was the buff-colored Hayley.

Shyness crawled over me like a thousand small, non-poisonous spiders: too uncomfortable to stand still for, but not actually dangerous. I hurried back to my room. I'd grown up and lived in the same suburban community my whole life. I went to high school with kids I'd been in first grade with—and they went through a lot with me and had my back for most of it. I didn't perceive, until that moment of walking quickly back to Washington Hall, how alone I was going to be in a place where no one knew me.

We lived two hours away, in Columbus, and Mom taught at Ohio State University. She wanted me there, but I was going to have to make my way in the real world one of these days and I wanted to get started. Two hours seemed like a good compromise: it wasn't so close to home that I'd be tempted to run home for dinner on a whim, but it was an easy bus ride home for a weekend. I had no doubt that Mom was going to keep my room just the way I'd left it, though she should really turn it into a home gym.

Also, Freytag University gave me a pretty good scholarship. My sister Amy was three years into her university term and I'd overheard Mom and Dad talking about taking out a second mortgage to pay for my college. I wouldn't do that to them;

they'd already spent the cost of a good college education on me for the doctors and the hormones and the surgery. Mom said I shouldn't have to worry about that at eighteen, but I did.

This wasn't the best school ever and it was so far out in the middle of nowhere that the campus dorms were the highest buildings as far as you could see, but it had a shockingly good Women's & Gender Studies department and even though I wanted to major in biology, I figured it had to mean there would be a kind of accepting vibe here.

If you'd asked me yesterday, I'd have told you I was good at making friends. But in the past I always had friends around me, so making more friends felt natural; when you were part of something, it was easy to invite others to join in.

I went into my room and closed the door and locked it. Then I went through the bathroom to the empty room and made sure that door was locked. I sat on the bed and curled my knees into my chest and just let the shy-scared-spidery feeling happen for a while. When it started to fade away, I got up and unpacked.

My clothes didn't all fit into my closet, so I borrowed space from my nonexistent roommate. I also hogged both sinks in the joint bathroom just because I could, not because I have that much bathroom stuff. I hung a poster in my room, the one of the Doradus-30 nebula that always reminds me how big the universe is, and then I went and hung my Evolution of Life poster in the other room. It was too bare in there otherwise.

Dinnertime came but I wasn't really hungry because I'd eaten with Mom and Dad a few hours before. I decided I should really get a mini-fridge for the room and maybe a hotpot or something. I set up my laptop and started looking at things I could buy for the room, and then checked out my class schedule and the various orientation events I was supposed to attend. At least it would be a busy next few days.

Just in case I had too much downtime and wasn't so good at this making friends on my own thing, I also looked at the university clubs. They were mostly really boring stuff about farming or cheerleading or ineffective social change, but one caught my eye: Real-world Gaming at FU.

There was contact information for a student named Johnny Han, so I sent him an email letting him know I was interested in joining. Hopefully by Real-world Gaming they meant something easy and not too geeky. I couldn't really pull off live-action role-playing without laughing and I was in no shape for parkour, but I played a lot of other games in high school.

I didn't miss high school. Not exactly. But I missed... something. Friends? I texted Nico: *Call?*

My phone rang two seconds later and I grinned. I'd been #3 on Nico's speed dial for the past four years.

"How's the middle of nowhere?" Nico asked.

"Shockingly well-populated. I haven't seen a single cow on campus yet."

"Crap, girl, why did you not come to school with me? I'm so bored."

"You've been there three days," I pointed out. Not like it mattered, Nico could get bored in ten minutes absent the right stimulation. That's what happened when you were the kid of an engineer and an astronomer. If Nico couldn't take something apart and put it back together again or fit it into the grand scheme of the cosmos, it was boring. Nico had bought me the Doradus-30 poster and told me that, like me, it was an "extremely luminous non-stellar object." We'd been sort of dating at the time and I hadn't been inclined to complain about the "object" part of that compliment.

"So bored," Nico repeated. "It's like a production plant of human beings out here and Mom won't stop checking on me."

"I've got an extra room if you want to drive out here for a few days."

"Anyone hot enough to drive out for? Other than you, of course."

I laughed. "I'll keep you posted. Don't tell me there's no one at OSU, you have ten times the options I do out here."

Nico laughed with me and, into the pause after the sound, I added, "I miss you."

"Miss you too, baby girl. Gotta run."

I said bye and clicked off and then just stared at my phone for a minute. Was Nico right? Should I have gone to OSU?

Furthermore, if there was someone hot out here, what would I even do about it? I'd barely managed to date Nico, let alone a total stranger.

CHAPTER TWO

Tucker

By the time she got back to campus, Tucker was starving. Trust Lindy to invite her over for a movie and only have popcorn and beer even though it was dinnertime. The Student Union's restaurant didn't close until ten, so she swung by to pick up something. With luck her roommate would be asleep when she got back and she wouldn't have to hear another story about the greatest high school production of Shakespeare's *Hamlet* in the history of ever.

Cheese breadsticks or hummus wrap? That was the real question. The garlic cheese breadsticks were loaded with butter and salt, making them taste like savory heaven, and they had the added benefit of making her highly avoidable until she'd brushed her teeth, just in case her roommate was still awake.

The Student Union was doing a booming business as new and returning students met and caught up on their summer activities. The whole place reminded her of a coral reef: schools of colorful students swarmed around the tables. Here and there were individuals, but most of them already seemed to be moving in packs.

Toward the back of the wide seating area was the huge table that the LGBTQIA students had commandeered last year as their go-to meeting spot. A few students sat there now and as she tried to identify them, the biggest guy at the table spotted her in line and waved. That would be Cal, who was built like a two-door refrigerator and who dressed as stereotypically gay as possible while looking like a football player. She grinned and raised a hand in his direction.

The line moved up a step. There was probably garlic in the hummus too and it would be better for her.

A word seared across her awareness and pulled her right out of her thinking with a jolt of anger. One of the girls behind her just ended a sentence with: "tranny." The offense of it put a bitter taste on Tucker's tongue and she turned her head sideways to hear better.

"I wouldn't either," another girl said. "Isn't the administration thinking at all? Any of us could end up in a bathroom with that person. Did you see his name?"

Tucker ground her back molars together. The fingers of her right hand curled into a fist. Using a male pronoun for a trans woman was so rude.

"I tried, but I was so surprised and the memo was just there for a minute," the first girl said.

"What did it say?"

"Just something about an MTF transsexual student and the dorms and a private bathroom. MTF, that's male to female, I looked it up."

Tucker's skin turned cold as she realized what must have happened. A trans girl had applied to live in the dorms and this little jerk in line behind her saw some notation about giving that girl her own bathroom because, of course, the freaked out, straight, cisgender world couldn't deal with the idea that one of their precious girls might accidentally walk into a women's room with another woman who, once upon a time, didn't have exactly the same body parts they all assumed they had.

She was afraid for this girl she'd never met, and so proud of her, even though her friends Claire and Emily would tell her that was a stupid reaction. Why be proud of someone who simply lived her life the way she had to? But it wasn't the transition that made her proud, it was the fact that this girl insisted on her right to be treated the same as any woman.

She could almost make out the reflections of the three girls behind her in the glass covering the hot food serving area. The details were lost, but she could see the shapes of their faces and hairstyles.

"What if he's one of our roommates? What does yours look like?" the girl with the skinny face and big hair asked.

"Oh it can't be mine," said round face, big hair. "She came back from the shower and changed in the room."

Their ignorance made Tucker want to spit. She almost hoped that roommate was the trans girl except for the danger she would be in from this weasel.

"I still just can't believe they let a transsexual in the dorms," said the girl with the mean face. "What if he's just there to peep at girls?"

That was it.

Tucker spun on her heel and glared at them. For a second she was too angry to speak and all the words she had to confront them with fell short of what she wanted to say. The words that did come out of her mouth surprised her, "Do you have something to say to my face?"

They all leaned back away from her as far as they could get without bumping into the people behind them in line. Like synchronized robots, their heads moved in unison; their eyes went down the front of her body, pausing at her breasts and then her crotch, before coming back up.

"It's not nice to eavesdrop," said Mean Face.

Tucker crossed her arms and stood up as tall as she was. This had the effect of hiding her rather large chest and showing that she was just two inches short of six feet.

"Do you want to repeat your nasty speculation to my face," she said. "I'm not here because I give a fuck about any of you. I'm here for an education like anyone else."

"You're not a tranny," Round Face said.

"The term is 'trans woman' or just 'woman,'" Tucker said. "And you don't know shit about what I am. You think you can pick a trans woman out in a crowd, well you can't. We look just like you."

They paused and took in that information and Tucker saw their eyes get impossibly harder and more distant than they'd already been. Never mind that she wasn't really a trans woman. The fact of the matter was that somewhere on this campus was a girl who just wanted a normal life and didn't deserve this hunt for her. If they believed Tucker was their target, at least they'd stop looking.

She'd come out as a lesbian in high school and stared down plenty of bigots; how different could this be?

"You're really a guy? Or are you turning into a guy? I don't get it. I can't even tell what you are," said Mean Face.

"You're full of shit," Tucker said. "You can tell that I'm a woman and it just freaks you out that I was born with a male body."

"No way," Skinny Face said.

Tucker leaned in and bunched the muscles in her shoulders in a way that she hoped looked sufficiently masculine to them.

"She is kind of big," Round Face said under her breath to the others. "And look at how square her jaw is and those big hands."

The line was moving forward again and Tucker had to take a few steps backward toward the registers to keep pace with it. The three girls let a wider gap open between her and them.

"You stay away from us," Mean Face said.

"You couldn't pay me to get near you," Tucker said and stepped out of line.

She crossed the room unsteadily because she was shaking from her shoulders to her knees. The LGBTQIA student table was on their feet by the time she reached them, having seen in her face that something was wrong. At this point in the year, the population of the table only amounted to three people: the hulking Cal; stocky, bronze Summer; and shy, peach-faced Tesh.

"What was *that*?" asked Summer with a scowl. She was by far the shortest and loudest member of their group.

"They were saying shit about trans people," Tucker told her. "I got so pissed I kind of came out to them."

"Like anyone doesn't know you're a lesbian just by looking at you," Summer told her. She waved a hand at Tucker's thick, bleached Mohawk, worn T-shirt, baggy men's jeans and boots.

"As trans," Tucker said.

"You are?" asked Tesh as she ran a hand through her short hair, making her face look even more pixie-like as tufts of hair stood up in light brown wisps.

"No, but I think maybe I should just be out as if I were. Will you guys cover for me if anyone asks and tell them that I am a transsexual woman?"

"Sure."

"Yeah."

"What?"

Tesh and Summer had been the female core of the LGBTQIA students since Tucker met them last winter. For months she screwed up their names because Tesh's deep blue eyes reminded Tucker of a summer sky and Summer's disposition was anything but sunny. She learned to keep them clear by associating Summer's temper with the heat of a scorching July day and linking the softness of Tesh's full name, Stesha, with her quiet demeanor.

"That's crazy," Summer said. "What's Lindy going to say when everyone thinks she's dating a transsexual?"

"She better not fucking care," Tucker said.

She sat down at the table and put her head in her hands. Tesh rubbed her back lightly. It drove her crazy that she lived in a world with this level of ignorance.

When she came out as a lesbian, it surprised no one in her family. Her mother didn't have the energy to protest. The fact that one of her daughters was attracted to women was so much less important than the fact that it made Tucker willing to try her hand at fixing things around the house, and that she wouldn't be coming home someday with an accidental pregnancy.

Tucker found it harder to get support for herself wanting to pursue a career in Women's & Gender Studies than it was to get support as a lesbian. In her family it didn't matter who you went to bed with: what mattered was your ability to make money and your spouse's ability to stick around and do the same. Tucker had been trying to talk herself into a practical career, not that she'd found anything that interested her, until she met Claire and Emily, and read Emily's book, and then she really wanted to study Gender Studies.

Claire and her girlfriend Emily were good friends of hers now, even though they mostly corresponded online and had only met in person twice. They'd taught her almost everything she knew about what it meant to be transsexual or transgender.

The smell of garlic wove through her folded arms and got her to lift her head. Cal pushed a plate of cheese bread in front of her.

"You've got to keep your strength up," he said.

Although the school's LGBTQIA group had held an orientation (or sexual orientation) session last week, Tucker already knew most of the group from Lindy, whom she'd been dating since January. Tucker was from one of the small towns near the university, so she came to the U for films, plays and other events when she could get away. She'd met Lindy at the screening of *Before Stonewall* and they'd started dating a week later. That relationship, plus the utter lack of any extra money for college, had been the deciding factor in Tucker's choice to come to Freytag.

Now in her junior year, Lindy lived off campus, but she and Tucker had come to enough meetings of the campus group last spring that Tucker knew them all and they knew her. Around the core group of Cal, Summer, Tesh and Lindy were about thirty other students who showed up to parties and movie nights and sometimes brought friends. Tonight, Tucker was glad it was just the four of them.

"What you did was really brave," Tesh said. "Though I can't say I've heard of a lot of people coming out as what they're not."

"Maybe more of them should," Tucker said.

CHAPTER THREE

Ella

My first course on Monday was also the one I most looked forward to: Machine Learning. I'm not much of a computer geek, so I was really happy to see there was a course that offered the fundamentals of how computers think without me having to learn a bunch of programming languages. I never planned to program anything mechanical, but I'd been reading some really cool articles about biological computers and I thought a basic understanding of computing would be one place to start.

At the start of my first year, I wasn't expected to know what my major would be or how that translated into a job exactly, but since I'd been around my mom at a university on and off for the last dozen years, I'd picked up some ideas. For example, I knew that if I started off going for a biology major and picked up some other courses in science that I liked along the way, I could very well end up with a double major, and that never hurt when looking for a job. Plus it gave me a good reason to take a bunch of cool science courses.

I started out a little early for class because I still didn't know my way around the campus very well. I had a map on my phone, but that's not the easiest thing to read while walking, so I got lost and had to ask directions from a hassled-looking older student.

The classroom was in the lower level of one of the buildings that hadn't been updated yet, with floor tiles stained a yellow tan and halls that smelled like metallic smoke. Inside, the room held the usual chairs and long tables, like in the science classroom in my high school, but across the back wall were thick workbenches with machine parts on them. I started to worry about what we'd have to do in this class. I have a bit of a knack for fixing machines that go wrong, but that's really from playing a lot of games on the Xbox, not because I know anything. This looked a lot more serious than the Xbox or the DVR.

Also, I was one of three girls in the class. But hey, at least there were other girls—though the other two didn't look like first-year students. They chatted to each other rapid-fire, like they'd been in a class together before.

"Hey, are you Ella?" a cheerful male voice asked from behind my left shoulder.

I turned and found myself facing a grinning Asian guy. He had a long face with a wide nose and a broad smile.

"Johnny Han," he said and stuck out his hand.

"Oh, I emailed you, but how do you know who I am?"

He tapped the side of his head and winked. The gestures were caricatures but they looked natural on him because of his good humor.

"Your name is on the list of students on the wiki for this class…" He paused and swept an arc with his hand indicating the room. "There are only three girls and I know the other two, so I figured you were probably the third. That doesn't make me sound like a stalker, does it? I was on the wiki for the assignments, I swear."

"I'm sure you were counting the number of girls in the class by accident," I told him, and then, "There's a wiki?"

"We'll show you, come sit with us, if you care to, that is." He had a fast way of talking that blended midwest with east coast broadcaster and a smidge of old-fashioned western.

I moved around the table to take the seat on his left. On his other side was another boy who leaned around Johnny and nodded in my direction with a slight smile.

"Shen Li," he said.

His accent was moderately thick Chinese, though I was guessing at the nationality because I knew "Li" was a Chinese name.

"Nice to meet you, Shen," I said, on the formal side because he seemed so composed.

"I keep telling him to change it to 'Shawn,'" Johnny said. He punctuated the statement to Shen with an elbow jab aimed at his ribs. Shen deftly twisted out of range.

"I like 'Shen,'" I said. "We have more than enough Shawns around here."

Shen gave me another half-smile. It wasn't the grand gesture of Johnny's grin, but it conveyed a lot more depth as his lips seemed to quirk down and up at the same time. He had darker eyebrows and eyes than Johnny and a square face with a flatter nose and a narrow but full mouth. Wisps of bangs hung down over Shen's forehead and his black hair was a little longer than Johnny's, who wore his spiked up.

"Where ya from?" Johnny asked me.

"Columbus," I said. "You?"

"Cleveland, but Shen's from distant China. His father is my father's cousin so they sent him over here to make sure I behave."

"How's that working out?" I asked.

Shen just shrugged but Johnny said, "He's worse than a nun."

"How many nuns have you spent time with?" I asked.

Johnny laughed and I got another little smile out of Shen.

"The game," Shen told Johnny.

"Oh yeah, you emailed me about the gaming club. We've got a game going on Friday if you want to play. It's an adaptation on the real-world assassination games only instead of using squirt guns, you use compliments. It's called Cruel 2 B Kind. I'll email you the info. Can you put together a team of three?"

"I don't really know anyone here," I admitted.

"If you don't have a team by Wednesday's class, let me know and I'll add you to the pool of lone wolves. We can assign teams from there. You play other games too?"

"Nothing hardcore, just a lot of the fantasy franchises on the Xbox and the usual tabletop stuff."

"Dance dance revolution?" Shen asked and I couldn't tell if he was serious about the dance competition game or if he was teasing me as a girl gamer.

"All my high scores are in Pretty Princess Magical Rescue Adventure," I deadpanned back.

"Me too," Shen said in mock surprise.

"I bet my unicorn can own yours," I told him.

"Tell me this is not a real thing," Johnny said. He looked back and forth from me to Shen but neither of us graced his question with an answer. After a while he said, "We have a sweet setup in our dorm's community room if you want to come by sometime. Are you in computer science? What dorm are you in?"

"Washington. I'm in biology, I think."

"Oh, yeah, sorry you're a first year, they're not going to stick you in the science geek dorm yet anyway. But come by sometime, it's always full of the gamers and we're a friendly group."

I just managed to get in my thanks when the professor started the class.

* * *

In the afternoon I had Calculus, which wasn't nearly as friendly as Machine Learning. The homework scared me. I try not to be a girl stereotype, but I'm not that facile with mathematics. I do all right when I bear down and apply myself, but it's usually not that interesting to me in the abstract. When I really understand what it means in terms of real-world application, then I'm in better shape. I spent a couple of hours looking up ways that calculus is applied to the study of population genetics so I'd be really clear about why I had to learn this stuff.

I debated going over to the gaming common room that

Johnny and Shen mentioned. Would it seem too eager to show up the same day they'd invited me? It was a good group of students to get in with because they'd be fun. I suppose I could have looked for a biology club, but really the only other group that I connected with was the LGBTQIA student union. I was tempted to find them and lean on my identity as a bisexual girl to get in—though I wondered how accepting they'd be of bisexuals, not to mention the other letter that included me, the "T."

I decided to do both. There was a social hour at the LGBTQIA student union office at eight p.m., so I could drop by the gaming room and have an excuse to leave if I wanted to, or I could stay and skip the office hours and go some other time. I looked at Johnny's instructions and the campus map a few times. There were three quads surrounded by dorms: the huge main quad where I was, a big quad to the northwest of me and one to the southwest, a small quad with only four dorm buildings around it—that's where they were. To get there, I had to go out the back door of my dorm, walk two blocks and turn left.

The evening air still had a bit of the muggy daytime humidity and the campus lights looked haloed against the cloudy sky. The air was heavy with the green smell of mown grass and that baked concrete smell that's more like a pressure than a scent. I'd have to remember to email Mom and let her know I wouldn't be on the Friday afternoon bus but rather the one on Saturday morning since I'd be here playing a real-world game with my new friends. She'd be glad to hear it.

I took out my phone and texted her: *going to meet new friends in communal game room.*

She texted back: *That's great, homey!*

My mom was not a big slang user, so that had to be an incidence of spell-checker revenge on her phone. I resisted the urge to reply, "*Yo, dog, thanks.*"

I looked up from my phone and tried to orient myself. Had I gone two blocks already? I thought so. I didn't really feel like asking for directions again and there wasn't any downside to getting lost, so I turned left and went into the first dorm I saw.

The game room was supposed to be the third-floor common room, but when I found that, it was a spartan square filled with silent students staring at books and tablets. Was I wrong about the dorm or the floor? Probably the dorm, but just to be sure I figured I'd go look at the room on the second floor. It was weirdly entertaining to be able to just poke my head into rooms full of strangers. I guess my shyness was starting to wear off now that I had new friends.

I took the stairs at the end of the hall to the second floor and looked for the common room but this floor wasn't set up the same as the third so I had to walk along the hall toward the middle of the building. A lot of the students had already decorated their doors with posters and stickers. This made for great juxtapositions like Justin Bieber and a nihilistic creed on one door, and Ke$ha and a feminist poster on another.

But the next door stopped me in my tracks. Someone had torn a poster off the door, its top still held in place by clear tape, and below the ragged edge of the paper they had spray-painted "Tranny" in big red letters across the door's surface. My heart and lungs stopped as if a huge steam engine piston slammed into my chest.

In the silence of not breathing, I heard voices raised inside the room.

"What were you thinking!" a first, nasal voice asked.

"She's the bigot," a second voice shot back. "Don't be mad at me."

I gasped in a big breath and then tried to exhale slowly and quietly so I could hear them.

"Do you think it was those girls?" the first voice asked.

"Or their boyfriends, or someone who heard them gossiping, who knows."

"I'm worried that you're not safe here. Let your roommate keep the room, come move in with me."

There was a long silence and then the second voice said. "Thanks, really, but I need to think about it. I kind of had my heart set on living on campus my first year."

Because she was still talking, I didn't realize how close to the door she was until it opened in my face. The woman who opened it was tall and looked even taller—her hair was some kind of bleached Mohawk that stood another three inches above her scalp. It wasn't made of aggressive, starched spikes, but rather a soft mop of wavy cream-colored hair. She had a square face with high, wide cheeks and blue eyes. Her complexion was that creamy, darker Germanic-white that I envied every time I looked at the random freckles on my pink cheeks.

"What?" she snarled at me.

I took a step back. "I'm sorry."

"You think there's something to see here? Did your friends send you over to look at the freak?"

I held up my hands. Was she the one who'd drawn the attention of the jerks who'd painted the slur on her door?

"No," I said. "I don't know who you're talking about. I got lost and I was walking through and I saw…that…and I just stopped because it was so unbelievably hateful."

The line of her mouth softened. "Oh shit, I'm sorry, I didn't mean to yell at you, it's just been a really long day. I'm Tucker."

She held out her hand. Her grip was strong and dry.

"Ella," I told her.

"I'm sorry I thought you were one of them because you're pretty," she said and grinned at me.

"Um, thank you, I think."

"I was going to get a Pepsi, do you want anything?"

"May I walk with you?"

"Of course, if you don't mind being seen with me," Tucker said.

"Why would I?"

I turned sideways to her and we walked down the hall together. The room with vending machines was only a few doors from Tucker's room.

"Did I see you in first-year orientation?" Tucker asked.

"I think I was sitting behind you for part of it," I told her. "I remember appreciating your hair. I'm sorry for eavesdropping, but I'm curious about what happened."

Three bottles dropped into the bottom of the vending machine one after the other as Tucker fed it random coins. I'm not really a big pop drinker, but if there's one thing I've learned from having an anthropologist mom it's that sometimes you need to mirror the local customs to show your respect and good intentions. I took the Pepsi that Tucker offered me.

"What all did you hear?" she asked.

"Something about your roommate," I told her.

Tucker turned back for her room and I fell in step next to her.

"She complained to residence hall administration that she doesn't want to room with a trans woman," Tucker said.

The content of the sentence was crappy so I tried not to smile even though my heart was pounding with excitement. How lucky was it to already find another trans woman when this was clearly a high-stealth, high-prejudice campus?

"I gather there aren't a lot of out trans women on campus," I said.

"None," Tucker said.

"I'm—" I started, then stopped because there was a tall, lean, angry-looking woman standing outside of Tucker's dorm room door.

"Who is this?" she asked.

"Ella, I just met her. She stopped to hate on my hateful graffiti, so now we're besties. Ella, this is my girlfriend Lindy."

Lindy was the same height as Tucker but she looked taller because she was rail thin. Tendons and veins stood out in her hands and forearms, and her cheeks had a hollowness to them. I'm a skinny girl too, but that's because all of my bones are on the small end of the spectrum and I have an athlete's metabolism without having to work at it, so I'm not opposed to skinny people—but I could see through the contours of Lindy's skin that her bones were medium to large and yet the skin stretched tight over them and gave her a bladed look. She was a handsome woman with an angular face, but her light brown eyes burned with frightening intensity. Wearing cargo pants with a dozen pockets that tucked into half-laced boots, and a tight gray shirt of some slick material, she looked like a character from a comic book or an opera, not quite like a real person.

"Hey," Lindy said. "Look, how long do you want to think about this moving in thing? Are you really going to protest it to the administration?"

"I don't want to, but it might be good for them to learn some things," Tucker said, but something in her tone was hesitant about more than just the administration. I thought that I wouldn't want to live with Lindy either, especially while just getting used to college.

"If you want to stay on campus, I have an empty room next to mine," I said. I was thinking that I'd love to have a trans woman as my roomie and the administration couldn't possibly get upset about that.

"You're a first year," Lindy said with disdain and clear disbelief that I could have access to an extra room.

"They say it was a paperwork screw-up. I'm on the third floor of Washington with a two-singles suite and a shared bathroom to myself."

"For serious?" Tucker asked.

"Completely. I was kind of bummed about not getting the roommate experience. Of course if you move in there, I'm going to reserve the right to complain about you."

"Will the administration even allow that?" Lindy asked.

"Won't know until we ask," Tucker said. She stepped up to Lindy and put a hand on her arm. "I really want the whole on-campus experience. It doesn't mean I won't be over at your place almost every night anyway."

Lindy's shoulders dropped a fraction of an inch. "I guess."

"And why don't I come spend the night tonight? I'll text my stupid roommate and let her know she can have the room to herself and I'll be moving out soon. Then I can talk to admin tomorrow, if that's okay with you, Ella."

I nodded. "You can move in whenever. If they're slow giving you a key, just knock on my door. My biology seminar ends pretty early tomorrow so I'll be around."

"Thanks," Tucker said. "This is really cool of you. You don't even know me."

"The RA said they might move someone in from the overcrowded dorm so I'm really just ensuring that I get a good roommate."

"Damn right you are," Tucker said and grinned.

I gave her my room number, full name, cell phone and email and left her and Lindy to packing a few things and clearing the essentials out of her room. This new friends thing was going great. Now I could add to my list one of the few other trans students at the school. This was the best getting lost on campus ever.

Outside the building I looked at my map, read the dorm name off the little plaque I hadn't noticed going in, and re-oriented toward the math and science dorm. It was starting to get dusky, the sun now behind the taller dorms, but it wouldn't be full dark for at least another hour.

I found the gaming community room easily once I had the right building. Unlike the other community room, this one was packed with about fifteen students clustered around two televisions with gaming consoles. One TV was showing a four-car racing game, and the other had a motion sensor hooked up to it so that people could play the popular dance games. I'm not a huge fan of those, but I did post a very respectable score in Fruit Ninja. Johnny and Shen didn't show, but the other students were friendly enough and by the time I was ready to walk back to my dorm, I felt that I'd found two places where I belonged.

CHAPTER FOUR

Tucker

Tucker tried to focus on the teaching assistant who was lecturing from the front of the room, but her eyes burned. She rubbed them, but that made them feel sandy like the inside of her brain. She'd been up way too late fighting with Lindy over the roommate thing, and then making up from the fight.

The making up made the fight totally worth it. She'd fallen into a doze just as the sun was starting to color the sky outside the bedroom window and dragged herself out of bed three hours later to get to this class.

Lindy had helped her get into this Women's & Gender Studies class, even though it had a prerequisite. The professor was Lindy's advisor and last year when Lindy was in this class, she'd managed to get a grant to present a paper at a conference. For a sophomore to already be getting grants was a huge deal, according to Lindy, and based on the way she seemed to get whatever she wanted in the department, she wasn't kidding.

Offered as a 200-level course to students in five other departments, including English, History, and Sociology, the class tended to be really big. Lindy said there were over eighty students in it when she took it. All students attended the same lecture once a week, but then they had two smaller classes, called recitations, with a teaching assistant. Because the lecture was on Wednesday and the recitations on Tuesday and Thursday, Tucker was at a recitation for the class before she'd heard the first lecture. Instead of the full group of sixty-some students, there were only twenty-two in the recitation.

She'd been assigned to the group whose TA was Vivien Yarwood and Tucker wasn't sure yet if that was an advantage. Vivien and Summer had a thing going on, but Summer never seemed quite able to say what sort of thing it was.

Tucker pulled a piece of paper out of her notebook and scrawled on it: *Are Vivien and Summer still together? Yes. No.*

Cal was sitting next to her and she put it in front of him. He looked at it for a minute, then picked up his pen and circled both *Yes* and *No.*

Vivien was attractive in an uptight white girl way. Her parchment-fair skin looked even paler under her red hair, which she'd pulled back in a loose bun. When she leaned against the desk and crossed her arms, the thick freckles on her forearms stood out. She'd rolled up the sleeves of her light blue button-down shirt and the effect made her arms look more delicate. Tucker had never seen Vivien and Summer together, but she could imagine how they'd make a handsome couple with Summer's stocky build, shorter black hair and warm russet skin highlighted by Vivien's pale and brassy tones.

After class she went to the administration building to ask if she could transfer into the dorm room next to Ella. When she first tried to describe the situation, the woman behind the desk looked at her like she was insane.

"I told a group of girls that I'm transsexual and now my roommate doesn't want to live with me. I'm sure you have her complaint on file by now," Tucker said. "But Ella Ramsey over in Washington says she has an empty single attached to her room. You can call her and confirm she's cool about me living there."

The woman typed into her computer for a silent minute. "I see," she said. Another minute passed as her fingers clicked the keys. Her eyes zigzagged as she scanned back and forth across the screen. Then she said, "Wait here."

She went into some back office for about ten years. Tucker dozed off in one of the unyielding plastic waiting room chairs, despite the way it was mistreating her butt and back.

"Excuse me," the woman said from near her ear, which made her jump but definitely woke her up.

"What'd they say?" Tucker asked.

"Just sign these papers and you're all set."

"Seriously?"

"There's nothing in your records about it, but I assume you've had the surgery, otherwise we can't let you stay on an all-women's floor."

Tucker's half-sleeping brain rolled over on itself. What surgery? She reviewed what she'd said when she came in. She hadn't said that she was trans, but she hadn't clarified that she wasn't either. What did her record look like now? Had they changed her status to "transsexual woman?" Did they even have such a coding?

And what gave this woman the right to ask about her genitals? Like she'd ask any other student if they had a penis or vagina or whatever. With a blush she realized that she'd asked Emily a similar question once, only to have Emily politely explain that the question was just as rude when asked to a trans woman as to a cisgender woman.

For a second, Tucker considered asking this woman, "Well, what do your genitals look like?" or "Tell me about yours and I'll tell you about mine." But she didn't want to risk losing the chance to sign a few forms and move out of her current room and into someplace infinitely more welcoming.

"I have a vagina," she said with a dry mouth.

The woman gave her a lemon-sucking frown and thrust the papers at her. "That wasn't necessary," she said. "'Yes' would have been enough."

"I'm sorry, I'm not used to being asked that," Tucker told her, with little sincerity in the apology. She signed the papers quickly.

"I hope you won't run into any more trouble in the dorms," the woman said in a steely tone that suggested she'd better not or she'd find herself short one dorm room. Considering what she had to scrape together to get a year in the dorms, even with the financial aid she had, it was a pretty good threat.

She hurried out of that building and stood blinking in the bright, late afternoon sunlight. Ella should be back to her room so she could start moving things over. She wished for a couple of big guys who could help her move and then realized she knew at least one.

She texted Cal: *Help me move and I'll buy you beer.*

Deal, he texted back.

He was a year older than her, but Tucker had a fake ID she used to sneak into gay bars sometimes. Granted the name on it was "Maria" and it said she was five four rather than five ten, but no one ever seemed to check the height. She and Maria, who'd sold Tucker the ID a year ago for fifty bucks, had the same eye color and hair color and broad cheekbones. As long as Tucker was in a group of women entering the bar on a busy night, the bouncers never looked hard. Buying beer was more of a challenge, but she knew one neighborhood liquor store where the aging owner hadn't updated his eyeglass prescription in about a decade. As long as she got there when he was behind the register, she was golden.

She texted back to Cal to meet her at her room in an hour and went to cram her stuff into boxes and plastic bags.

* * *

Cal showed up with Summer and Tesh, which meant a single trip across campus with most of Tucker's worldly possessions. She and Lindy had already taken a few boxes of books and essentials to Lindy's house the night before and now Lindy replied via text that she'd drive over to Ella's dorm and meet them there. And that's how Tucker found herself knocking on Ella's door at the head of a caravan of four people loaded with a variety of boxes, duffels and black plastic bags, resembling a homeless LGBTQIA United Nations.

Ella opened the door within seconds of Tucker's knock, probably because no place in her room was far enough from the door to make it take more than a few steps to reach it. She looked as shockingly pretty as she had the first time a door opened between them. It was the combination of high cheekbones and classic features, plus great makeup, and an inner light that shone through her intelligent green eyes.

Tucker didn't usually go for pretty; she preferred strong good looks, but the superficial beauty of Ella's face had a matching thoughtfulness behind it that she wanted to know more about.

From over Tucker's shoulder, and some distance above it, Cal intoned, "Ours is not a caravan of despair."

Ella laughed. "Oh good. Let me go around and unlock the door. You won't all fit in my room."

A moment later her head popped out from the next door down.

Tucker followed her inside the small room. Compared to her last dorm room, this was heaven: a really bare heaven. The long, narrow room held a single bed that took up almost half of its width, a dresser pushed against the same wall as the bed, a little bedside table, and a desk near the door. Tucker thought she could just fit a small bookcase on the wall of the room between the closet and the door to the bathroom. Currently, the only thing in the room was an "Evolution of Life" poster showing eras of plants and dinosaurs leading up to modern plant and animal life.

"Oh sorry," Ella said when she saw Tucker looking at it. She went to take the poster down. "I was decorating so it wouldn't look so empty."

"You can leave it," Tucker told her. "It's sort of cool and I should probably know that stuff."

Everyone tried to cram into the room and set down their baggage, but this created a traffic jam that pushed Tesh through the bathroom into Ella's room. Lindy showed up and commandeered Cal and Summer to go down to her car and get the other stuff. Tucker struggled to stow the various boxes and bags in the most efficient way that would let her get back into them later when she had time to unpack.

"You owe me next house party," Cal said as he set another big box on the bed. His face was blotchy with the exertion of carrying it up from Lindy's car and sweat stains showed on his peach T-shirt.

"I sure do."

"We should order pizza and have a room party," he announced.

"Because we love being all on top of each other so much," Summer said. "Why don't we just meet up in the Union like always?"

Tucker dug herself out of the box pile and slid around people into Ella's room. Ella was sitting in her desk chair talking to Tesh, who was perched against the desk itself.

"Did you meet everyone?" Tucker asked, dropping down to sit on the foot of the bed. "I'm being a horrible roommate already."

"I met a few."

"This is the core group of the LGBTQIA student organization on campus," Tucker said. "I met them all last spring since this is the nearest queer oasis to my home town."

She watched Ella's face closely as she talked. So far she seemed cool with lesbians, and at least the idea of trans women, but hadn't given up any intel about her own sexual orientation.

"I was thinking about going to that open house last night," Ella said.

"You didn't miss much," Tesh told her. "A few new students showed up, which is always nice, but out here in the boondocks you don't get a huge group of incoming students wanting to wave their hands around in week one and yell 'Look at me, I'm queer.'"

"What's the makeup of the group?" Ella asked. "Mostly gay and lesbian or some bi and trans also?"

"The first," Tesh said. "We've got a few bisexual folks and I'm sure someone's a closet crossdresser, but that's it for the T."

Ella turned to Tucker. Her eyebrows were up and their front ends dipped toward each other, creating worried creases in her forehead. *Celadon, that was the right word for the color of Ella's eyes,* Tucker thought as Ella stared at her.

"You're trans…" she said.

"Actually I'm not," Tucker said. "I'm sorry if you were counting on that, like it made me a super cool roommate or something. I just told a bunch of girls that I was because they were being real jerks about trans stuff and I thought they should have to face a real person for once and not just their stupid ideas. I figured I'm tall enough and big-boned enough that they'd believe it."

She knew she was rambling, but Ella looked so discomfited that she wanted to keep going until she could erase that look and replace it with the light, smiling Ella.

"It's okay," Ella said, with a strange, resonant tightness in her voice. "You don't have to be trans to be my roommate."

"You just thought it was cool?" Tucker asked.

"Something like that." Ella looked at the poster on her wall, the one with the dense cluster of bright blue stars surrounded by gold and red space dust. Her expression was sad and wistful.

Summer, who'd overheard part of the conversation from the doorway, cut into their deadlock with the blunt question, "So are you a lesbian or what?"

"I'm…I think I'm bi," Ella said. "I don't know. I kind of feel up in the air but…that makes me sound like the worst kind of bi-curious girl, doesn't it?"

"Yes, yes it does," Summer said and Tesh shot her a disapproving look.

"You're fine," Tesh told Ella. "You take all the time you need to figure things out. Some of us just need a little more time than others before we're ready to make a declarative statement to the world about what we are."

Lindy shoved into the bathroom behind Summer and called into Ella's room. "Hey, are we getting dinner?"

"I was just going to head over to the dining hall," Tucker said. She couldn't afford to buy dinner at the Union every night, or even most nights, especially if she didn't want to spend every school break working.

"Come to the Union, I'll buy," Lindy said. Either she was reading Tucker's mind or perhaps she'd seen the sorry state of the contents of Tucker's wallet.

"Well, if you're buying."

"Before you all go," Ella said. "Do any of you like playing games? I need a team of three to play Cruel 2 B Kind on Friday. It's like Assassination but with compliments."

"Like what?" Tesh asked.

"Assassination is a game that people play with squirt guns where you go around in teams and try to kill other teams by jumping out and squirting them," Ella said. "But apparently when they played it here a few years ago some students who weren't playing got soaked and complained, so in this version you 'kill' people with compliments."

"That sounds awesome," Tucker said. "I don't know how good I'll be, but I'd be happy to be on your team, roomie."

"I'm in too," Lindy said quickly.

"Can you have more than one team?" Tesh asked.

"I'll check tomorrow but I'm sure they'll say yes."

Tesh looked at Summer who nodded and then shouted over her and Lindy's shoulders into the other room, "Hey, Cal, you free Friday?"

"Yeah," he yelled back. "Is there food?"

"We're going to play a game, we need you to hide behind."

He laughed. "Sure thing."

The whole crew emptied out of Ella and Tucker's rooms and into the hallway except for Ella. She stood in her doorway looking small inside the wooden frame.

"I'll be there in a few," she said. "I just want to finish this problem I was working on."

They went down the hall in a straggle and then split into small groups as they walked across the quad toward the Union. Tesh and Lindy were talking about a movie and Cal was a few steps behind listening in; Summer fell in next to Tucker.

"You think she's really bi?" Summer asked.

"As opposed to lesbian?"

"Straight."

"I haven't met any straight girls who just want to hang out with us," Tucker pointed out.

"Do you think she's had a girlfriend or even kissed a girl?" Summer went on. "I mean, maybe she really is just bi-curious like she said, but I'll bet you as soon as someone's really interested in her, she's going to pull away."

Tucker shook her head. "You don't know that."

Summer's dark brown eyes warmed with mischief. "We need a single girl we can get to hit on her and find out."

"What about Tesh?"

"She says she met a girl over the summer but won't tell me who it is yet, like I'd be jealous or something." Summer frowned.

She and Tesh had been together the latter half of their first year at Freytag and the beginning of the second until, with surprisingly little drama, their dating slid into a comfortable friendship and they started to date other people.

"Too bad Alisa's not around," Summer added.

"Where is she?" Tucker asked. Alisa was Lindy's ex before her.

"She's here," Summer said. "I saw her across the quad, but she won't come to the table. She's probably mad that you and Lindy are still together. I don't think she liked Lindy going after you and was hoping it wouldn't last."

"She didn't 'go after' me," Tucker protested. "It was mutual."

She jammed her hands into her pockets as they crossed the corner of the big quad toward the Union.

"Figure of speech," Summer said. "And anyway, you two were like horny rabbits the first few months. I think it bugged Alisa. I saw her watching you a few times and she looked pretty upset."

"Yeah, Lindy said she was being weird possessive."

Summer shook her head as she held the Union door open for Tucker. "Let it be. People gotta process their own shit in their own time."

They were halfway through dinner when Ella joined them with a tray of cheese bread and a salad. She slid onto the bench next to Tucker and tore off a strip of bread.

"Want one?" she asked Tucker.

Tucker was already stuffed, but she took one anyway because she could always find room for garlic cheese bread.

"So what's your deal?" Summer asked, leaning across the table and half into Tesh so she could face Ella directly. "*Have* you ever dated a girl?"

Ella blushed and Tucker jumped to her defense. "Hey, you didn't quiz me when I showed up to my first meeting."

"That's 'cause you were clearly staring at anyone with boobs," Summer said.

Tesh looked across the table at Ella and said softly, "Summer likes to pick on the shy girls. Sometimes it works out for her."

Ella smiled, though the discomfort on her face didn't vanish.

"I get it," she said. "I've kissed two girls, but it was more like an experimenting thing than dating."

"Boys?" Summer asked.

"Kind of the same boat. I went to this really small, tight-knit high school and we all knew each other for years and years so when it was time to start dating it seemed really awkward."

"How small?" Tucker asked, eager to get the topic off Ella's dating life, even though she was fiercely curious.

"Two hundred students total. It was a magnet school—lots of geeks."

"Damn, that's as small as my high school and I come from a town of five thousand," Tucker said. "And I know what you mean about knowing everyone."

She caught Summer's eye and shook her head. Summer rolled her eyes.

"Well honey, you just let us know when you're ready for us to fix you up with someone," Summer told her.

CHAPTER FIVE

Ella

Wednesday during Machine Learning, I told Johnny and Shen that I had not just one but two teams for Cruel 2 B Kind.

"Two days and she's already angling for a promotion," Johnny said. "Give me their info and I'll make sure they get instructions. You can also forward them to this website." He wrote an address on a piece of paper. "It has all the basics. We've got eleven teams so far. It's going to be a good year."

"Are you on a team?" I aimed the question at both Johnny and Shen. Maybe a little more at Shen.

"Nah, we run the game. Someone has to uphold the rules," Johnny said.

"We played early last year," Shen said.

"How did it go?"

"We were winning so hard that two other teams called a truce with each other and set us up," Johnny told me.

I looked at Shen, who was looking down with a thoroughly satisfied smile on his lips, and wondered how much of the winning came from him.

In my room that evening, I looked up the website for the game and read through the rules. It was hard to settle down to do homework. Do they even call it homework when you're not at home anymore? "School work" sounded like elementary school and "dorm work" was pretty stupid. Anyway, I got some of it done but my concentration was not good and I could hear Tucker banging around in her room. I'd recovered from my surprise the evening before when she said she wasn't trans—or at least I'd started the recovery process.

It was hard to understand why someone would say they were if they didn't have to. She'd signed herself up to get hassled in ways she didn't even realize.

I got up from my chair and knocked on the door to her room.

"Come on in," she said.

She stood in front of the dresser at the foot of her bed, wearing loose, faded jeans and a T-shirt that might have started out black but was now a charcoal color and frayed at the neck and sleeves. She had a bunch of clothing strewn across her bed and was doing a strange combination of folding some and jamming other pieces into drawers. I didn't see the logic, but it had to be there, right?

Two posters graced the walls next to my evolution poster. One said, "Women's Rights Are Human Rights" and the other had a picture of two very cute women kissing.

"How's the room feel?" I asked.

"It's cozy. We really lucked out, huh? Normally you have to be a junior to get a suite like this."

She folded a pair of worn jeans and put them in the drawer and then tossed a pair of cargo shorts in next to them. On top of the dresser was a four-foot high stack of paperback books with creased spines. I didn't know how she managed to have so many books or why she bothered to bring them to college with her rather than buying eBooks so she wouldn't have to pack so many.

I wanted to know what made her say she was transsexual if she wasn't. That seemed plain crazy to me, but also too personal a question. It was possible she did have some gender dysphoria and just hadn't completely come out to herself. I didn't want to freak her out by asking about her directly, so I picked a related question.

"What were the girls saying, the ones you came out to, if it's okay to ask?"

"Oh yeah, it's fine. They weren't targeting me, I was just in line with them, and, well, it makes more sense if you know that I have a good friend who's a trans woman so I know a bunch about all that and these girls...it sounded like one of them was working in admissions and saw a memo about a trans girl moving into the dorms and was freaking out about it."

I swallowed around the dry clot of sandy fear in my throat. The subject of the memo had to be me.

"What did she say?" I asked.

"The usual dumb shit about not wanting to be in the bathroom with a...well you know...a trans person," she said and folded another pair of jeans into the dresser drawer. "I can't repeat all of it, it was pretty stupid. Like they kept referring to this girl as 'he.' I don't know how much you know about the trans community but that kind of misgendering on purpose is total bullshit. It's really disrespectful."

I was glad Tucker wasn't looking at me because I felt like if she did, she'd see right through my skin and my defenses and know everything about me. She'd see my history written in my body. And she'd see my gut-twisting fear that there was a whole group of girls on campus who were on the lookout for a trans girl and they were all set to make her life hell—they were looking for me.

When I came out I'd had a really lucky situation, relatively speaking since it's kind of hard to call coming out transsexual "lucky." I was pretty young when I first started telling Mom that I was a girl, and she was open to the idea, plus she explained it all to Dad for me. They both had a lot of questions and concerns, but they agreed that I could go on hormone suppressors and block male puberty from happening to me. I lived my first two years of high school as a very girlie boy and then over a summer, with the help of hormones, went into puberty as a girl and that's how I went to school my junior year.

I attended a very cool alternative high school with about two hundred students so my parents were able to talk to each teacher and we held a town hall meeting in the school common room for everyone. My closest friends, Nico especially, took on the few people who thought it was weird or unnatural and explained transsexualism in great detail to them so that I didn't have to, and by the time I came back to school as Ella, the response was overwhelmingly positive.

I know it helped that I'm on the small side and I have big eyes and people tend to see me as cute or pretty. It helped that I had Nico, who came out as genderqueer before I ever came out. And it helped that half of our group of friends were geniuses who could figure it all out really quickly or who were too into their own subject matter to care.

This was the first time I really felt afraid for my safety. The kids who were willing to get into Tucker's dorm and spray-paint a slur on her door in the middle of the night intended that act of hate for me.

Tucker switched to a box of books and went about unpacking them, finding places for them on the dresser or on the nightstand by her bed. She kept talking as she organized the books with more care than she'd shown any of her clothes.

"I figured, what if the girl in admissions really had seen something," Tucker said. "What if there is really a trans girl student here this year? The last thing she needs is to overhear the shit that I did. I know I don't understand viscerally what it means to have gender dysphoria or to have people always questioning who you are, but I do know what it's like to have people be assholes to you just because of who you are. And I just got really pissed and really afraid for this girl and so I said it was me. That way they'll direct their bullshit at me and I know I can take it."

She glanced over at me and put down the books in her hands.

"You're crying," she said.

I wasn't really. The tears were in my eyes but none had fallen—okay maybe just one. I waved a hand in front of my face and tried to keep my voice level as I said, "That's so heroic."

"Well, I hope it works, so if anyone asks, don't tell them I'm not transsexual, okay?"

I crossed the small room and put my arms around her. After a second, her arms wrapped around my shoulders. My chin rested in the warm curve where her neck met her collarbones and she smelled like applewood smoke and molasses. Her breasts felt heavy against my chest just above mine. I stepped back but my body didn't seem to want to let go of the memory of hers.

She grinned at me. "I should be heroic more often," she said.

I smiled back and went to perch on the edge of her desk. I opened my mouth to tell her why she was even more of a hero to me than she knew, but what held me back had nothing to do with Tucker and everything to do with Lindy. I didn't like the way I'd seen her looking at me when she thought I wasn't paying attention. I got the impression she resented me for inviting Tucker to live here when she wanted Tucker to be with her. And I suspected that if I told Tucker she'd eventually tell Lindy and who knows what would happen then.

Tucker had given me a gift of unfathomable value and I wasn't about to waste it.

* * *

After staying Wednesday in the dorm room, Tucker said she was going to spend the next night or two at Lindy's. I was glad for the quiet. Much as I liked having the coolest roommate in the world, I needed a day or two to get my mind around what she'd shared with me and to figure out if she was really that amazing or if she just had some kind of martyr complex. Maybe playing an assassination style game with her would give me some clue.

The email about the game came on Thursday afternoon around twenty-four hours before the start time. It felt very secret agent—like it should self-destruct after I read it or something:

Dear Kind Assassin,

The playing field for our game tomorrow night, Friday, will be the triangle created by Tyler and Jefferson avenues and the south edge of the main quad. Any team moving outside of this area during the two-hour play time will be considered dead. The game will run from 7 p.m. to 9 p.m. and we'll all meet at the Union afterward to debrief and display booty.

Players must bring a piece of personal booty. You won't get this back, so choose something slightly significant but not majorly important to you. If you are killed, you must surrender your booty to the team that killed you.

Your weapons! You have three verbal weapons you can use to "kill" other teams. These are:

Welcome your targets to beautiful FU.
Tell your targets "You look gorgeous today!"
Wish your targets a happy made-up holiday.

These are used in a rock-paper-scissors fashion so that:
Welcome beats Gorgeous
Gorgeous beats Holiday
Holiday beats Welcome

When you "kill" a team, that team becomes part of your team. Your entire team must stay within eyesight of each other throughout play, though you may stand apart to be less obvious.

When you make a kill, report this via text to Game Master Johnny Han. If you have questions during play, please address them to Game Master Shen Li.

You must be within five feet of your target team to kill them. You can't shout across the quad and randomly down other teams.

We'd like to thank the game's creators Jane McGonigal and Ian Bogost.

Everyone have fun!

It sounded awesome and there was nothing in the rules that said we couldn't strategize ahead of time. I texted Tucker: *check your email for game rules. strategy session?*

She texted back: *Yes! @ Lindy's. Come over?*

I wrote back: *sure, address?*

She sent me the number and street and I looked it up on the map. It was two blocks north of campus and an easy walk from my dorm. I should have asked if I could bring anything. I headed out of my dorm and onto Tyler Ave., which ran all the way along the east edge of campus and was populated with stores that catered to students, including a bunch of restaurants. I'd already discovered the creamery that made its own ice cream, but that was a couple of blocks south and I was headed north. This end of Tyler had a pizza place, a clothing store, and a Vietnamese deli. They served bánh mì so I went in and picked up a few sandwiches. No one ever resented a guest showing up with food, right?

A block over, the shops catering to students gave way to a residential area that looked to be mostly duplexes, triplexes and a few small apartment buildings—the low kind with eight or twelve units. Lindy lived in one of the big old houses that was converted into a triplex. She had the top unit and Tucker's text said to come up the back stairs, so I did.

The second flight of back stairs looked like someone just tossed boards together and hit them randomly with a nail gun, but I survived the ascent and knocked. Tucker opened the door.

"I brought sandwiches," I said and held up the bag.

"Oh, Lindy was making some kind of salad," she said. "But these will go great with that. Are some vegetarian?"

"Two are tofu, one beef and one pork."

"Great, come on in."

I handed her the bag and stepped through the doorway as she moved into the room. Inside was a vaulted area, basically a single room under the roof. At the far end was a kitchen and, in the middle, a place with a couch and television. In front of the door I'd come through was an entryway/study with a coat rack and a small desk. One door led off each side of the single, vaulted room and I guessed one was a bathroom and the other a bedroom.

Lindy stood in the kitchen space at the far end, chopping something on a large cutting board set on the countertop. I paused in the middle of the room, near the couch, and looked around. The décor was early eclectic with an accent of hit-or-miss. There were beautiful built-in bookshelves with some classic-looking books, a few new books with bright, glossy spines, a variety of pieces of wood or stone, a Greek goddess statue, and a thick layer of dust over all of it. The television was also dusty but had a scattering of recently touched DVD cases around its base. The couch looked about fifteen years old and sagged in the middle but featured a thick, folded wool blanket on the back and a few rather nice Navajo-style throw pillows. The rug under this area showed a fine Turkish pattern and if it was genuine it probably cost a few thousand dollars. The kitchen continued the combination of careless affluence and affected poverty with islands of obsessive neatness.

"Ella brought sandwiches," Tucker said.

"Bánh mì from the Vietnamese place," I added. "Two are vegetarian, they're the ones with the green tape."

"Thank you," Lindy said. "That's very thoughtful. I was just making a lentil and kale salad, but we can eat that as a side. It will keep."

She over-enunciated the words, but her tone was friendly enough. I couldn't get a good sense of her. In my high school we had more than enough geeky kids and brilliant kids with various emotional challenges. For all I knew, Lindy could be some kind of high functioning, undiagnosed Asperger's. She did seem to have some issue with eye contact, tending to either stare at me or not meet my eyes.

Tucker got me a glass of water and set the beef bánh mì on a plate with a bit of kale salad. I know beef isn't a traditional option and I felt a little guilty about ordering it, but it was my favorite. I wondered if Shen liked bánh mì. Yeah, it was Vietnamese and he was Chinese, but hey, I'm from the Midwest and I like a lot of different cuisines. Of course I wasn't sure Midwestern cow town bánh mì could compare to anything you could order in China.

When I took my plate to the living room area, I discovered that the couch was even older than it looked. I sank a good six inches due to compressed springs. I set my water on a coffee table that looked like an expensive mission-style antique that

got in a fight with a wood chipper. Tucker took the middle of
the couch and Lindy the far end.

"You called this meeting, team leader, what's on your mind?"
Tucker asked after we dug into our sandwiches. "This is great,
thank you," she added, lifting her sandwich in appreciation. She
had taken the pork sandwich, not the tofu.

"Well, I was thinking we should decide our protocol for
which weapon we'll use and in what order. The 'weapons' are
to either welcome people to Freytag, to tell them 'You look
gorgeous today' or to wish them a made-up holiday."

I paused and looked at Tucker. She swallowed a mouthful
of sandwich and asked, "Let me see if I get this? We run up on
people and say one of those three things and if they're another
team and they didn't see us coming, then we beat them. But if
they see us coming and say their weapon-phrase at the same
time, then we have to beat them rock-paper-scissors style with
ours?"

"Yes, like that," I said.

"Let's try it," Tucker suggested. She held up her fingers
counting down three...two...one.

I said, "Merry Chrisnukka!"

She declared, "Welcome to beautiful Freytag U!" at the
same time.

"Who wins?" Lindy asked.

"I do," I said. "Holiday beats Welcome. I kind of figured
that most people would start with Welcome, so we should tend
toward Holiday, unless the other teams are likely to figure that
out too."

"I think it's fair to assume most teams will be as new as we
are," Lindy said. "Why don't we start out using Holiday and
Gorgeous."

"Should we have a hand signal so we don't say out loud
which one we're going to use? Like one finger or two or three?"
Tucker asked.

"Yes," I agreed. "But let's do it in reverse order so one means
Holiday. That way if they think we're going to do Welcome...
oh wait."

"They'll do Holiday," Lindy finished. "So one should be Gorgeous."

"So then two would be Welcome and three would be Holiday."

"I'm going to need a cue card," Tucker said. "What are we going to use for our holidays?"

"Kwanzakka?" Lindy offered.

"Arborween?" I suggested.

"Hallowgiving, Lesbian Day," Tucker said.

Lindy and I laughed. "I like that last one," Lindy said.

"I'll make a list," Tucker offered. "We can put the holidays on one side of a card with the numbers, for quick reference."

"We should practice our number system after we're done eating," I suggested. "And you two can pick where we should be when the game starts. I really don't know the campus very well."

We ate in silence for a few minutes and then Lindy said, "Ella, I hear you're in biology. I'm glad to see more women interested in science. What drew you to it?"

"I'm just one woman in science, but thanks. It's just always interested me. As a kid, I brought stuff into the house from the yard and so my parents got me a bunch of books about bugs and how things work and evolution. Lucky for me, I was more into evolution and genetics than bugs, though I suppose I wouldn't feel that way if I was really into bugs. Tucker tells me you're a little bit famous because you've already presented a paper at a conference?"

Lindy shifted away from me, or toward the arm of the couch, it was hard to tell with Tucker between us, but her eyes darted down and then around the room before coming back to my face.

"Yes, it was very exciting but now I have to figure out what I'll do next. Academia is so fickle like that, you know, they always want the next great thing."

"But she's working on it," Tucker said and gave an encouraging pat to Lindy's leg.

"No pressure, ha ha," Lindy added with a forced laugh. "But tell me more about your field of study. Are you one of those people who doesn't freak out about Frankenfood?"

"Not as such. I think paying careful attention to genetic modification is important but we've been tampering with genetics through plant and animal breeding programs for millennia. A lot of what people take for granted as natural today isn't at all...it was just created by people long enough ago that the popular mind forgot we did it. There's this real romance about a lot of stuff being natural that actually isn't."

And I was off and running. I can talk about genetics for a good long while and Lindy seemed genuinely interested. When we finished eating, Tucker took the plates and washed them while we kept talking.

I started to see what Tucker liked about Lindy—when you had her full attention you really felt like someone important. Even though she was clearly against genetically modified food, she had a way of asking questions and really taking in the answers that made me want to not only explain my side but listen to her side too. I didn't want to stop the conversation, but I finally had to shake myself out of that limelight so that we could practice our hand signals for the game.

* * *

I thought the Game Masters picked Friday night for the game just because it was a good social time for the players, but when we showed up to our spot on campus, it was clear that they were better masterminds than I thought because the quads were packed with students. No one had classes for the next two days, so coursework was on hold, and the weather was still warm enough that people wanted to be outside playing Frisbee, reading, or just hanging out.

"How are we going to find anyone in this?" Tucker asked.

"We don't need to," I told her. "We just need to be really kind to a whole bunch of people. That's the brilliance of using compliments instead of squirt guns."

It was five minutes to seven and we were on the southwest side of the north quad. From where we stood, we could easily see fifty people playing and lying around and walking from one place to another. Much harder was determining who of those fifty was in a three-person kill squad.

"If we just start walking around welcoming people, we'll be a target," Lindy pointed out.

"We need camouflage, but not the military kind. Come on."

Now that I was part of something and had a team, my old self-confidence had returned. Well, most of it. A thin line of fear tugged at me at times through the day as I wondered which of the people around me were the ones who wanted to ferret out the trans girl and harass her, but that didn't trouble me tonight. I walked up to two guys playing Frisbee.

"Hey, can we join you for like ten minutes?" I asked. "We're part of this thing and we need a cover."

The guy standing near me with the Frisbee laughed. "Sure, honey." Then he yelled to his friend, "Duke, come closer, these girls want to play."

We formed a fairly loose pentagon and tossed the Frisbee around. I felt certain that we could have been at least twice as far and still caught it with ease, but standing closer made it easier for us to compliment targets as they walked by us.

As people came near us, Lindy would flash a number of fingers and we'd chime out cheerfully:

"Happy Solar Power Day!"

"Oh cool, is that today?" the guy passing us said. We just grinned and waved.

"You look gorgeous today!"

That made a group of girls giggle their way around the corner.

"Welcome to beautiful Freytag University!"

That was greeted by thanks and cheers.

"Wishing you a beautiful Arborween!"

"Oh shit!" the guy passing near me said. "No way! Is that a made-up holiday?"

"It sure is," I said cheerfully.

"Ugh, I surrender."

I handed the Frisbee back to the guy who had it originally and told him, "Thanks for letting us play, honey." He blinked but didn't seem to get that I was just returning the endearment he used on me.

The other two members of that team formally surrendered and then their team lead, the guy I'd hit with my holiday greeting, asked, "Whose idea was it to hide out as Frisbee players?"

"Me," I said.

He handed me his booty, which looked like some kind of high school sports medal, and the other two also gave me theirs. I was going to need a bigger bag to carry my catch if I got much more.

"Brilliant idea," one of the guys said. "We're Team Death Socks. Let's get into some cover and we'll call in our kill."

Due to a stalemate between some mildly obscene and truly obscure names we ended up being named the Woolf Pack. I'm pretty sure that when we said the team name to the Death Socks guys they didn't get that Woolf had more than one "o" in it, even though Lindy said, "like Virginia Woolf."

"What's your strat?" the Death Socks lead said.

We explained our hand signals and handed them some extra reminder cards I'd printed up.

"Now that there are more of us, we're going to have to use more natural cover," he said. "Come on."

I cleared my throat. "I think we defeated you so you're supposed to do things our way now."

"Whatever," he replied, but he waited and he didn't even look annoyed about it.

"I know we're not supposed to go in the buildings, other than the Union, per the rules," Lindy said. "But did they say anything about going *on* the buildings? There's a fire escape on the back side of Russel that would give us a pretty good view if we can get over the trees."

"It will make us visible," I said. "We could get trapped."

The Death Socks lead turned to one of his guys and asked, "Jake, you have any smokes on you? We could disguise ourselves as smokers using the fire escape."

"Yep, got 'em. Let's go…uh, when you're ready, boss." That last bit was directed at me.

I grinned at him. "Lead on, lieutenant."

We ducked behind one of the dorms and around the side of a big parking ramp. My heart was pounding much faster than I thought it should. After all, if we were spotted all that would happen was a fierce greeting and complimenting, but I wasn't ready to die yet, even in a game.

We ran along, crouched behind a retaining wall, and came out behind Russel. Lindy pointed to where the fire escape ladder had slipped its mooring and hung nearly to the ground. Tucker gave me a leg up since I was the shortest of them all and then we were scrambling up. Jake already had a cigarette in his mouth and he'd given one to a teammate so by the time we made it to the third-floor level of the fire escape we had a good cloud of smoke going.

"Get a little behind each other if you can so we don't look like six people," I suggested.

Lindy stepped behind Tucker and put her hands on Tucker's hips. The three guys looked but didn't say anything. Maybe I should have okayed the name "Team Grrrl Power." It was better than "Team Vagina Dentata."

"What do we see?" I asked.

For a few minutes we all just looked. I think Jake may have been actually smoking too but I wasn't going to complain since he made our literal smoke screen. A few times I thought I spotted a group of kind assassins, but then the groups would split up or turn out to have numbers not divisible by three.

"Well, we could just hide up here and take our survival points," one of the guys said.

"No way, let's give it a bit more time," I said. "The larger the groups get, the easier they'll be to spot. Let's say twenty minutes and then we're out of here regardless. In the meantime, let's figure out how we're going to get down from here and do an ambush, right?"

"We could travel single file like the Sand People," Tucker said.

"What?" Lindy asked at the same time that I said, "That's great."

"You weren't joking?" Lindy asked her.

"Only half," Tucker said. "After all, they do travel single file to hide their numbers."

Lindy didn't get the *Star Wars* reference but I flashed Tucker a smile.

"If we get down from here, we can go in a line across the back of the building and catch anyone walking between Russel and Washington to the North Quad," Jake said.

"I like it. Now we wait, okay?"

We waited maybe ten minutes. Jake started to look like he was getting sick of smoking. Then we saw a big group of students pour out of the Student Union. I counted twenty-one. They started moving in a mass toward the center of the quad and then stopped.

"We have to take them," Jake said.

I nodded.

The group turned north.

"That's it, let's go. Operation Sand People is on!"

We scurried down the fire escape like there was a real fire and jogged in a line across the back of the dorm. Lindy got to the edge of the building first and peeked around.

Then she turned to us. "They're coming. We're doing Gorgeous on my mark."

I held my breath. I thought for sure they were going to hear my heart beating, or Jake shifting impatiently behind me so that his boot scuffed on the concrete. A slow breeze carried the scent of cigarette smoke from him to me. I moved a halfstep forward and brushed Tucker's shoulder by accident. She reached back and found my fingers with hers and gave them a quick squeeze.

"Go!" Lindy said in a whispered shout and we surged around the corner.

I bounced up on the balls of my feet and spread my arms overhead and yelled, "You look gorgeous today!"

A few of the startled crowd said "Happy" or "Welcome" followed by things like "damn" or "crap."

The surrenders started coming in. Now I was worried because a group of twenty-seven people was pretty obvious even on a busy Friday.

"We need sentries," I told Jake. He had a much louder voice than I did.

"When you've surrendered, go to the outside and keep watch!" he bellowed.

Lindy was getting a lot of booty for being the first one around the corner with the Gorgeous attack. Some of the guys got booty from people who were friends of theirs, and Tucker and I each picked up a few items. Okay, I got more than Tucker but only because I have a more traditional cuteness and even a non-spiky Mohawk on her could be intimidating.

With so many people, we couldn't rely on hand signals anymore, so we just set an order. We'd do Gorgeous again, then Holiday with Chrisnukka, then Welcome, then repeat the cycle. The new teams were pretty sure the remaining teams had to be in the north area, so we continued in that direction.

We were an army of complimenters and many startled students were the recipients of twenty-seven voices calling them gorgeous or welcoming them or wishing them a happy holiday. We went up to each group sitting on the North Quad and used our weapons of kindness on them, leaving a lot of laughter and giggling behind. We turned at the end and started down the other side. Even if we didn't find the other teams, it was a heck of a good time.

"You look gorgeous!" we shouted.

But at the same time nine people jumped up from where they'd been reading or chatting on the grass and yelled, "Welcome to beautiful Freytag University!"

Their compliment beat ours. We were down.

Tesh, Summer and Cal were in that group. We should have recognized them, but they wore actual disguises, including hats and sunglasses, and at that point we'd become mad with power and weren't really playing attention. I gave my booty, a blue-footed stuffed bird, to Tesh.

The lot of us set off south again to meet up with our game masters and hear how the scoring played out. The winning team was Team Covalent Bonds, but there would still be prizes for high-scoring players and runner-up teams. I thought we had a good shot at getting the prize for the biggest kill and that was plenty for me.

Jake fell in beside me while we were walking.

"Hey, that was really well played," he said. "Have you played this before?"

"No, but I played a lot of games in my high school. Have you played it?"

"I was in the one they did last year but it wasn't nearly this big. I think we had twenty-one people total. So, what program are you in?"

"Biology."

"Really?"

He looked so surprised that I said, "Don't tell me you thought I was in Home Ec."

"They have that here?" he asked.

"No, they don't."

"Are you teasing me because I did the 'girls don't like science or games' thing?" he asked.

I liked him better. "Guilty. I get the science thing a lot. You'd think it wasn't the twenty-first century or something."

"Does that mean I'm screwed if I ask you to coffee or something? I mean, do you have a boyfriend?"

I checked him out again peripherally. He was pretty good looking if you liked your guys to have that triangular and lean muscled swimmer body. Okay, he was quite good looking, but I just didn't feel that into him. I tried to imagine what we'd say at a coffee shop and kept blanking, and then the mental picture flickered and was replaced with an image of me and Shen in a coffee shop. I liked that a lot better.

"There's someone I'm interested in," I said.

"Is it her?" he pointed at Tucker.

I was startled that he'd pick another woman, but there was a way Tucker had of filling up a space with her energy. Or he'd seen her take my hand—that was a simpler explanation. Of course it might just be his way of trying to find out what my sexual orientation was since I clearly hung out with lesbians.

The curious thing was that the answer to his question about Tucker wasn't "no." I could still remember the hug from the other night and I wanted to do that again for a lot longer, but I wasn't even going to try as long as Lindy was on the scene. Okay then, I was interested in two people. But I wasn't going to tell Jake that.

"It's a guy," I said.

"If he doesn't work out, Johnny and Shen know how to get in touch with me."

If he didn't work out, no way was I going to ask those guys for Jake's info.

"Thanks," I said. "It was fun being on a team with you."

We all poured into the Student Union and took up half the tables on the ground floor. Johnny and Shen had already ordered a bunch of pizzas and everyone fell on them while the guys read a long list of awards. Team Woolf Pack did take Largest Single Kill and second place Survivalists. Lindy won the award for most points due to her excessive amount of booty.

I watched Shen help Johnny hand out the ribbons and admire the various booty items. Shen still smiled more with his eyes than his mouth, but his eyes were smiling a lot. Compared to Johnny, he was quiet, but he didn't seem particularly shy. As he counted the booty items, he grinned at a few and cracked a joke I couldn't hear that made all the students around him laugh.

"This was a great game, thanks for inviting us," Lindy said when she got back to the table after accepting her ribbon.

"Congrats on your win," I told her.

She held up the ribbon, which was the kind of blue "1st Place" ribbon you get at a State Fair for a kid's event. "I shouldn't feel as happy about this as I do," she said.

"Are you kidding? I'm putting our Largest Single Kill ribbon on my dorm room door—on the outside—just so everyone knows how awesome we are."

CHAPTER SIX

Tucker

At first, Tucker thought living next to Ella was going to be more of a problem than she expected, because Lindy kept asking her about every conversation they had and trying to get her to stay the night every night. Frustrated and feeling claustrophobic, Tucker spent a whole weekend working at the hardware store in her hometown so she could have space away from Lindy, even though the owner told her she should be focusing on school. She'd worked at Shipley's Hardware on and off since she was fifteen, and the familiar smells of oil and paint blocked out Lindy's nagging jealousy.

The fourth time Tucker answered Lindy's question with, "Ella and I talked about the cute boy in her Machine Learning class…again," Lindy calmed down.

"Seriously," Tucker said while she and Lindy were sitting together on the couch after dinner. "Is she ever going to ask him out? I get that it's weird with his cousin around all the time, but I think she should just text him or something. We all have his phone number from the Cruel 2 B Kind game. It's been over two weeks and she hasn't even used it. Maybe she could ask him to come fix her computer or something."

Lindy made the sound of agreement that meant she wasn't really listening, followed by, "I have a movie picked out for us."

"I can't stay for a whole movie," Tucker told her. "I have to get to work on this paper for Gender Studies; I was at the shop all weekend fixing jammed weed-whackers. Anyway, don't you have writing to work on?"

"I was working on that all day," Lindy said. "I need a break from it. I'll find something to watch by myself."

Her sentence ended on a down note that was half-pout and half-sigh and made Tucker want to curl up next to her on the couch. She kissed Lindy and picked up her backpack.

"I'll text you good night," she said.

Halfway back to the dorm, Tucker remembered a story Lindy had told her earlier in the evening about how Lindy had taken her car in to the shop that morning and gotten stranded while they fixed some stupid issue with her thermostat. She'd said that she walked around boring downtown Freytag for a few hours and not gotten home until after lunch. If that was the case, how could Lindy have been working on her writing "all day?" Maybe she'd meant all afternoon. That had to be it.

She also wouldn't let Tucker look at her work. Was she even getting work done? Lindy said she'd had issues with depression and anxiety in the past. Was she going into some kind of down spell? Tucker wasn't sure what to do for her.

It was early enough that she could go for a run before settling down to work on her paper. She had two more weeks until it was due, but she wanted to get it right. She went to her room and picked up her gym duffel, then knocked on Ella's door.

"You know you have Shen's cell phone number, right?" Tucker told her without any preamble. "You should text him that you need someone to come fix your computer."

"They'll both come," Ella said, standing in the doorway with a bemused look. "But thanks for thinking of me."

"You need someone to run interference for you. What's Johnny's type?"

"Female humanoid, I think, but I never asked. He could be gay," Ella said.

"Well, that narrows it. Find out. Cal is single and I'm sure we could come up with an eligible woman, so that solves that. I'm off to the gym."

"Have fun."

Tucker walked the few blocks to the gym, changed and went to the track that ran around the second floor above the swimming pool. She preferred to run barefoot and that made it tough to run outside.

She did an easy two-and-a-half miles while her brain churned through the last few weeks with Lindy. It had to be something about the start of the school year that had her down because she'd been pretty cheerful all summer. After Tucker had the first draft of this paper done, she'd spend more time watching movies with her and see if they could talk about depression or whatever the issue was.

Lindy was her first real girlfriend, so she didn't exactly know what the protocol was for addressing problems that impacted the relationship. She'd fooled around with a good female friend of hers in high school on and off, but then that friend kept having boyfriends. And she'd had some hookups early in her senior year when her reputation as a lesbian was all over town, but nothing long-term. Now that she had a girlfriend, she didn't really know where to look for advice. Tesh was too quiet and Tucker would feel weird asking her, and she didn't trust any advice that came from Summer.

She grabbed her towel off the bar and wiped her face and neck on the way back to the locker room. One of the sports practices must have let out because the place was full of women. She threaded her way over to her locker without looking at any of them. As a lesbian, she was always overly conscious of looking at straight women in various states of undress; she didn't want them to think that she was getting ideas when she really wouldn't give them the time of day.

Most of the women she saw around campus weren't that interesting to her, but somehow as soon as she was out as a lesbian, they all assumed she was checking them out.

"Oh my God, it's that freak," a sadly familiar voice said from the end of the locker row. She looked up into the ferret-like eyes of Mean Face.

"This is the one I was telling you about," Mean Face said to a half-dozen of her friends who were gathering around you. "The one who was born a man."

"What's he doing in here?" one of the girls asked.

"This is for wo-men," another said, really slowly as if she didn't speak English.

"I'm going to tell the staff," a third girl chimed in and headed for the doors.

Tucker was acutely self-conscious of her sweaty T-shirt and shorts. She was taller than most of them, but there were at least six women in various stages of half-dress holding towels over themselves and glaring at her. That struck her as particularly ludicrous since a few of them came around the lockers just to glare at her when she hadn't even been able to see them.

"Do you all get how horrible you are?" Tucker asked.

"You're the one invading *our* space," Mean Face said.

"I'm not invading anything," Tucker told her. "I'm a woman in the women's locker room. Now if you'll get out of my way, I'm done here."

Tucker pulled her gym bag from the locker and threw her street clothes in it. She could walk back to the dorm in her shorts and T-shirt. She grabbed her boots with the socks stuffed in them and slung the bag over her shoulder.

"She has really big boobs," one of the girls said to another. "How do you think they do that?"

"Surgery," another said. "Boob job. I saw a show on TV. And they do the dick too."

"How?"

"They gut it like a fish and turn it inside out like a sock," Tucker said angrily. It was a paraphrase from Kate Bornstein and the humor was clearly lost on this crowd.

Shocked giggling and disapproving sounds rippled through the group as Tucker pushed past them and into the long hallway heading out. Angry tears burned in the back of her throat and she needed an hour-long shower to remove the disgust she felt.

Beyond the glass doors that led out of the building, the evening sky had turned to full darkness. She stopped and sat on a bench just inside the door to put on her boots, even though they looked ridiculous with her gym shorts. No one would see her in the dark outdoors. While she was tying the laces, no one came to throw her out of the building. She hoped the girl from the locker room had found an official sort of person who told her she was being ridiculous. More likely she'd given up and wandered back to trash talk with her cohort.

Normally Tucker didn't worry about walking across campus after dark. She'd been tall from a young age and never developed a general fear of strangers that the other girls in her high school seemed to have. She trusted her ability to scream, fight and run if she had to. But tonight she was on edge, and she was about to cross campus in short athletic shorts and a tight T-shirt over her sports bra because she hadn't wanted to change in front of the mean girls. She reached into her bag for the pepper spray her mother insisted she carry. Holding it ready in her hand, she gripped her gym bag loosely in the other.

The night air was cool now but not chilly. The smell of turning leaves mixed with a lingering warm grass scent. She loved this season and the rest of fall with its crunchy fallen leaves and crisp air, fresh apple cider and pumpkin muffins at the local bakery.

As she walked, an acrid smoke smell drifted across the evening air. It didn't belong here, being too early in the season for anyone to burn leaves, and it smelled like a chemistry experiment gone bad. She walked faster to get free of it, passing behind the smallest of the university's three quads, and came to the dark gap between two buildings that would take her to the big quad and her dorm. Running steps sounded behind her and she turned.

His fist caught her high on the left side of her head. Tucker staggered sideways as the already dark landscape blurred. His hand closed on her left arm and he shoved her into the shadowed area between the empty class buildings. He shoved again and her momentum slammed her against the brick wall of one building. The impact ran up and down the nerves of her arm, delivering a mix of pain and numbness.

"Fucking faggot," he said. "Don't ever go near my girlfriend again."

Her tingling fingers registered that the pepper spray canister was gone. She must have dropped it next to the building when she hit the wall.

Could she scream and get help? They were tucked into a dark well where the lights from the paths on either side of the buildings didn't reach. This wasn't the most used part of campus after dark, but maybe if she was loud enough someone would hear.

She glanced at the hulking form of the guy who'd hit her. He positioned his body between her and the nearest path so the light was behind him and his face masked in shadows, but he was clearly one of the school's athletes.

She opened her mouth to scream and his thick fist rammed into her stomach. Bile burned in her throat as her gut clenched around the impact, but her legs didn't buckle. She coughed and tried to gasp in a full breath.

"Pat, that you?" another voice asked from the direction of the path.

"Over here," Pat said, "Don't use my name, you idiot."

His words sent a jagged flash of fear through her body. She wiggled her fingers trying to get full sensation and control in them. Did these two actually plan to get away with assaulting her?

"You get that freak?" the nameless guy asked.

"Right here. What should we do with it?"

He punctuated his question with another punch that hit the side of her head and knocked her shoulder into the wall again. Tucker wanted to shout back at him. She wanted to scream with rage, but she knew better. She had to minimize the number of times they hit her so she wouldn't be too hurt to run when she got a chance.

She couldn't run yet. Her head was spinning from the second punch and as soon as he heard his friend approaching,

Pat moved in front of her, standing out from the wall. If she ran forward or tried to dart left, he could reach her. And if she tried to turn and run, his friend could tackle her.

She crouched down and put her left arm up to protect the side of her head, hoping that in the darkness they couldn't see her right hand combing through the gravel for the spray canister. Her fingers dragged through the rough stones but found nothing.

"Aw, it doesn't want you to hurt its face," the nameless guy said in a mincing tone. "Maybe we should break its nose. That'd probably make it prettier."

Pat laughed and the dry, cold sound hit Tucker as hard as his fist and scared her worse. She tried to search through the gravel systematically, but her fingers were shaking hard and scattering the little stones everywhere.

"You think those tits are real?" he asked.

"Do you care?" the other guy asked. "What if it still has a dick?" He paused and spat.

When he spoke again his mouth was only a few feet away from her ear. "Do you still have a dick? You want us to cut it off for you, save you all that trouble? Put you out of your fucking misery?"

A hand grabbed the hair at the back of her head and forced her face up. She saw the squinting eyes of Pat and they looked gray-black in the darkness. His other hand grabbed her breast and squeezed it roughly.

"Fucking boob job," he said. "See if it has a dick."

Tucker's whole body was shaking now. Her mouth was dry as sandpaper or she'd have spat in his face. She wanted to tell him to fuck off, but she was afraid if she spoke he'd hear her teeth chatter and know she was afraid.

And she was afraid, but the rage kept burning through the fear. If they decided to go ahead with their sadistic plan to see what kind of genitals she had, she figured the likelihood that they'd try to rape her was high. She made herself take her focus off them and listen for sounds of other students or campus security. The minute she heard footsteps, she would start yelling even if they hit her again.

The nameless guy reached for her crotch.

Her hand closed over the pepper spray canister.

He was so close she smelled the bitterness of his sweat. Near the ground, her fingers turned the canister and felt for the groove that meant it would be pointing away from her. His fingers poked at her while her index finger found the groove in the front of the canister.

"Nothing here," he said. "Hold it still, I want to see what it looks like."

She took a deep inhale and held her breath. His eyes were narrow with muddy-colored pupils and she met them for a second as she raised the canister and pressed the button. The stream of pepper spray hit him full in the eyes and he screamed with a high-pitched yowling sound like a cat.

She twisted left just far enough to see where Pat's face was and directed the still streaming spray there. He was staring at his friend and the spray caught him mostly on the right side of his face, but it was enough. His hand dropped from her hair and went to his face.

The two of them rolled on the ground, coughing, choking and howling. Tucker straightened up from her crouch and waited a moment for the world to settle itself around her. Her head throbbed from where she'd been hit and her right arm felt bruised in a half-dozen places. She felt ready to scream, puke, and cry. She took a couple of quick breaths through her mouth then leaned down to grab a handful of Pat's hair.

"Should I break *your* nose or chop off *your* dick?" she snarled at him. "You worthless piece of shit."

He was coughing hard enough that she couldn't be sure he heard her so she dropped her hold on him and kicked him hard in the crotch. Then she kicked the other guy too. Their howls went up in pitch.

She wanted to kick them again and again, but this dark alcove wasn't safe. Pat might have told more than one friend to meet him here. Tucker picked up her gym bag with her left hand and started walking slowly toward her dorm. The lawn wavered like the deck of a ship but as she walked it evened out.

Her legs didn't hurt, and she was grateful for that, but every step sent jolts of pain across her right shoulder and up into her skull.

She fell into a rhythm of taking careful steps and breathing. Nothing felt seriously injured, broken or torn, and what hurt most from the whole experience was the conversation the jerks were willing to have over her, as if she wasn't human. She had to turn her mind away from it or she wouldn't make it back to her room without falling apart.

In her dorm, outside the elevator, she paused and put down the gym bag so she could pull the pepper spray canister out of her clenched hand and tuck it into the side pocket. Her right arm didn't want to move any more than it had to. She rode up to her floor but went past her own door and knocked on Ella's.

"One sec," Ella called and then swung the door wide. Her lips parted in shock. "Tucker, oh my God."

"You should see the other guys."

Ella stepped to the side and let Tucker move slowly into the room. As soon as she crossed the threshold, Ella took the gym bag out of her hand and dropped it by the foot of the bed. She swung the wheeled chair out from her desk.

"Sit."

Tucker did so and held onto the arm of the chair with her good hand just to make sure she was completely steady. Ella bent and looked into her eyes and then at the side of her head. Her full lips pressed together hard, making a straight, pink line, as she examined the damage.

"Who hit you?" Ella asked. "Lindy?"

"No! Two guys, outside the gym."

Ella's fingertips brushed high on her cheek. The touch quivered. Ella's other hand gripped the edge of her desk, as if she could use that to pull herself and Tucker to safety.

"We should call emergency services," she said.

"I really don't want to go anywhere," Tucker told her. She felt the burn of tears start in her eyes and tried to blink them back.

"How do you feel?" Ella asked.

"Like I got hit," Tucker said and managed part of a laugh. "Twice. In the head. And my arm hit the wall. I think I'm going to have some bruises but nothing's broken."

As a kid, Tucker had broken her foot and her wrist pulling reckless stunts and she didn't feel the sickening pain now that accompanied those breaks. Her shoulder just throbbed, a big, dull mass of pain.

Ella walked to her desk and typed something into her computer, then scanned down a page. She turned the lamp toward Tucker.

"Look up," she said. The bright light hit Tucker's eyes and made her blink.

"Your eyes look okay, decent pupillary response," she said. "Nausea? Dizziness?" She turned the lamp away.

"No. I was dizzy but it cleared up fast."

"Stay put. I can clean you up, but if you start to feel worse you have to tell me."

"Yes, Nurse Ella."

That almost got a smile, but Ella's mouth stayed compressed, lips stitched together with anger or fear or furious disapproval.

Tucker remained in the chair and watched Ella go into the bathroom and come out with two washcloths. She also got a little white case, a first-aid kit, from her dresser and opened it on her desk.

"You've got a pretty bad cut on your cheek," Ella told her. "I gather one of the guys was wearing a ring."

"Yeah."

"You want to tell me everything that happened?"

Tucker sighed and tried to hold still as Ella dabbed the damp washcloth on the part of her cheek that stung the most.

"It was that girl from the Union. The anti-trans one. The ringleader of that little group. She was in the locker room and she started going off. One of the girls left the locker room to get someone official and I guess when she didn't find anyone, or at least anyone who would listen, she went and told her meathead boyfriend, who decided to try to scare me or something."

"I'd be scared," Ella said in a barely audible voice.

The way she said it made Tucker want to wrap Ella in her arms, and that made her feel better than just about anything else could. She lifted her hand from the chair and rested it on Ella's shoulder. Ella's lips turned up but she stayed focused on Tucker's wound.

"He'll think twice about picking on anyone of the LGBTQIA flavors again," Tucker said. "He and his buddy caught up with me halfway back from the gym, in that spot by Davis Hall where the lighting is shitty. And the first guy called me a faggot and shoved me into the dark spot."

"How does that figure?" Ella asked.

She dabbed gently at the blood, working her way along the painful part of Tucker's cheek. When Tucker flinched, she put her other hand on Tucker's jaw to keep her from turning away and her fingers felt ice cold. The golden curtain of her hair half-obscured her face, but the parts Tucker saw, the cute, broad nose and rounded chin, were white as snow.

Tucker said, "That's what I wondered. Then he hit me again and they got really creepy talking about what they should do next."

"You *have* to report them to campus police," Ella insisted. "I wonder if they can identify one of the guys from the cut from his ring."

Tucker grinned, even though it made her cheek ache. "It's going to be a lot easier than that to find them."

Ella opened a tube of ointment and dabbed it along the cut. It stung some, but the pain was nothing compared to the rest of the evening.

"When the first guy hit me, I dropped the pepper spray I had out, but then I found it in the gravel. And it's the kind with the purple dye in it. Campus cops are going to have no trouble finding them. You should have seen them drop when I sprayed them, and then I kicked them both in the fucking balls."

Tucker glanced up to see Ella staring at her wide-eyed. "Wow."

"I got the spray out because I was in my shorts and it was dark. And then he was waiting to grab me, the stupid shit."

Ella turned back to the first-aid kit and pulled out a bandage pad and some tape. She cut it down to size and then taped it carefully on Tucker's cheek.

"I think that's as clean as I can make it without hurting you worse. You're going to have a bruise I'm sure, but probably not a black eye. I hope you didn't want to look too tough."

"This is fine," Tucker said.

"You need to call the campus emergency line. I'm going to see what I have for bruising."

"How many first-aid kits do you have?" Tucker asked.

"Only two, maybe three…I wanted to be a doctor for about ten minutes before I realized genetics is so much cooler. But no one knows what to get a future geneticist for the holidays so I get all this medical gear."

Tucker went carefully into her room and sat on the bed for a minute staring at the phone. Then she took a long breath, grabbed the orientation packet she'd tossed on her dresser and dialed the number on the back.

"These two guys grabbed me outside of the gym, punched me a few times and slammed me against the wall," she explained after the woman on the other end had clarified that she wasn't in immediate danger. "I had my pepper spray out for walking in the dark so I got them pretty good. They should be showing up in the health center any time now with purple dye all over them. I just wanted to report it. Oh and they called me a faggot and said a bunch of anti-transgender stuff, so it was a hate-motivated thing."

"I understand," the woman said. "Do you need medical attention? You sound like you're in shock."

"I'm back in my room and I want to stay here," Tucker told her. "My roommate is doing first-aid."

"I'm sending campus police over to take a statement and make sure you're okay. What room are you in?"

Tucker told her and was assured that they were on their way. When she hung up, Ella was standing in the doorway. She had an array of items held on a box lid that she was using as tray, including a bottle of painkillers, a white tube of some kind of cream, and a pint of ice cream with two plastic spoons.

"I hope you don't mind excessive amounts of chocolate and caramel," she said.

"I love it."

Tucker pushed two pillows against her headboard so she could sit up comfortably and Ella settled cross-legged against the wall halfway down the bed. Tucker took a big spoonful of the ice cream. It was thickly creamy with a soothing cold that she needed very badly.

"Now the painkillers," Ella said and handed her two pills. Tucker downed those and accepted the ice cream back for another big spoonful.

"I also have something for bruising—want me to look at your shoulder?"

Tucker looked down at her thin T-shirt. It had been off-white and was now smudged with dirt and flecked with blood on the left side. Her right arm still had the kind of grinding hurt that indicated a deep bruise and she wasn't sure she wanted to try lifting it. A flash of helplessness hit her and she bit her cheek to keep from crying. She shook her head at Ella.

Ella set down her spoon and edged across the bed toward Tucker. "If it hurts that much, we should look at it," she said, quiet but resolute.

Tucker shook her head again. She didn't trust herself to talk. She'd felt so tough and protective minutes ago and now she was struggling not to cry in front of Ella.

Ella's fingers touched the collar of her T-shirt. "May I?" she asked.

Tucker managed a tight nod. Ella lifted the collar and peeked under. "It doesn't look too bad," she said. "I can see the bruise forming and…" She shifted her head so that her hair brushed the side of Tucker's face. "Oh, that's ugly. We need to ice that and you should let me put some arnica cream on it."

Wisps of Ella's hair were tickling her collarbone and the gentle touch of her fingers distracted Tucker from the throbbing in her shoulder. She wanted Ella to keep touching her.

"Okay," she said.

She sat away from the wall and pulled the bottom of her shirt up, but halfway she realized she couldn't get it over her head without using both arms and her right arm was still in protest. She was stuck with her left arm hanging half out of her shirt.

"Hold still," Ella said, laughing.

She straddled Tucker's lap, took hold of the shirt with both hands, and worked it over Tucker's mobile shoulder and head, and then let it slip easily down her sore arm.

Tucker abruptly didn't care at all about the pain. She turned her right shoulder toward Ella. "How bad is it?"

"When all the blood comes up, that's going to be one hell of a beauty. You should totally Facebook it—unless your mom's on Facebook," Ella said. "Is it okay to touch?"

"Don't poke it!"

"Hah." Ella leaned back and snared a white tube of cream from the box top tray. She put a thick glob of it on her fingers and with feather touches began spreading it on Tucker's shoulder.

Tucker sat very still. She didn't want Ella to realize how close their bodies were. Warmth radiated from Ella and a sweet scent like baby powder and blackberries. She felt so light and small across Tucker's lap. It wasn't just her size, but there was a way that she carried herself deep inside so that even touching Tucker she held herself away. It was the exact opposite of Lindy's demanding presence and just as compelling. Tucker wanted to pull her close and break through that distance.

A knock sounded on the door and Ella jumped. She scrambled back off Tucker.

"Blanket," Tucker said and pointed at the lopsided afghan at the foot of her bed. Ella picked it up and helped Tucker drape it across herself so she wasn't just in running shorts and a sports bra.

Two campus police were at the door. Ella let them into the room and then tucked herself into the small space by Tucker's closet. The first one in was a woman, on the tall side with maple skin and dirty blond hair pulled back into a high, severe ponytail. Behind her came a stocky guy, oak-skinned, black-haired, who looked uncomfortable about being in a dorm room with three women and stayed near the door with his thumbs tucked into his belt.

The woman introduced herself and the guy, and then started taking Tucker's statement, starting with a series of questions about how she was doing physically and if she needed medical attention. She made sure they understood that the men had referred to her as "it," and made anti-trans statements, and that they grabbed her breasts and crotch.

"I don't know if that counts as sexual assault or a hate crime or both," she said. "But it's really important that's included."

The woman cop nodded. "I have it all in my notes."

They asked a few times if she wanted to go to the hospital but finally relented and strongly suggested she visit the campus health center in the morning.

When they were gone, Ella slipped into the other room and came back with a lumpy package wrapped in a shirt.

"Frozen soup," she said. "It's the closest to an ice pack I've got."

"Thanks." Tucker propped it between her shoulder, a pillow, and the wall and leaned back gingerly. The ice felt just a little less wonderful than Ella's touch.

"Tucker," Ella said as she picked up the softening ice cream. "Maybe it's time to tell people you're not really trans."

"I don't think it would matter. They've got it in for me now and that one girl's going to be pissed that I pepper sprayed her boyfriend. If I tell them, they'll be even madder that I lied. It's kind of a done deal at this point."

"I guess so," Ella said. "But I don't want to see you get hurt again."

"Me either!"

They passed the pint of ice cream back and forth until most of it was gone. At that point Tucker just wanted to turn off the light and close her eyes. She crawled under the blanket and lay back. Ella turned off the light and then seemed to stand for a long time in the doorway before she went back into her room, but later Tucker wondered if she'd just imagined that.

CHAPTER SEVEN

Ella

Just after midnight, I went back and checked on Tucker again but she was sleeping. I thought I should go to sleep too, but I didn't want to turn off my light. Pacing the room didn't help. In compromise, I switched off the overhead light and left on my desk lamp. I got Erasmus the stuffed tortoise from the top of my dresser and brought him to bed with me. Lying on my side with his furry body held to my chest, I looked at the poster of Doradus-30 and tried to imagine I was floating in that cold, vast space with stars being born out of the fiery clouds of matter around me.

Out of the darkness came a huge fist that smashed into my face. I jerked up with a yelp. The little light on my desk illuminated an empty dorm room. My heart pounded. I must have fallen asleep and dreamed it. But the fear felt so real—as if there was still someone waiting just out of sight to hit me.

Minutes passed and Tucker didn't knock on the door. She must have been deeply asleep or maybe I hadn't actually yelled aloud and only thought I had because I was dreaming. I wanted her to come through into my room and comfort me, but that was hardly fair. She was the one who'd been hit tonight, not me.

Erasmus lay on the floor next to the bed where he'd fallen when I sat up. I leaned down to get him and when my fingers touched the soft, brown plush of his shell, I just started crying. I held him hard against my mouth so I wouldn't make a sound and curled my knees to my chest.

They called Tucker "it," I'd heard her tell the cops. They called *me* "it."

What if they found me walking across campus some night and not Tucker? I didn't carry pepper spray. I wasn't strong like she was. I would have curled into a ball and prayed that they didn't kill me.

Would they have killed me?

Would they have killed Tucker?

I wanted to run into her room and cling to her and make sure we were both okay. But I couldn't.

I cried into Erasmus's furry shell until it was damp and matted. My head ached and my eyes felt like sandpaper even though they were wet. Forcing myself to uncurl, I got off the bed, grabbed a tissue from the box on my desk and blew my nose, then sat down in my desk chair.

I both wanted to talk to someone and didn't. If I tried to talk to Mom or Dad, they'd just freak out and I didn't want them to pull me out of school. I had to prove to myself that I could make it in the real world. I could text Nico but I didn't want to put this on ze. Nico acted tough, but I knew it was an act. Sometimes I thought Nico was more vulnerable than I was, even as I envied zir flamboyant gender play, because Nico was the one who heard this kind of shit on a regular basis.

For the last few years I'd been able to just walk around in the world as a regular girl. But Nico and other trans folk who either chose not to play the gender binary or couldn't pass— they got treated in terrible ways. What kind of coward was I that I couldn't even handle tonight?

I wrapped my arms around myself and took long, slow breaths. When my hands stopped shaking, I opened up my microbiology textbook and woke up my computer. After about an hour I went into the bathroom and washed my face, then took the trek through the silent dorm halls to get myself some caffeine from the vending machine. I didn't plan to stay up all night, but every time I thought about getting into bed again I just didn't want to.

When the sky outside the window started to get light around six a.m., I could finally get up from the desk and fall into bed to squeeze in a few hours of sleep before I had to go to class.

* * *

I stopped back in my room after my late morning class. Lindy's voice came from the other side of Tucker's door. The words weren't clear, but her tone was pleading and fussy. I backed quietly out of my room and headed for the dining hall. I'd wanted a quiet lunch alone in my room, but I didn't want to have to run into Lindy in full rescue mode. Mostly I didn't want to have to try to talk to Tucker now with Lindy watching.

Every time I looked at Tucker, I remembered her sitting against the wall by her bed in a bra and shorts looking vulnerable and humming with anger all at the same time. I didn't even have a way to think about what I wanted, but I felt paranoid that Lindy would see it in the way I looked at Tucker.

When she didn't know I was in my room the week before, I'd heard Lindy accuse Tucker of wanting to date me. I didn't know if that was true or not, since I'd also heard Lindy accuse Tucker of having a crush on Summer and on her writer friend Claire.

I was not the best judge of relationships. I hadn't ever really had one. I could look at my mom and dad and see some of the things that make relationships work in the long term, at least with sane adults, but that didn't really help with the whole dating part of things.

It was hard to want to be in a relationship back when my body wasn't right. I know a lot of people have to deal with their body not being the way they want it to be, but gender is such a big thing in our society that it can be a deal breaker. When I looked like a boy, if I asked a girl out she'd be thinking we were in a heterosexual relationship and that I should do all the boy stuff and that wasn't me. And if I wanted to go out with a guy, he'd have to be bi or gay, but if he was gay then he'd also expect me to act like a guy.

It's ridiculously tough to say to someone, "Hey, I know I look like a guy, but I want to go out with you as a girl, okay?"

At thirteen and fourteen when my friends were starting to go out with each other, I was willing to just skip it. And then there were those weird middle years of fifteen, sixteen and seventeen, where I looked like a girl but still had that boy part. Nico never cared about that, and that's one reason we managed to date off and on for a bit. The trouble was that even if Nico didn't care, I did. I just wasn't ready to get into a relationship where we might get sexual and all I had to offer was something I wasn't. Plus I know there are some people who fetishize the hermaphrodite look—ugh. I mean, it's cool in art, but it's not cool when you're talking about my body because then you just don't really get me. When it comes to a relationship that I'm in, I'd rather be part of it.

I also really wanted to come out to Tucker and at the same time I was afraid to—not just because of Lindy, though that was still a top reason, but I didn't know how Tucker would feel when she understood that the person she'd gotten beat up for was me. Would some part of her blame me for what had happened to her?

I went to the dining hall for lunch, then read in the library until my afternoon class. That ended at 3:30 and I headed to the Union just in case Lindy and Tucker were still back at the room. Usually they went to Lindy's apartment, but I didn't know if Tucker's injuries would change that pattern.

Summer and Tesh sat at The Table with big mugs of tea and books spread out in front of them. Only Tesh was actually looking at an open book. Summer spotted me as soon as I walked through the front doors and waved me over. Her black hair was just long enough to pull into a tight, high ponytail, which made her welcoming grin dominate her round face. As

I sat down, Tesh closed her book and widened her smoke-blue eyes expectantly.

"How's Tucker?" she asked.

"Bruised and angry, but she seems pretty good otherwise."

"I wish I'd been able to see her pepper spray those assholes," Summer said. She was still smiling as she said it, which made her look a little crazy.

I shouldn't have been surprised that they had the whole story less than twenty-four hours after it happened. News traveled with dizzying speed in the LGBTQIA group—it was worse than my high school.

"Those fuckers. They found them and they're already out of their dorm rooms," Summer continued. "And they're banned from campus, on top of the assault charges. If they even try to show up around here, they're screwed."

I raised an eyebrow at her.

"Someone posted their pictures online," Tesh told me. She didn't have to add that the someone was probably Summer.

"Don't you think that could backfire?" I asked.

"How?"

"Because they attacked Tucker as a trans woman. I'd be worried that some people might actually side with them."

"Shit," Summer said. "That's messed up. Anyway, the post is just about two guys jumping a woman outside the gym, it doesn't have the details."

"But it will," Tesh pointed out. "You know those girls who've been harassing her will be all over it if they find it."

I felt sick inside. The hazy, terrified sensation of last night returned and it reminded me that I was running on three hours of sleep.

"If there's news online about an assault on campus, I should go let my folks know not to worry," I told the two of them. "Even though they know I'm the last person to be caught coming out of the gym, since I never go into it." I shouldered my bag and headed for the door.

Back in my room I wrote a quick email to my mom and dad letting them know that I was doing fine. I didn't mention the assault on campus, but I gave enough detail of the last few days that if they did see it, they would know it wasn't me.

I slept for a bit and woke around dinnertime, but I didn't want to go to the dining hall or the Union. I had enough food to make a dinner for myself and if I didn't turn on the lights and worked by the glow of my laptop, I could pretend I wasn't there even if someone knocked on my door.

* * *

Shen and Johnny were always happy to see me in the gaming room in their dorm, so I spent Wednesday night there. The loudness of the room was a buffer against my thoughts and I knew none of the topics that could come up in conversation would have anything to do with Tucker or anti-trans attacks or me.

When I came in, Shen and Johnny shoved themselves apart on the couch and invited me to sit between them. Johnny insisted it was so I'd have the best view of the TV screen. The two of them were nearly inseparable. They had most of their classes together, took meals together, roomed together and as far as I could tell, worked out together when they managed to actually make it to the gym.

Not that I'd been stalking them, but it was pretty easy to pick up their movements—in the gaming room, their conjoined twins status was legendary and spawned a variety of jokes ranging from pooping together to the notion that they'd have to date the same girl if they were ever going to get any action.

Apparently this idea occurred to them too because that night when Johnny went to get more pop, Shen asked, "Do you study in the library?"

It took me a minute to realize he was asking me because he was still looking at the TV screen.

"Sometimes," I told him.

"So do I," he said. "Mostly on Wednesdays and Thursdays."

I waited but he didn't say anything else. Was he inviting me to come study with him?

"Do you prefer to study alone?" I asked.

"It's good to have someone to talk to during study breaks," he said. "Unless you prefer to study alone."

"Oh no, I'm a social studier."

That sounded stupid to me so I tried to come up with something else to say, but then Johnny came back and I thought that maybe Shen didn't want him to know about the study... date?

CHAPTER EIGHT

Tucker

The days after getting jumped outside the gym seemed to Tucker like one long chorus of: "Holy [noun of your choice], what happened to your face?"

The most common answer she gave was, "Two guys tried to beat me up for being trans and I pepper sprayed the shit out of them."

The trip to the health center confirmed that she hadn't fractured anything in her cheek or shoulder, and she didn't have a concussion. The school had discovered the guys who'd attacked her about ten minutes after she called the incident in. They were still on the ground outside the gym when a passing coach found them coughing and whimpering. Long story short, the two of them weren't going to Freytag anymore. Pat didn't dispute the charge that he'd shoved Tucker up against the wall, only said that it was necessary because she was creeping around to look at his girlfriend. That didn't fare well as an excuse.

The administration told Tucker she could take a few days off classes if she wanted, but she liked her classes and said that wouldn't be necessary. They also offered a few sessions of counseling but she couldn't imagine trying to tell a well-meaning stranger the whole story about saying she was a trans woman when she wasn't and then being harassed like she was one.

The anger was the hard part. It came over her unexpectedly, randomly, and she wanted to punch someone over and over until bones broke. On Tuesday she started shaking in her Women's & Gender Studies class and had to step out into the hall and gulp air until she no longer felt electric currents traveling from her jaw down to her fists.

She needed to move and to work out the rage in her blood so she took Cal up on his offer of going to the gym to work out together on Wednesday and she didn't try to change in the locker room. Cal was over six feet and easily two hundred pounds. No one came near them in the weight room or when Cal lamely stretched while Tucker ran.

Taking Cal with her meant that she had to listen to him complain about not having a boyfriend, but for once it was comforting. Some part of her knew she was avoiding thinking about Monday night. Her shoulder still hurt and she cut her run short because of it. The jarring motion of her steps on the track turned the dull ache into a painful throb. At least Lindy was being super attentive, bringing her dinner every night and suggesting movies they could watch to keep her mind off it.

When she showed up for Women's & Gender Studies on Thursday, they had a guest lecturer. The TAs had arranged to have two of the smaller recitation groups meet at the same time, and Vivien was the one introducing the guest speaker. Tucker watched Vivien walk up to the front of the room with small, precise steps, but when she got up to the front, her hand gestures were loose and expressive. What was it like with her and Summer? Was she delicate like her stride, or passionate like her hands? Tucker made herself focus on Vivien's words.

"Some of you may have already heard that a female student was attacked while walking across campus last week," Vivien said.

Tucker straightened up in her seat and glared around the room, but no one looked in her direction, not even Vivien. Her hands clenched around the sides of the desk and from his seat next to her, Cal put a hand over hers and gave her a quick squeeze. She pulled her hands away before anyone could see the interaction.

The info posted by Summer online had only said that a woman was assaulted by two men as part of a hate crime, nothing that would identify who or where. And the administration said they'd keep Tucker's identity private.

Vivien continued, "This is Selima Page from the Sexual Assault Response Network of Central Ohio," Vivien said. "She's here to talk to us about feminism and women's safety."

Selima was a heavy woman who carried her weight easily. She reminded Tucker of a darker-skinned, less exhausted version of her mother.

"How many of you think that the feminist movement is a thing of the past and that women and men are now roughly equal?" she asked. About half the hands in the room went up.

"All right," she went on. "Let's do a little exercise." She drew a line in chalk down the middle of the board and stood on the right side of it. "I'd like the men in the class to tell me all the things you do to ensure your personal safety."

A few hands went up.

"I lock my door," one guy said.

"I never leave the gay bar alone." That came from Cal and got a general chuckle from the class.

Selima dutifully wrote both on the board. "Okay, what else?"

The room was silent.

"Anyone?"

"I don't leave my iPod out in my car where someone can see it," one guy offered.

"Personal safety," Selima reminded them. She waited another half minute and then stepped to the left side of the line. "Women in the class, what do you do to ensure your personal safety?"

"I get my key out and carry it pointing out from my fist if I'm walking alone at night," one woman said.

"If I see a strange man coming, I usually cross the street," another said.

"I carry pepper spray," Tucker added to the list.

"I don't wear a short skirt if I'm going to a dance by myself."

"If I see a group of men coming toward me, I step into an open store."

"I get out my cell phone and pretend I'm on a call."

"My mom and I got a pit bull for the house because we live alone."

"I always tell my roommate when I'm going to be back so she knows to look for me if I don't."

"I took self-defense classes."

The answers went on until the entire side of the board was full.

"Well, hell," one of the guys in the class said. "That sucks."

"And that's why we still need feminism," Selima said. "Because too many people believe they can have access to women's bodies wherever and whenever they want, politically or personally. All too often, no matter what women do to prepare themselves, they're not ready for the violence that comes at them from our culture and sometimes from their loved ones. We need to change our culture so that it doesn't teach men that it's an option to attack women."

Tucker thought she should say something about how the attack wasn't just about men and women and sexism but was also transphobic. But in order to say that, she'd have to reveal that she was the one attacked and she didn't want to.

When she came out as a lesbian in high school, she didn't give a shit how anyone reacted. A few times kids called her a dyke and she marched down the hall after them and demanded they meet her face-to-face and tell her what was their problem. They always backed off.

Why was this different? Was it because she wasn't really trans or was she more afraid of being harassed for being trans than for being lesbian? Or maybe it was simply the fact that she'd already been attacked and hurt because of this and she was afraid of provoking another attack.

When class was over and most of the students gone, she went up to Vivien and Selima at the front of the room. Cal followed her.

"The attack was about transphobia," Tucker said. "It wasn't just about a couple of guys attacking a woman walking alone."

"What?" Vivien exclaimed.

"I wasn't attacked because I was a woman, I was attacked for being openly transsexual," Tucker said. The words felt thick in her mouth, but she voiced them clearly enough.

Neither Vivien nor Selima knew who had been attacked and she watched the realization change their expressions. Vivien's went from intense to alarmed, her face shading a paler white, and Selima's broader features narrowed from curious to troubled.

"Oh honey, how are you doing?" Selima asked. "Have you talked to someone about this?"

"I'm okay. Pepper spray really helps with the whole trauma thing."

That got a smile from Selima. She was a honey-eyed woman with her black hair pulled back in a thick braid.

"It helps," Selima said. "But you still need to reach out, get support."

"My friends are helping a lot," Tucker told her, but she thought she might need to cast a wider circle. Her friends here didn't understand the anti-trans aspect of the attack. Like Vivien, most of them reacted to it like she'd been attacked because she was lesbian or because she was a cisgender woman out alone after dark.

"People keep thinking the attack was anti-woman, not anti-trans," Tucker added.

"Transphobia is still based in sexism," Selima said. She picked up her notes and started to sort through them, but her purse got in the way. She held it out to Cal, "Would you be a dear and hold this for me while I get myself organized?"

He took the tasseled and frilled white leather bag and held it carefully a few inches away from his body.

Selima's lips parted in a grin. "Sweetheart, you're perfect. See, it's dangerous in our culture for a man to even associate himself with the trappings of femininity. To keep sexism in place, you have to keep men and women clearly separate. Transsexualism is a huge threat to that."

She retrieved her purse from Cal and said, "Thank you, dear." Pulling a card out of its front pocket, she offered it to Tucker. "I've got to get back to my office but if you need anything at all, call me. You look like you have good friends here, but please never think you have to go through something like that on your own."

Tucker took the card and watched her bustle out through the door.

"Lindy told me you were attacked for being an out lesbian," Vivien said.

That bothered Tucker for two reasons: that Lindy and Vivien were talking about her and because Lindy knew the information she was disseminating was wrong.

"I think the guys were confused about why they were supposed to be upset," Tucker said. "I heard some of the girls saying a lot of anti-trans stuff so I came out to them as a trans woman just to confront them, and then they got all crazy in the locker room and this girl told her boyfriend something that got him really riled even though I didn't do anything and..."

Tucker trailed off. She'd been about to say "I'm not even really a trans woman" but the expression on Vivien's face had changed so much in the past few seconds that she had to stop and look at her again. Vivien's eyes went from open to narrow and cold, and she glanced up and down Tucker's body the same way the women in the Union had: breasts, check; genitals? Dubious.

"Perhaps you shouldn't have been in the women's locker room," Vivien said.

"Are you serious?"

"Women have a right to women-only space."

"I *am* a woman," Tucker said.

Vivien picked up her bag and walked out of the room.

"Whoa," Cal said. "What the fuck was that about?"

Tucker shook her head. She didn't trust herself to talk without yelling or crying.

She went back to her dorm room with a pain burning in her throat and called Claire once she was safely locked in. It went to voice mail and she realized she couldn't leave a message without it sounding like she was crying, because she was. She ended the call.

Tucker had met Emily and Claire when she and Lindy drove up to Madison, Wisconsin, to attend the world's leading feminist science fiction convention last spring. She hadn't even known there were feminist sci fi conventions, but it seemed like a really cool place to be and Lindy got a grant to present her paper there. A moderate fan of the new *Battlestar Galactica*, after Lindy made her watch all of it, and *Firefly*, courtesy of Cal who had a huge crush on Nathan Fillion, she felt a little out of place in the more hardcore fan events but was immediately drawn to all the panels about feminism and gender.

While Lindy sat schmoozing other academic types in the bar on Friday night, Tucker went to some of the readings, including one by Emily Hesse from her recently released semi-autobiographical novel, *Being Emily*. Tucker bought a copy of her book and read most of it that night. Once she started, she didn't want to put it down; she'd never understood before what it would be like growing up in a body that wasn't your gender. Lindy came back late enough and drunk enough that she just let Tucker go on reading.

The next afternoon, she saw Emily in the hotel lobby. Her curly brown hair was in a longer bob than her author photo, but she had the same long, high-cheeked face and warm eyes. She was also an inch taller than Tucker, which Tucker loved, even though in the book she'd read how Emily wasn't that happy about being a tall girl. Tucker thought tall girls were the best.

"I really liked your book," Tucker told her and immediately felt like a dork.

Emily grinned. "Thank you. Claire helped a lot with the words part of it. Have you met her?"

The diminutive woman with long hair dyed black and thick, dark eyeliner held out her hand as Emily introduced her.

"I'm Tucker," she said. "I came up with my girlfriend. She did the paper on 'Treacherous Women Tropes in *Battlestar*

Galactica.' I didn't realize…there was just a lot that I never thought about before I read Emily's book. Like what it must really be like to grow up in a body that doesn't match how you see yourself."

"Most people don't," Claire said. "Come sit with us."

They headed into the restaurant/coffee shop section of the hotel and by the time they got to a table, Emily and Claire had acquired four more people who all wanted to talk to them. Tucker ended up squeezed into a booth with Claire next to her.

"I really liked what you said last night about how important it is to fight for femininity, not just for women's rights," Tucker told Claire. Now that she'd been introduced, she remembered the extended comment Claire had offered from the audience after Emily's reading the night before. "I never thought about it that way. I try hard to keep people from seeing me as girlie and I guess I did always think that femininity was weaker."

"Just like people used to think of women as weaker," Claire said.

"Yeah, that was really wild to see the parallel."

"You came out young, didn't you?" Claire asked.

"How can you tell?"

Claire laughed. "Because you're already out, you've got a girlfriend and you look like you're still in college."

"High school," Tucker said. "I graduate next month."

"I rest my case."

"I don't so much feel that I came out as I just never realized there was another option for me. I never got why the other girls gave a damn about boys. When Emily came out to you, was it like it is in the book?"

Claire shook her head but she was smiling so the gesture came across as only half-negative. She ate a french fry from one of the plates the table was sharing and pushed the plate closer to Tucker.

"Everything took longer in real life than it takes you to read it," she said. "I think it reads like I just got cool about transsexualism really fast, but it seemed like it was forever in my mind. Particularly wondering what it meant about me."

"And you two are still together," Tucker said, gesturing across the table toward Emily.

"We're working on being together again," Claire explained. "I saw some other people the last few years, but I like Emily best. I think I needed to be able to choose her again as Emily, not as Christopher."

"That's so cool."

"Hey, what are you doing after this?" Claire asked.

Tucker shrugged. She wasn't into all the academic panels and hadn't seen anything else that caught her attention on the schedule.

"There's a Mystic Warlords of Ka'a tournament in the gaming rooms, want to swing by with us?"

"What is it?"

"It's a made-up game from a TV series that someone made a real game from and they're testing their prototype. I'm not into the card game scene normally, but I'm a freak for anything real that originated as joke in another context."

"I'm in," Tucker said.

From there it was natural to swap contact info and book recommendations. They stayed in touch online. And then Claire was awesome about answering the million more questions Tucker had about trans women after she attended the Columbus Pride festival that June.

She felt stupid asking the questions, but she would have felt worse if she hadn't asked them. Small town Ohio wasn't a place where she ran into trans women, as far as she knew, and all she'd seen was the bit parts on TV where trans women were trotted out for a laugh or beat up to provide drama in a crime show. There was something about Emily that she really wanted to understand. The night after she met her, she spent a long time staring at herself in the bathroom mirror in the hotel room she and Lindy shared.

She and Emily were about the same height. Tucker might be an inch shorter, but her shoulders were wider because she liked to swim and her bones were thicker than Emily's. Between the two of them, Tucker was the one most likely to be seen as male, and she liked it that way. She enjoyed that when she was working at Shipley's Hardware, strangers were as likely to call her "sir" as "miss." Not that she wanted to be a guy, but she liked it as a neighborhood she could visit.

She hadn't thought about how hard it was to go the other way. She had to dress pretty butch before anyone gave her shit about it, and then it was usually one of her sisters who complained. But understanding how hard it had been for Emily to come out and all the secrecy she'd gone through showed Tucker how tough it was to transition or even just to make a day trip from the vast continent of male over to female.

When she heard stories of women in other countries being oppressed by a brutal regime, she just wanted to go over and get all of them and bring them back to the US and help them have good lives. She felt the same way about the women like Emily who were trapped in maleness. Although she couldn't say exactly what it was, she felt there was something important about those women, not unlike her growing up lesbian. Every kind of woman should have a shot at a great life—and men too; but she didn't worry as much about them.

The cell phone sitting on her dorm room desk rang and Tucker stared at it for a moment before her brain clicked to the present and she realized Claire was calling her back.

"Hey, are you okay?" Claire asked as soon as she answered. "You didn't leave a message."

"Things are kind of fucked up," Tucker said. Her voice was still rough from crying and she had to clear her throat before she could continue. "I got attacked by these guys—"

"Just now? Did you call nine-one-one?"

"Monday night."

"Oh sweetie, are you okay?"

"Yeah, I had pepper spray and everyone's being really great about it except…" She paused and took a long inhale. She hoped this didn't sound stupid. "They came after me for being a trans woman."

"Okay?"

"It's a crazy story," she told Claire.

"Those are my favorites," Claire said, so Tucker started with the girls in the Union and told her the whole thing.

"…and then today in my Gender Studies class, it was like nobody got what really happened and when I told the TA she blamed me. She said maybe I shouldn't have been in the women's locker room because it was women-only space. It was insane."

"Oh sweetie," Claire said again and there was a long pause on the other end of the line. Finally she said, "Are you writing all this down?"

"To document it?"

"Yes, but also just to process it and to remember it. And it will help if you need to take legal action. But right now I want to make sure you're really safe. Are you?"

"Yeah, I'm just pissed. Cal's been walking me around campus and Ella bandaged me up really well."

"Ella…she's your cute roommate?"

"Yeah."

Tucker was glad Claire couldn't see her blushing. She'd sent a few long and complimentary texts to Claire about Ella right after she got the offer to move in and they included a lot of description about how Ella was really pretty, but not like stupid Barbie pretty, just beautiful and with an inner strength. Yeah, she'd gone over the top with the Ella texts.

"Tucker, you realize you didn't mention Lindy."

"She's been really stressed out about her next presentation, but she brings me dinner and stuff. She's trying, she's just not always paying attention. Anyway, the guys who attacked me got thrown out of school."

"Maybe you should come out as cis," Claire suggested. "You'll be safer if people know you're not trans."

"I was going to tell Vivien, the TA, but then she got so shitty about it. And what if it was really true? The only way she's going to learn is to have to deal with a trans student, or at least one she thinks is. There's still a girl here who is, you know. What if she's in that same class?"

"Just take care of yourself. You sound spread thin emotionally. If Lindy isn't taking care of you, make sure you have other support around you. And call me more."

"Okay," Tucker said. "Thanks a bunch. Give Emily a hug for me."

Claire would be graduating from the University of Iowa that spring and planned to move back to the Twin Cities where she hoped to get a job at a local literary journal. She wanted a few years out of school before she thought about going for a graduate degree and this put her near Emily, who still had another year and a half at the U of M due to the year she took after community college to work full-time and complete her transition.

Tucker went to the top of her dresser and found her copy of Emily's book. She wanted to share it with Ella. By the way Ella reacted to Tucker's story about coming out as trans, she thought that Ella would like it. She had trouble reading Ella's reactions sometimes. She seemed to be pretty up on trans issues but not very political. Or maybe she was just shy about discussing her politics. Tucker wished she knew how to draw her out more. Maybe the book would be the thing.

She knocked on Ella's door. Holding her phone, she thought about texting her and asking her when she was coming back to the room. She wanted to talk to her more than anyone else on campus right now and the thought scared her. Claire was right, it was weird that she listed Ella as one of the most supportive people around her rather than Lindy.

There was something to Ella's soft, inquisitive way of listening to her; it gave her the impression that Ella knew a lot more than she let on. She hadn't freaked out when Tucker showed up bruised and bleeding at her door. She hadn't pestered her with a million questions or turned it into a "who's been more victimized by life" contest like Lindy did.

Tucker wanted to stay in her room and wait until Ella came back, but already there were two texts from Lindy asking what she wanted for dinner. She sighed and went back to her desk to put the books she was reading into her backpack.

CHAPTER NINE

Ella

After dinner on Thursday I went back to the room, but Tucker wasn't there. She wasn't in the Union either so I headed for the library to see if I could find Shen.

Shen didn't say where in the library he studied and the building had three floors plus a basement. I figured I'd walk around the first floor and then pick a spot in the open study area near the door and start studying. If I didn't see him in an hour, I'd head up to the second floor and so on.

I sat down with my tablet and my notepad and started looking at the biology text on the tablet. I loved being able to carry a bunch of big textbooks on my tablet but preferred the feel of paper note taking. It felt like my fingers helped my brain learn the material. Maybe someday I'd pool my money and get a smartpen so I could write and upload it to the tablet as text.

After about fifteen minutes I looked up and scanned the room. No Shen. I went back to reading and looked up again about ten minutes later. Still no sign of Shen and, as it turned out, there was one major flaw in this plan. A moment after I was absorbed in the book again, I felt someone sit down next to me. I looked over to see a total stranger smiling at me.

"Hello?" I said.

"You looking for someone?" he asked.

He was tall and lean with Finland-meets-England ruddy tan skin and short brown hair in a messy style—if that was an intentional style.

"A classmate," I told him.

"Are you sure it's not me?"

He was trying to make a joke, or a come on, or a joking come on. He sprawled out in the chair with his legs stretched close to mine and one arm thrown along the back, making his already long body look bigger.

"Pretty sure," I said with the emphasis on "sure."

"You should give me a try," he said.

"Have we met?" I asked, trying subtly remind him that he was a total stranger to me and his presence might not be welcome.

"Yes, just now."

"I don't know you," I persisted.

"I'm Mike," he said.

"What I mean, Mike, is that you're someone I don't know who just interrupted my studying and I'd like to get back to my book now."

"You don't have to be like that," he said, getting up from the chair. "I was just trying to be friendly."

I didn't answer that and he got up and stood there for a few seconds exuding hurt just to see if that would work. It didn't. I knew better than to look up from my tablet again and in a moment he gave a loud sigh and walked away.

This sort of thing happened to me fairly often when I went anywhere alone, which was one reason I rarely did. I could walk into a coffee shop and be checking out the décor and a complete stranger would come up and say something about the weather or ask what I was reading or, most awkward of all, tell me how pretty I was.

I felt like saying, "I'm not sitting here being pretty for you. I just won the genetic lottery and I like wearing makeup so I look pretty to myself." But I usually said, "Thank you" and then "I've got a lot of studying to do." If that didn't work, I just got up and left.

I remembered being fourteen years old and going into a coffee shop and reading for a whole hour and no one ever talked to me. I could stare around the room all I wanted and the only thing that happened was that people would look away from my direct gaze. Not that I sat around staring at people, but I liked to check them out and hypothesize about their genetic heritage or think about human evolution in general. Why did we grow bodies that could make us that big or that small? How did we escape having long necks or tiny forearms?

By the time I was almost fifteen, as if someone had flipped a switch, the world began reacting differently to me. I shouldn't make it sound that cosmic: the switch was hormones. At fourteen I was able to go from just taking the blockers that prevented me from entering male puberty to taking female hormones. This was a compromise with Mom and Dad. I wanted to start at twelve or thirteen, they wanted me to wait until sixteen, just in case I realized this wasn't the path for me. We fought about it some and hammered out a date we could all live with.

Back then I couldn't understand how they could be so cool and so pigheaded at the same time, but that was because I could tell I was lagging behind the other girls and it was driving me crazy. I don't know whether it's worse being a late bloomer and not knowing when you're going to hit puberty or knowing it's there waiting for you and you just can't have access yet because someone else decided it was too soon. At least I knew that mine was coming.

And once it happened, I could sort of understand Mom and Dad's fears—but I was never going back. The trouble is that gender dysphoria is not something you can see so Mom and Dad thought they had a son. They'd spent ten years thinking they had a son before my continued insistence that I was a girl wore through Mom's defenses and she realized what I was trying to tell her. So then I'm a boy in their minds and I'm changing who I am—or that's how it seems to them because they've never experienced the feeling of their self-perception and their body not matching up. They wanted to make sure I wasn't "changing" something I couldn't change back, but to me it was never a change.

It's hard to describe to them or friends or anyone what it's like. It's kind of like the phantom limb thing where a person loses their arm but they keep feeling it should be there, it's actually hurting but they can't do anything about it because it's not really there—but the brain keeps sending the signal anyway, "Hey, move your arm." Well, my brain kept saying "Hey girl" and the limb was my whole body.

I hit puberty at seven a.m. on November 13, six months after my fourteenth birthday. That was the morning I first took hormones. Nothing big happened, I just added a pill to the GnRH and the multivitamin Dad made me take. It was rather a letdown.

Everything started to change the following spring. I was still going out in public as a boy. I mostly wore jeans and T-shirts with geeky stuff on them and kept my hair shaggy but on the short side. I looked a little young for my age in general and with the hormone blockers I looked extra young, so mostly people thought I was a twelve-year-old boy instead of nearly a fifteen-year-old girl. My guy friends assumed I was going to come out as gay at any minute since I had a lot of female friends and a reputation for being a sensitive guy and a great listener. That didn't bother me since I did think some guys were cute, I just didn't want to date any of them while I was still a guy. I didn't actually want to date a girl either with a boy's body so I cultivated an asexual, late bloomer identity.

That spring I had to start binding my breasts under my T-shirt in order to keep passing as a boy. We planned that I'd grow my hair out over the summer and come back to school for my junior year as myself, as Ella, but it was getting harder to hide the way my body was changing. The shape of my face slowly altered and I began to put some padding on my butt and hips.

My friends didn't really notice, or at least they weren't aware of noticing, because they were so used to the way I looked that I don't think they saw changes: the way you don't see a friend losing or gaining a little weight. But if I went into a store on my own, I could be called "miss" by one person and a minute later it was "young man" from someone else. That lasted until the summer when I started to grow my hair out and didn't hide having breasts anymore.

At fifteen I'd lost the ability to sit quietly in a coffee shop for an hour without someone trying to strike up a conversation with me, but compared to everything I gained, I really couldn't complain.

I shook myself out of the memories and looked at the time on my tablet. I'd spent forty-five minutes on the first floor, I could legitimately start moving up through the library without feeling like I was here just to stalk Shen.

The second floor of the library had two study areas. I looked into the larger one first but didn't see him so I headed for the little one: a service room before the library was renovated. Now the space had a couch along one wall and a small table with three chairs at either end. Shen was tucked into the near corner with his books spread out on the table there.

"Oh hi," I said. "This is a cool space."

He looked up. "Ella. I am hiding from my cousin. I'm glad you found me."

"You're safe, I doubt he's left the gaming room."

"He is quite loud and talkative."

"Well, I didn't want to interrupt you…"

He smiled. "Your interruption is welcome." He pulled the chair next to him back from the table. "Will you join me?"

"Thanks." I sat down and tried not to grin a bunch. I had no idea what to say now that I was here. "I've been wondering where you're from," I said and then immediately felt dumb.

"China," he said deadpan, but I caught the mischievous glint in his eyes.

I flipped my hair over my shoulder and widened my eyes, "Oh my gawd, is that, like, really far away?"

He laughed. "You got me. You want to know what city? Kunming. Southern China. Very beautiful. Cool summers and soft winters. And yes, I miss it."

"What do you think of America? Are we still the land of opportunity?"

"More like land of innovation and favorable exchange rate," he said.

"So you'll go home after you graduate?"

"It depends where the jobs are in three years. Where do you come from?"

I oriented myself toward a direction I hoped was easterly and pointed. "About two hours that way."

"Closer," he said.

"Much."

"You didn't want to go far?"

"Not yet," I said. "Someday I'd love to travel."

"Will you be a scientist?" he asked and we got talking about biology and career aspirations. From there somehow we got on the topic of gaming and the kinds of characters we like and the games. He liked the science fiction games and playing characters who were part or all machine.

"Machines are very elegant," he said. "But it's best when a character is both the messy human and the disciplined machine. The struggle is good between the two. Johnny and I go to movies on Fridays. What is your feeling about the Resident Evil movies?"

"Guilty pleasure," I said with a grin. I am a sucker for women-with-guns movies.

"Perhaps would you join us?"

"I'd love to, but are you sure Johnny won't mind?"

"Of course not," he said.

And with that we went back to studying. Or at least it looked like he was studying, I was staring at the words on my tablet without reading any of them and trying to figure out what the deal was. Did he like me? It seemed that way when he asked me to come study with him, but then why would he invite me out with both him and Johnny? What if Johnny was the one who liked me and Shen just offered to invite me when Johnny wasn't around so it wouldn't embarrass him? Or what if both of them just wanted to be friends and were inviting me to their weekly movie night because they thought I was fun?

I wondered if it was true that they'd have to date the same girl. I didn't want to date Johnny, but we could work that out later if it turned out this was really a date.

* * *

When I went back to my room, I wanted to talk to Tucker and ask her what she thought about that interaction with Shen. And I wanted to know how she was doing, but she still wasn't there. I was starting to feel like I would never see her again.

Finally on Friday afternoon when I got back from class I heard music coming from her side of the door. I tapped on the bathroom door to Tucker's room so she'd know it was me. I'd already told her to just ignore me if she was working on something and when I didn't hear a response in a few seconds I went back to my room. I got a glass of water and, since I was caught up on my schoolwork, I flopped down on my bed to do a little pleasure reading.

Minutes later, I heard a tap on my room's inner door. "Come on in," I called.

Tucker came in and sat on the foot of the bed. The cut on her cheek had a thick scab over it.

"You should keep a bandage on that for a few more days," I told her. "Unless you want it to scar."

She laughed a little. "You're sure you're not pre-med?"

I blushed and turned around to fish in my dresser for the Neosporin. There was only one reason I knew a lot about scars and it had nothing to do with studying biology. Maybe it was time to tell Tucker that chapter of my history.

"At least let me put some Neosporin on it," I said.

She didn't protest as I put a dab of the cream on my finger and rubbed it along the cut on her cheek. I replaced the tube in my dresser and sat back down in my desk chair.

"How do you feel?" I asked.

"Sore. And tired of answering that question," she said.

"Well then, let me change the topic." I was still debating how to come out in my head, so I picked the next thing on my mind. "How do you know if a guy likes you?" I asked.

She raised her eyebrows at me. "Hell if I know."

"Well, I mean, anyone?"

"They laugh at all your jokes," she said. "And smile a lot. Or they corner you during a party and fuck your brains out, it kind of depends on the person."

I couldn't think of a thing to say about that because I was trying not to think about Lindy…yeah, no. Ugh. Tucker, on the other hand—the idea sent a wave of heat from my knees up to my scalp.

"What are you up to?" I asked her, in order to change the topic again, and reached for the glass of water on my desk.

"Working on the Gender Studies paper. I can't seem to say what I want to. Vivien, my TA, totally pissed me off yesterday. She said maybe I shouldn't have been in the women's locker room as a trans woman, that it was women-only space. Can you believe that?"

I forgot about the water I was sipping and inhaled sharply, giving myself a fit of choking. Tucker grabbed the glass so I wouldn't drop it and waited while I coughed myself back into clear breathing.

"Sorry," I managed. "Swallowed wrong. Go on."

"That was it," Tucker said. "As soon as I said the attack was anti-trans she was done with me."

I was sitting completely upright from the coughing attack and I crossed my arms and held them tightly against my chest. In a way it was even more frightening than the idea of being attacked for who I was—the idea that allies could turn away for the same reason.

"That's awful." I pushed the words out of my mouth. I didn't know what to say. It felt like I was comforting someone who should have been me and at the same time I was over here being as upset as if they'd come after me and not Tucker.

I had to get her to stop pretending to be me, even though she didn't know it was me. Could I do that without coming out to her myself?

But the truth was, I really *did* want to come out to her now. We'd been friends and roommates for only a month, but already I felt as close to her as I'd been to my best friends in high school—well, except Nico.

Coming out was always a weird thing because it could completely change how someone thought about me, and I didn't feel like I wanted to come out to a lot of people. It was a really personal thing and I'd always been a girl in my own experience so there wasn't that much to reveal. But it wasn't about revealing, it was about sharing. In our late-night chats Tucker had already told me a bunch about growing up with a single mom and not having a lot of money and how that shaped her experiences. Telling her about how I'd been born and grown up was the same order of information—the kind of detail your close friends know and love you all the more because of it.

"I had no idea how much anti-trans feeling is still out there," Tucker was saying. "I mean, I have the ability to undo my coming out, but so many people don't and they have to put up with this shit. I don't know why it bothers me more than anti-lesbian stuff. I guess I feel like it's a different kind of ignorance. Plus as a lesbian I really could hide that if I wanted, but trans people don't always have that choice."

"Not always," I agreed.

"Oh hey, I have something for you," Tucker said. She went back into her room and reappeared through the doorway a moment later with a book in her hand. "I thought if you have time you might want to read this. I know the woman who wrote it, she's really cool, and it's about her coming out as trans, and I think if you read it then it'll help you understand more about what's going on with the transphobic shit on campus and all that."

The familiar cover made me smile. "I've read it," I told her.

I'd read all of them. There weren't so many trans books in the world that you couldn't blow through all of them in under a year, even with classes and homework, and then wish for more.

"You have? What did you think?"

"Tucker…can I trust you to keep something confidential, just between you and me?"

"Of course. You want me to swear to it or something."

"I trust you," I said, and I did.

Now I just had to remember what my coming out speech was.

A loud knock sounded on Tucker's door and we heard Lindy's voice calling her name. Tucker got up but before she could cross back into her room, Lindy was knocking on my door and saying loudly, "Tucker, are you in there?"

I nodded at Tucker and she opened my door. "I'm here."

"Why are you always in her room?" Lindy asked.

"I'm not. I've been at your place all week. We're just catching up. We're friends, you know, we do that."

"Well, are you coming back to my place?"

"Sure," Tucker said, though she didn't sound enthusiastic. "But not right away."

"Were you there this afternoon? Did you move my papers?" Lindy asked.

"No."

"Someone moved them. Someone's been through them." Lindy's words rose in volume.

"It wasn't me," Tucker shot back in frustration. "Who else have you had over?"

Lindy's face was turning red and she sputtered with her answer, but before she could get actual words out, someone farther down the hall called, "Hey, is that room 226?"

The voice was beautifully familiar and reminded me of home. I pushed past Tucker and Lindy into the hall. Nico was standing three doors down under the watery golden glow of the overhead light, looking to me like an Afro-Asian god/dess.

"Nico!"

Nico came down the hall and caught me in a crushing hug. After a moment, I was held at arm's length while Nico looked me up and down. This gave me a good view of Nico's current look as well.

Nico's presentation changed like the seasons—regular and yet unpredictable. Over the summer the highly feminine garb of our senior year had been falling away and now Nico looked like a very pretty man wearing dangling jewelry on one ear and serious guyliner—or was the look sort of a neo-butch lesbian play? I couldn't decide. With Nico, that was usually the point.

The quarter-inch buzz cut of Nico's black hair suggested masculinity, but the jewelry was highly feminine. The rest of Nico's outfit included heavy black leather boots with a girl-style narrow foot, worn boy-style jeans and a T-shirt under a bright blue-green Nehru-style Indian jacket that wasn't buttoned.

"Ella, baby doll, what the hell? I read about this online! Who got attacked? Are you safe?"

I shook my head in a frantic "no" motion and looked at Tucker and Lindy, who had both stepped out into the hall. If Nico had heard that a trans woman was attacked on my campus it would be logical to think it could have been me, but Nico was a half-second shy of outing me.

Nico looked from me to Tucker to Lindy, back to Tucker, back to Lindy, then said, "Hey, I'm Nico."

"This is my roommate Tucker and her girlfriend Lindy," I said. "Nico's a friend of mine from high school."

"You drove all the way up here to check on her just because a woman was attacked on campus?" Tucker asked.

"Oh, I messaged her first," Nico said. "But someone has been unusually tight-lipped on the Interwebs the last few days. You can't tell me something isn't wrong." That last was directed at me.

"It was Tucker," I said. "They attacked her."

"Holy beans, you're the cis girl who came out as trans?" Nico grabbed Tucker's hand and shook it heartily. "Majorly cool, man."

I was used to watching people watch Nico and learning a lot about them by their reactions. Tucker looked confused but had a lopsided grin that widened as Nico shook her hand. Lindy's face mixed distrust and wariness. I could watch her trying to work out what to ask Nico without sounding too horribly rude.

"So are you Ella's boyfriend?" Lindy finally asked.

Nico looked at me. "You have a boyfriend?"

"You know I don't," I said. "At least not yet."

The air in the hallway thickened. Nico's eyes looked intense with the weight of unasked questions that had nothing to do with dating and everything to do with why I wasn't out and whether or not I was safe. Lindy's face was a narrow mask of suspicion. And Tucker was trying to smother her smile so it wouldn't look like she was laughing at Lindy's discomfort—which she was.

"I thought you said you hadn't had a girlfriend," Lindy persisted with her questions by directing this one at me.

"I haven't," I said.

An edgy silence fell over our group and I just had to break it. I didn't like Lindy very much, but it was too hard to watch her try to work out what she could or couldn't ask.

"I love that look," I told Nico. "It's so dyke George Clooney in drag. How does it play at OSU?"

"Drives everyone crazy," Nico said with a grin. "I went back to using per instead of ze."

"I thought 'per' didn't carry well in loud places," I said. Nico cycled through gender-neutral pronouns as often as through looks.

"Yeah but with 'ze,' people kept screwing up and reverting to 'he.' And it would have been cool if they then turned 'zirself' into 'herself,' but they didn't. Gender's just stubborn like that. I figure with 'per' at least they'll turn it into 'her' when they screw it up and that counterbalances the pretty boy butch look."

I laughed. "I wanted you to try 'yo.'"

"That's next when I get sick of 'per.'"

"You can use 'yo' as a third-person pronoun?" Tucker asked.

"Some kids started doing it spontaneously," Nico told her. "Like, 'Have you seen yo?' and 'Isn't that yos jacket?'"

"Sweet," Tucker said. "Are you here for the weekend?"

"As long as my baby girl will have me," Nico said with a sidelong look at me.

"You two really never dated?" Lindy asked.

"Oh we dated, I was just never a boyfriend or girlfriend," Nico said. "And anyway, it didn't last."

"Too much geek all in one place," I said in answer to Tucker's raised eyebrows.

"Well, if you're here tomorrow night, come to the party at Cal's," Tucker said to Nico. "It's just a casual thing."

"Thanks," Nico told her. "That'd be cool."

Tucker put her hand on Lindy's arm and pulled lightly so they moved down the hall past us to the door to Tucker's room. She opened it and Lindy went ahead of her into her room. Tucker turned back to me and her eyes were full of questions.

I shook my head at her. I wanted to come out to her so badly, but not with Lindy there. If it had only been Tucker, me and Nico, that would have been the most perfect coming out ever, but no. I went into my room with Nico right behind me.

"You have not been telling me the full story," Nico said.

I put a finger to my lips and crossed the room to my iPod and speakers. I turned on music and kicked the volume up high enough that Tucker and Lindy couldn't hear us, but not so high that we couldn't talk normally.

Nico sat on my bed and scooted back to lean against the wall. "Not the full story," per repeated. "What *is* up with those two? That angry one is like a violin string about to snap. And Tucker, hot damn, you just said she was cute, but she's like: oh. my. gawd."

"Well, I was going to try to take a pic to email you, but I hadn't figured out how to set it up to look casual. I couldn't really be like, 'Hey, Tucker, I want to show my friend Nico how adorable you are.'"

Nico paused and raised an eyebrow. "Yeah you could. As long as that possessive Polly wasn't with her. So you're not out to her either?"

"Again, Lindy," I said by way of explanation.

Nico nodded. "I get that. Still, girl, I panicked when I saw that article online."

"There's an article?"

"On a trans news blog I follow about how a trans girl was attacked up here. My heart seriously stopped."

"I told you I was okay."

"You know you always say you're 'okay' when you're freakin' losing it, right?"

"Oh."

"So?"

I climbed onto the bed, crawled over to Nico and curled against per chest.

"I'm so glad you're here," I said and started crying.

Per arms tightened around me and I felt the comforting pressure of per cheek on the top of my head.

"I got you," Nico said quietly and let me cry.

CHAPTER TEN

Tucker

"I've never met anyone genderqueer who was so…good at it," Tucker said. She and Summer were sitting on the porch at Cal's place waiting for more party guests to arrive.

"Well, what did Ella say about her dating life? She said she'd kissed girls and something about it being about the same with boys, but then Nico said they dated, right? Maybe we can figure it out that way," Summer suggested.

"You haven't even met Nico yet and you're already trying to figure per out."

"Oh and you didn't, Ms. High and Mighty? Nice use of the gender-neutral pronoun; how long did you have to practice that?"

"Okay, yeah, I wondered about Nico," Tucker admitted.

"See!" Summer pushed off the ratty outdoor couch and went to get another beer.

Cal lived in the bottom half of a duplex with a broad, broken-down front porch and a worn deck off the back. His roommate was in an ongoing relationship with a girl who lived across town and he was gone more weekends than he was home, so Cal's place became a frequent gathering spot for the LGBTQIA Alliance parties. They were only a block off campus and this was Cal's second year renting there. The upstairs unit was also rented to Freytag students so they didn't complain about the noise as long as they could come down and raid the beer cooler on the back deck.

The weather was still nice enough that on the screened-in porch, Tucker wasn't cold in a T-shirt and could enjoy the soft wind moving around her. A rich, sweet, jasmine smell carried from the little white flowers climbing a trellis in the neighbor's yard and mixed with a sharp metal tang from the half-cleaned bike parts in a heap against the porch wall. Tucker inhaled deeply. It reminded her of working in the back of the hardware store with the windows open.

Her phone vibrated and she read the text from Lindy: *Where are you?*

Cal's. You coming? Tucker typed.

Is Summer there?

Yeah, why?

Vivien asked, Lindy wrote.

Tucker didn't recall Lindy having any classes with Vivien this semester. What was going on? Did Vivien want to know about Summer because she was trying to meet up with her? But why not just text her? Or was she trying to avoid her? Summer hadn't mentioned Vivien recently and Tucker wasn't sure if those two were still hooking up or not.

She typed to Lindy, *Is she looking for Summer or avoiding her?*

We're on our way, Lindy replied.

Hearing familiar laughter, Tucker looked up from her phone to see Ella and Nico coming up the walk together. A few inches taller than Ella, Nico had an arm draped easily around her shoulders. Tucker's chest clenched. She wanted both to join them and to push them apart.

They opened the door to the porch and she stood up.

"I'll give you the tour," she offered.

Ella looked better than she had all week. Tucker had only seen her in passing until Friday, and her face had been shadowed with fatigue and worry. Now her green eyes were bright again.

She was in dark jeans and a gray T-shirt over a white waffle-weave long underwear shirt. The effect of the slightly butch outfit made her look even smaller and more delicate than usual. Nico was in a denim jacket over a shimmering multicolored shirt with slender pants tucked into heavy boots. As before, Nico struck Tucker first as a guy who was cross-dressing, then as a woman who was passing as a pretty man wearing male-style eye makeup. In the time it took them to walk across the porch and into the living room, Tucker changed her mind about Nico's gender three times.

"There's beer on the back deck in a cooler, and another cooler of water and pop, plus some other drinks in the fridge." She didn't have to point out the food since it was spread over the dining room table and buffet.

Tesh sat on the couch by the front windows, her short brown hair sticking up wildly in many directions as it often did after a long day of running her hands through it while she studied. Cal was in the big armchair next to her, his tall body bent toward her with one elbow propped on a thick armrest. Summer came into the room from the back deck with three beers in her hands.

"Hey guys, this is Ella's friend Nico from OSU. Nico, that's Tesh on the couch and Cal next to her and this is Summer."

Summer put two beers on the coffee table in front of Tesh and Cal and held the third out to Nico.

"Want one?" she asked.

"Sure. Thanks."

Ella rolled her eyes and Tucker wondered if she often got overlooked next to Nico. They were both striking but in such different ways. Nico clearly dressed to draw attention. It was hard not to want to look at per.

"Since when do you drink?" Ella asked Nico.

"I'm a college student now," Nico said and took the bottle Summer was offering.

"You want anything?" Ella asked Tucker.

Tucker held up the half full can of Pepsi she was drinking and shook her head. Ella went toward the back of the house. Summer dropped onto the couch in the middle, next to Tesh, and patted the open space on her other side. Nico obligingly took it.

"What's Nico short for?" Summer asked. "Nicholas?"

"Nope," Nico said.

"Nicole?"

"Still no."

"Nikhita?"

Nico shook per head. "If you must know, my birth name is Nehal, but my little sister started calling me Neho and it just morphed."

"Is Nehal a boy's name?" Summer prompted.

"It's unisex."

"Seriously?"

"Look it up," Nico said and gave her a wide grin.

Summer paused and smiled back at Nico because it was almost impossible not to smile at Nico up close. Nico's thick lips framed the sort of bright white teeth you usually saw on TV and with per high, wide cheekbones even a small smile looked like an invitation to mischief. Per had warm brown skin and hazel eyes outlined with kohl and weighted down gently by well-shaped black brows. No matter what gender you read into per, Nico was a beautiful person.

"Okay." Summer switched tracks. "So was Ella out when you two dated?"

"Out as what?"

"Bi, right? What else?"

"She has a lot to come out about. She didn't tell you about her embarrassing Bollywood phase? I'll bet she still has a sari in the back of her closet. You should ask her."

"I do not," Ella said. She'd just returned from the kitchen with a bottle of orange soda. There were four folding chairs around the room and she carried the nearest one to the side of the couch where Nico was sitting so she could be on Nico's right.

Tucker leaned against one of the wooden columns that separated the living room from the dining room and sipped her warm Pepsi. She disliked not being the one Ella gravitated toward in a group.

Lindy came in the back way with Vivien. Tucker heard their voices in the kitchen and then they pushed through the swinging door into the dining room. Lindy paused at the table, but Vivien came to the archway between the rooms and leaned against the column opposite where Tucker was standing.

The muscles in Tucker's arms and across her shoulders tightened. What business did Vivien have coming to this party after how cold she'd been in class? Lindy must have invited her, since they'd come in together, which meant this was all Lindy trying to kiss up somehow. Why did Vivien care about a party of undergrads anyway? Weren't there enough queer people at the graduate level in this school?

"Hey," Summer said to Vivien and Tucker couldn't tell if that was meant as a warmly casual greeting or not. It sounded pretty distant for Summer and gave Tucker no clue about where they stood romantically. On the bright side, Summer was never one to withhold information so Tucker could just ask her later when they were alone and get the scoop.

"Nice place," Vivien said.

"It's Cal's," Summer told her. "You've met Tesh. And that's Nico and then Ella; Nico came up from OSU to visit Ella." To Ella and Nico she said, "Vivien's a grad student in Women's & Gender Studies."

Lindy came into the living room balancing a plate of food in one hand and holding a beer in the other. She gave Tucker a quick kiss on the cheek and took the empty chair between where Tucker was and Cal. She was in worn, gray jeans and engineer boots, along with a brown sleeveless T-shirt that brought out the olive tones in her skin and showed off her ropey arm muscles. A wave of desire rolled through Tucker's gut. Lindy's strong arms and hands were one of Tucker's favorite things about her.

"Glad you could make it," Cal said to the room at large.

Introductions managed, Summer turned back to Nico. "Okay, now, seriously Nico, it's driving me crazy, are you a boy or a girl?"

Nico's smile widened. "Both," per said.

Cal laughed.

Summer pushed on, "But, how can you be both, is that like a hermaphrodite?"

"Intersex," Cal said.

"Genderqueer," Ella suggested.

"Don't be rude," Tesh told Summer. "That's a really personal question."

Nico said, "I never talk about genitals on the first date."

Cal choked on his beer, grabbed a napkin, and held it to his nose as he sputtered.

"That's a good policy," Tucker said in a light tone. Nico seemed good at handling perself, but Tucker didn't want per to have to spend the next hour dodging questions about gender.

"Okay fine, no genitals," Summer said. "But what is genderqueer anyway? Is it mostly a style or like a political thing or what?"

"Some of each," Nico said. "By screwing with the gender binary you make more space for people to be themselves."

"Screwing with the gender binary is something you have to be in a very privileged position to do," Vivien said. She'd crossed her arms across her chest and was leaning with her back against the edge of the square pillar. When she pinched up her eyes like that, she looked like a predatory fox. "Most people can't afford that luxury."

"Then those of us who can should do more of it," Nico replied.

"Why don't you spend some of that energy helping out the women in third world countries stuck under horrible regimes?" Vivien asked.

Tucker wondered what the hell Vivien's deal was. She was already harsh and opinionated in class and that kind of worked when she was teaching, but this was a casual party. With a sinking feeling, Tucker wondered if her own presence had something to do with it. Was Vivien aiming some of her anger at her?

"How do you know I'm not?" Nico asked. "You just met me. I could be good at dressing fabulously *and* fighting for international women's rights. And don't you think at some level enforcing and policing gender *is* the issue? If anyone can be anything, then there can't be any gender-based oppression. Patriarchy is a system that oppresses men too."

"You must be one if you think that way," Vivien said in a cool, disconnected tone.

"See how you think it's okay to try to force me into the gender binary?" Nico told her.

"A man would think he should have access to anything he wanted," Lindy pointed out. "It's natural to think you grew up male if you think you can just be any way you want to be. You never suffered under the oppression women suffer in this culture."

"Hey, I think I can be any way I want," Summer said. She leaned forward and put her beer down on the table with a loud thunk. "It's not just about men and women, you know. You're just blowing past all the race and class issues people live with."

"And do you really want to get essentialist like that?" Nico asked. "All men are a certain way?"

"She's not saying it's their biology," Vivien said. "But in our culture men are raised with privilege. Look at the fact that there are more people transitioning from male-to-female than the reverse and tell me that men don't have things women don't have."

Her gaze cut sideways and brushed over Tucker as she talked and then Tucker knew it was about her as much as it was about Nico. Probably more about Tucker when it came down to it. Had Lindy told her that Tucker wasn't trans or did Vivien still think she was and wanted her to know that Vivien thought of her as a man with privilege rather than a woman caught in a particularly shitty situation?

Nico shook per head and gestured widely with per hands. Per said, "I'm not disputing that people assigned male or perceived as male on average make more money in most of the world. Everybody knows that and it's ridiculous. But if nobody knew who was assigned male at birth, how would they even know who to pay unfairly?"

"Not everyone wants to be genderqueer. What about all the women who just want to go on being women but be equal?"

Vivien asked. She unfolded one arm and jabbed the air with her index finger as she talked.

"It's also about femininity," Ella said. Her voice was quieter than the others in the room, but clear enough that everyone heard.

"That's what Selima was saying," Tucker added. "The guest speaker in our class. She said that it's dangerous for men to be feminine."

Ella nodded to her and continued speaking, "I think maybe at some level it would be good if feminism was about raising up women but also femininity, no matter where it is. Sometimes it's the delicate and the weak and the yielding aspects of life that are the most important. Power isn't all about muscles and weapons—microbes can make or break civilizations."

"Are you saying all fungus is female?" Nico asked, casting a sideways grin at Ella. Tucker got the impression this was a topic that Nico and Ella had talked about before and felt a pang of envy that she hadn't been part of those conversations.

"At least the yeasts and molds," Ella told Nico as she smiled back at per. "I've seen some pretty male mushrooms."

"I think I dated a few of those," Cal said with a hearty laugh. Tesh slapped him on the arm, but not very hard.

"You say you're against the gender binary, but by playing with gender like that, you're just making it more real," Vivien continued, unfazed by the humorous attempts to move the conversation to lighter topics. "You can't blend male and female unless they exist as separate and are capable of being blended. You can't be genderqueer unless there's a norm that your queerness is defined against, so in a way you keep reinforcing the gender binary."

"I can be both genderqueer and feminist," Nico said. "I can be for the eradication of patriarchal power and sexism in our culture and still screw around with gender as a personal choice about how I want people to see me."

"But you want more gender rather than less."

"Maybe both of those are the same thing," Cal offered. "More gender means more self-expression and if you did away with gender you'd also see more people just expressing themselves as people. It's a win either way. We're on the same side."

He got up from his chair and picked up empty beer bottles from the coffee table. "Who needs a fresh drink? And there's ice cream in the freezer."

"I'll serve ice cream," Ella said as she hopped up. "Who wants?"

Hands went up around the room. Ella followed Cal into the kitchen. Tesh got off the couch and Summer gestured Vivien over to the now empty spot on her left. Vivien hesitated but went to sit next to her. Lindy got up and pulled another folding chair next to her, near where Tucker was standing.

"One sec," Tucker told her. She went across the room to Nico's end of the couch and crouched down. "Are you the reason Ella knows so much about trans politics?" she asked Nico quietly.

Nico looked at her for a long time. "No," per said finally. "Ella's cooler than that. You want to know why she thinks the way she does, you ask her."

Tucker went back across the room to sit next to Lindy and talk about things they'd already talked about a hundred times, but she watched Nico out of the corner of her eye. Ella seemed so comfortable around Nico. Maybe there wasn't a direct connection between Nico being genderqueer and Ella knowing about trans issues, but an indirect one. Did Nico represent some kind of freedom to Ella?

Was it possible that somewhere in her psyche Ella wanted to be less of a girl? Could she wish she were androgynous or bi-gendered or genderqueer like Nico? Or were her long hair and makeup a response against some push inside herself? Maybe she secretly felt like a guy and was reacting against it. Maybe that's what she'd been about to tell Tucker when Lindy and Nico showed up; maybe that was why she'd already read Emily's book. But that didn't make any sense. If she was thinking about transitioning from female to male, wouldn't she cut her hair and butch up a little?

* * *

The next week started out slowly. Tucker's Monday classes weren't particularly exciting and after that she went over to Lindy's to watch TV. When the sun went down, the temperature grew crisp but not so cold that Lindy had to close the windows. They sat on the couch together under a blanket with their arms around each other. Those cozy hours felt more like the first months of their relationship. Lindy was in a playful mood and cracked jokes at all the commercials and tickled Tucker when she had nothing clever to say, until her sides ached from laughing.

Tuesday after Women's & Gender Studies, she was stretched out on her bed in her room with a book propped open in front of her when her phone chimed.

The text from Summer said: *Where u?*

Tucker replied: *Room*

Summer said: *Omw, you need to see this*

Summer showed up so quickly after the last text that Tucker knew she'd been texting while already in the dorm and on her way up to Tucker's room. Her chest rose and fell quickly and her face was darkened with exertion or anger or both.

"What's up?" Tucker asked.

Summer tapped her phone screen a few times and then held it out so Tucker could read the document on it:

Last week there was an incident involving a transsexual student in the women's locker room. The University policy is that transsexual people are asked to use the facilities that correspond to the sex on their birth certificate.

"What the hell?" Tucker said.

"That was in the faculty and staff email news bulletin this morning," Summer said. "That's about you, isn't it? One of those bitches in the locker room must have complained to someone for real."

"Send that to me, I want to show it to Claire."

Summer tapped on her phone and kept talking. "We're going to do something about this, right? I mean, it's like saying lesbians can't use the women's locker room."

Tucker nodded. She liked the analogy. Claire would have advice about how to fight against it. She watched the email from Summer pop up on her phone and forwarded it on Claire with a short note. As she finished typing, Ella knocked on the door between their rooms.

Tucker opened it. "Hey," she said.

"Summer texted me to come over," Ella said, looking from Tucker to Summer.

Summer handed her the phone. "Read this shit."

Ella's eyes scanned the screen and her skin went from pale to paper white. "Oh," she said.

"We think one of the women from the locker room complained," Tucker explained.

Ella nodded and gave the phone back to Summer.

"Isn't it just total crap?" Summer asked her.

"Yes, it's bad," Ella said. She wrapped her arms around herself. Tucker tried to catch her eye to figure out what she was thinking, but she was looking down at a spot between the foot of Tucker's bed and the wall.

"Screw them," Tucker said. "Claire will know what we can do about it."

"Of course this way we could find out about Nico, if Nico comes up again," Summer said. "Unless Nico already got his or her birth certificate changed."

"You can't change it," Ella said quietly.

Tucker looked at her. "What?"

"In Ohio, you can't change the sex on your birth certificate."

"No shit?" Summer asked.

Tucker wanted to ask how she knew that, but now wasn't the time. She tried to imagine Ella as a boy. What if she was FTM? Tucker didn't like the idea as much as she thought she should. She liked Ella the way she was. To have her be that markedly different, to have her be a guy, it felt unnatural. But if it was who Ella needed to be, she'd just have to get over herself.

Ella shook her head at Summer.

"That seems cruel," Summer said. "I'm willing to be an ass like anyone else and drive Nico crazy with questions, but to never be able to change that…I mean, what if you looked completely female and it still said male on your birth certificate? It wouldn't even be safe to use the men's room."

"That's what I'm going to do," Tucker said. "I'm using the men's bathrooms around campus from now on and just let them ask to see my birth certificate."

That made Ella smile for the first time since the conversation started. "You are, aren't you?"

"Absolutely."

But Tucker worried about the woman at school who really was trans. What happened when she heard about this? Would she feel like she had to go back to her dorm every time she wanted to use the bathroom? And what if she didn't have a suite like Tucker did and had to share the bathroom with her floor? What was it like to feel afraid every time you went to the toilet?

"Tell me what Claire says," Ella said. "I'll be in my room." She went back through the inner door.

Tucker tapped Summer on the shoulder so she'd look up from her phone where she was quickly messaging more students.

"Hey, what's up with you and Vivien?" she asked.

Summer shrugged. "She got weird."

"Clingy weird or distant weird?"

"Distant. Like she'd break up with me if we were going out, but we're not, so she's just not really talking much. And I don't feel like processing it out. You should see this hottie in my finance class. She's got that buttoned-up thing going on. I can't decide who's hotter, her or Ella."

"Don't even think about it," Tucker said.

"You calling dibs? Does Lindy know?"

"I'm not calling dibs, she's just off limits for you. There is no way I want to hear your freaky sex noises through the wall."

"We could go back to my place," Summer pointed out.

"She's *not* on your list," Tucker said. She stared at Summer until Summer looked away.

CHAPTER ELEVEN

Ella

Nico's visit over the weekend worked; I felt better. The nightmares left me alone and I was sleeping well again until I saw the policy notice that Summer found. I didn't want it to be a huge issue. I preferred the bathroom in my room anyway and it's not like I used the women's locker room, but it scared me because someone in admissions knew what was on my birth certificate—maybe many someones. The people who put me in a junior/senior level suite rather than a shared dorm room knew. Did they care enough to try to track me down and find out which bathroom I was using? I spent Tuesday wishing it would just blow over and no one would notice.

No such luck with Summer around. She'd already sent it to a friend on the school paper minutes after she saw it. By Wednesday morning it was up on the school newspaper site and the comments were piling up. I didn't bother to read them. It was pretty much the same conversation any time the "bathroom issue" came up. Unfortunately it was a lot harder to avoid the conversations in the Union.

"Check this out!" Summer waved me over to where she and Cal were sitting at the table in the after-lunch lull. I'd waited until an hour after lunch in hopes I could get something to take back to my room without running into anyone I knew.

I sighed and walked over to the table. Summer had a photo of Tucker that she'd posted herself that morning. In it, Tucker was standing in the doorway to the men's room in the Student Union with the door closed just enough that you could clearly see the Men's sign. She was grinning and waving. Summer had added a caption in white text below it, "Come at me, bro!" and looked ready to post it to every social network she knew.

"That's great," I said, but my voice came out flat. "Are you sure that's a good idea?"

"What's the worst that can happen? If they ask to see her birth certificate and find out she's a woman using the men's room, they'll just tell her to cut it out. They'll be more embarrassed than she will."

I shuddered. And a horrible part of me was glad that it would be Tucker and not me. If they did discover that she was using the men's room as a cis woman, Summer was right, they'd just tell her stop—but what if she had been a trans student?

"I have to go," I told Summer and hurried out of the Union. I wasn't hungry anyway.

I thought about leaving Friday after my classes and going home for the weekend so I could get away from it all, but I was supposed to go to a movie with Shen and Johnny. If I got a bus early Saturday, I could be in Columbus in time for brunch.

I texted Mom and asked if she could pick me up at the bus station late Saturday morning. I wanted to feel a little more protected for a while, but what I told her was that I needed a rescue from my hyper-social friends. That was true enough.

She wrote back: *Sure, honey, we'll be your knight in shining armpit.*

* * *

By Friday I was ready for classes to be over and to get away from school for a while, but I was also looking forward to going to the movie with Shen and Johnny. Well, mostly with Shen. And the theater was off campus so I didn't have to worry about the stupid bathroom thing.

The days weren't cold yet, but the nights were starting to have a chill and the bright leaves that turned weeks ago were falling. Johnny, Shen and I walked from campus to the movie theater and Johnny pointed at the bright red trees we passed on the way and asked if I could name them. I didn't bother to explain that microbiology was a far cry from botany, and the truth was I'd been on enough walks with Dad that I did know some of them.

"Maples," I said. "And I think that one's an oak, but I'm really better with microbes than plants. The red color shows up in trees that are rich in sugar, I remember that."

Seeing the bright colors made me doubly glad to be headed home this weekend. The bus trip down would be gorgeous and I was sure Dad would want to hike with me on Sunday. Not that I'm a big outdoors girl, and I have nothing to compare them to, but I'm pretty sure the fall colors in Ohio beat just about anywhere.

We watched Alice blow away about a million evil zombies and ate too much popcorn and drank too much pop, but since you can't eat too many M&Ms, we were fine in that category.

"Is it hard to understand people when they're talking so fast and there's so much action?" I asked Shen as we were leaving.

"I understand fluent English," he said. "I started taking it in school at age six. I also speak fairly poor Thai. Sometimes I increase my accent or act like I don't understand, but mostly that's if someone is being obnoxious or just for fun."

I laughed. "You look so serious all the time—it's hard to tell when you're joking."

"I only look serious because I'm standing beside this guy," he said and shoved Johnny lightly.

"I feel a little stupid for knowing just the one language," I said.

"Me too," Johnny said with a laugh. "My worthless cousin won't teach me to swear or pick up girls in Mandarin. Hey, do you guys want to stop for ice cream?"

We'd come to the creamery on the strip of restaurants that catered to the campus population. They made their own ice cream and you could have them custom mix any flavors with any number of nuts, candies, chocolates and other items. I think they even carried bacon bits. I'd discovered the place the second week of class and usually kept a custom pint from them in the mini-fridge.

"Of course," I told them.

I got a small dish of salted caramel ice cream with a prolific number of items mixed into it: more M&Ms, almonds, and toffee pieces. Shen ordered strawberry with fresh strawberries and blueberries. We found a table while Johnny was still putting in his order.

"It took me a while to catch on," I told Shen. "But I think you're actually the funny one."

"Oh yes," he said with a little smile. "I am so very much more funny than Johnny; he's the loud one." His face grew serious. "He has a harder life than me. He tries to make fun, but he's not lighthearted."

"What do you mean?"

"His parents came over before he was born so he is an American and also Chinese and he wants to please his parents and rebel against them and be American but also make fun of America. He's torn in two ways, maybe more. I'm a good Chinese boy, so it's easy. I'm just the one thing, like you."

I thought about that. Was I just one thing?

"Yes," I said. "I see what you mean—to do what I want and to make my parents happy and fit in culturally, it's all the same thing. It's harder when those don't match."

Johnny arrived at the table with a bowl heaped higher than either of ours, including a mountain of whipped cream and a river of hot fudge.

"I know you're talking about me," he said as he threw one leg over a chair and sat.

"It's all I ever do," Shen told him. "I was just telling Ella how bad you are at *Assassin's Creed 3*."

"Lies," he said around a mouthful of ice cream.

"He is truly awful with a musket," Shen said to me, but I could see from the glint in his eye that Johnny was actually very good at the game.

"When did you start gaming?" Johnny asked as the next huge spoonful of ice cream, whipped cream and chocolate sauce made its way toward his face.

"Junior high, I think. A few of my friends got really into the online games but their parents were limiting the time they could spend on the computer, so they talked a bunch of us into doing the classic pencil and paper *Dungeons and Dragons* and it was really fun."

"Were you the only girl in the group? How was that?" Johnny asked.

My cheeks got hot. "It was mixed," I managed to say after a long pause. "There were more guys than girls, but I wasn't the only one."

I *was* the only girl in the group who looked like a guy at that point, but my friends were pretty decent about me wanting to play female characters even though they all still thought I was a guy. It was toughest on the game master who once had my character hit with a curse that turned her male. I rallied the group into a campaign to find a wizard who could turn me female again. I think that actually helped when I did come out to that group of friends two years later; they were already used to fighting for my right to be whoever I wanted to be.

We went on to talk about the games we'd played and the ones we liked best and why—but Johnny's question brought up dual tracks of uncomfortable wondering in my mind. I wanted to spend more time with Shen, but I also wanted to spend an awful lot of time with Tucker. If she hadn't been with Lindy, would I want to be more than friends? And if so, was that fair to Shen? Even if it was fair and I could see more of Shen without feeling guilty, when and what did I tell him about me?

* * *

The bus down to Columbus wove through beautiful forests and relatively plain fields, though one housed a spectacularly blazing orange pumpkin farm. Mom picked me up at the bus station and we went to grab lunch at her favorite bakery and sandwich place. They usually had two great soups, homemade bread and fantastic pastries.

"Do you think I could have two of those?" I asked Mom as I pointed to the apricot brioche.

"For your lunch?"

"No, for dessert."

She rolled her eyes. "One of these days that metabolism of yours is going to catch up to you."

"Oh right, look at you."

My mom wasn't skinny but she still fell on the slender side of the spectrum compared to a lot of women in their early fifties.

"I had to give up pasta to look like this," she protested.

She put in our orders, including my two brioche, and took the number-on-a-stick thing to a table by the windows. I carried the two mugs we'd been given over to the coffee station and filled them. Mine got a ton of cream and sugar and Mom's just a dash of cream.

"Thanks," she said as I set her mug down in front of her and settled into my seat. "What do you think about your classes now that you've had some time in them?"

"I still really like microbiology and that machine learning course is really hard but I'm learning a ton. I'm not sure I could do the next level of it, too much programming, but it's helping me understand some questions I had. Calculus is only tough when I let it get abstract. As long as I can translate it into practical stuff I'm okay, plus I think Shen would tutor me if I asked."

Mom's eyebrows went up.

"He's in the machine learning class with me. He and his cousin are really funny. They're the ones who organized that big game on campus I told you about."

She took a sip of her coffee and waited. While she was working on her Ph.D., Mom had to interview all kinds of people from different cultures and socioeconomic classes. Her ability to wait for the answer she knew was there trumped any other technique I'd seen for getting people to talk.

"I can't figure out what their deal is," I said. "Shen asked me to come study with him—well, he didn't even really ask, he just kind of slipped it into a conversation like it would be a good idea. And then he invited me to a movie with him and Johnny, so I don't get if that was a date or not and if he likes me or if Johnny does or if we're all just friends."

"Would I like these young men?"

"You'd love Shen. His parents sent him over here from China to watch over Johnny and get an American degree and he's very polite but also really funny in this subtle way. He's actually sort of courtly. I really like that. And shy but not awkward. And Johnny—he's funny and kind of loud, but he's also really smart, though I think sometimes he tries to hide that."

"It sounds like they enjoy spending time with you," Mom said.

I nodded. "I also kind of like Tucker but she's in a relationship. But I'm not sure how good her relationship is."

"This is your roommate?" Mom asked. "The one who came out as transsexual even though she isn't?"

"Yes."

"Do you think maybe that's why you have a crush on her?"

"Um, what? No," I said.

"There could be some transference going on."

A lock of sandy blond hair was curling the wrong way from her chin-length bob and she tucked it back behind her ear. She turned her head so she was staring out the window, as if the lack of direct pressure on me would make her comment less obnoxious.

"Mom, cut it out," I told her. "Don't psychobabble me."

"I just want you to be aware of what might be happening before you make any big choices," she said. "If you're worried about not fitting in, maybe dating a girl isn't your best bet."

"Mom!"

"On the other hand it would probably be easier to come out to her. Have you thought about how you're going to talk to whoever you choose to date?"

"Of course I've thought about it, but it doesn't seem fair. It seems like it's a really…medical thing to talk about."

The server showed up with our food and I dug into the steaming bowl of French onion soup. I knew why that was the first question on Mom's mind when she heard I liked someone; the media was full of stories of the "deceptive" transsexual who tricks men into having sex with her and then usually gets killed for her trouble. The thing is, that image was total bullshit. It was some crazy paranoia cooked up by a culture that couldn't handle that sex and gender just weren't as cut and dried as some people wanted to believe.

But there was a real fear that some people, men in particular, if they thought I was a guy, would beat me up or worse. I understood what Mom was getting at, I just thought it was completely unfair. No other girl I knew had to think about having the most embarrassing and scary conversation possible with a guy she liked. I mean, how was I even supposed to talk about it. Just thinking about saying "Oh hey, I want to tell you I had genital surgery" made my cheeks burn with embarrassment.

Maybe Shen and I could just keep it at the casual friends level for a while. But even then, was I setting him up to feel deceived if I later told him and we'd already spent all sorts of time together?

This was another one of those issues I never had to deal with in high school because everyone just knew and if they didn't like me, well then they didn't have to hang out with me. It made it hard to find people to date because most of the guys had known me in my guy drag. I went out with a girl for a bit and then there was a friend of a friend who was cool about everything and we went out for a few weeks, but I never found myself all that interested in him. And I had this creepy suspicion that he was "putting up" with my trans status because he could get a pretty girl on his arm. It was like I was some kind of discounted designer purse. Well, except he'd never carry a purse.

It was too bad Nico and I couldn't seem to keep dating. We'd try it and sometimes it worked and other times we'd just end up cracking jokes and laughing together when we tried to make out.

I met a couple of guys at parties over the last year who wanted to make out, but I never felt like I wanted them to know a lot of personal information about me, so it was easy not to tell them. If a guy doesn't already know that some of the women in the world were born with "boys'" bodies, then late at night on a Saturday when he's tipsy is not the most effective time to deliver that educational unit. And I don't think it's deceptive to not want to tell strangers or new friends a long story about the state of my genitals.

"It's kind of a mess," I told Mom. "I don't know what I'm supposed to do. There isn't really a guide book for this."

She put the fork down to the side of her mostly-eaten salad and touched my hand. "Just watch out for yourself," she said.

"I won't put myself in danger, I promise. Plus, Tucker will look out for me. I am going to come out to her. I almost did this week but her girlfriend came over all upset. I think there's something not right going on there."

"What kind of not right?"

"I can't tell. It's like, sometimes Lindy is fun to be around and other times she's cagey and strange."

"Does she drink?"

"I don't know."

Mom pushed her salad aside and tore one of my brioche in half.

"Hey, get your own," I said.

She ignored me and took a bite of the gooey middle part where the apricot and glaze pooled together.

"I'll get you another when you finish all this," she said around a mouthful of pastry.

I grinned at her. "I have pocket money, I can get my own, I'm just defending my territory."

"Poorly," she said. "Now I'm not a psychologist, but I'd be wondering if there wasn't some kind of addiction or alcohol issue going on with Lindy the way you describe her being inconsistent like that. Do you think Tucker suspects that?"

"I think she's too nice to think that," I said.

"Codependent?" Mom asked.

"Maybe, though I'm not really sure what that means. And I don't want it to sound like Tucker's got problems because she's really awesome."

I hadn't told Mom the part about Tucker being grabbed outside the gym. There's just a level at which I didn't want her to worry about me, but I realized I was going to have to in order to ask the next question.

"This other thing happened to Tucker," I said. "Two guys grabbed her and shoved her into a wall because they thought she was trans."

I downplayed the incident because I didn't want Mom to worry about me or to freak out and pull me out of school. I'd already spent enough time going over what could have happened if two huge guys started hitting me; she didn't need to run that scenario too. It was over, the guys weren't coming back to campus and I'd ordered myself a canister of pepper spray like Tucker's.

"Oh honey," Mom said.

"It's okay, she pepper sprayed them in the face and they got kicked out of school."

"I want you to get pepper spray too," she said. "Don't walk alone after dark. And if you don't feel safe, think about transferring to OSU. You wouldn't have to live at home. We'd give you money to get an apartment."

"Mom, please. I'm not going to spend my whole life living close to home."

She'd finished the brioche half and was eyeing the other half so I picked it up and put it on her plate. She cut off a small edge with her fork and ate it.

"Ella," she said with a long sigh. "I saw the news about the facilities policy. Arinya came to my office to tell me and ask if you were okay."

Arinya was Nico's mom and also worked at OSU, so she was a quick walk across campus from my mom—plus, she was way more overprotective than my parents. I don't know what kind of crazy Google searches she had set up that flagged the story about the facilities policy at Freytag, but I was sure that was how she found it. No way would Nico share that with per folks knowing how often our moms talked.

"I'm fine," I said and tried not to look away from Mom while I said it. Having an anthropologist parent made me very careful about social cues even before I got adept at navigating gender roles. "We think someone complained about Tucker being in the women's locker room."

"OSU has a much better policy and they have gender neutral changing rooms and bathrooms."

"I'm not gender neutral," I said.

"I know, honey, but it's a tough issue and gender neutral facilities are a good compromise."

"That's why I have a suite in a senior dorm. They didn't want me using the bathroom with *real* women."

She didn't bother to respond. There wasn't a good reply to it anyway. She just looked at me and didn't even pick at the remnants of the mangled brioche.

"I want you to seriously think about transferring to OSU," she said.

"I don't want to go to OSU," I said. I didn't say: *I don't need to go to college with my mommy there to protect me.* "I like my classes, I like my friends, I'm fine where I am."

"Your credits would transfer and you'd have your own apartment near campus. Just think about it."

"I'm getting another pastry," I said and got up from the table.

I went to the counter and ordered another apricot brioche, this one to go. I didn't want to keep sitting there and listening to Mom's suggestions about how to live my life: I shouldn't date women so I could be more mainstream; I should move home so they could watch over me; I should be happy to have the opportunity to use gender neutral bathrooms. Right.

We went back to the house and I said I had studying to do so I'd have an excuse to sit in my old bedroom until I'd calmed down some. Then I made a point to help Mom with the chores before I fired up the Xbox, just so she wouldn't think I was sulking or withholding and try to engage me in some other deep conversation.

It was so relaxing to be back in a space where I felt completely safe that I ended up going to bed early and sleeping for nine hours. Then it was off to the woods with Dad to kick through the leaves before it was time to catch the bus back to campus.

CHAPTER TWELVE

Tucker

Now that Tucker was angry at Vivien, the focus for the paper for the Women's & Gender Studies class came easily. She wrote about bathrooms and locker rooms and the importance of making facilities safe for trans women.

She turned in the paper on Tuesday and invited Lindy out to an official dinner at a restaurant to celebrate. She'd set aside enough of her money from her hardware store job to be able to treat and picked the modern Italian place that Lindy liked at the end of the strip of restaurants near campus. They ordered a huge portion of spaghetti with mussels, clams and calamari. Tucker wished she could also get them a bottle of wine, but they were too close to campus for her to use her fake ID. Everyone here was on the lookout for underaged students trying to buy booze. She had to remember to make a run with Cal to get beer for his house party week after next.

"This is great," Tucker said midway through her first plate of pasta. "Thanks for coming with me."

"Silly, why wouldn't I?" Lindy asked.

"You've been so busy."

Last weekend, Tucker had been on her own because Lindy was concentrating on the paper she had to write for midterm. It was an extra quiet weekend because Ella had gone home and stayed over at her folks' house on Saturday night. In the middle of all that quiet, Tucker wondered if Lindy had overhead Ella talking about her plans and that's why she didn't try to monopolize Tucker, but that had seemed overly paranoid.

Lindy had started a few arguments by saying that Tucker was spending too much time with Ella. Tucker protested that it was a nonissue because she was dating Lindy exclusively and Ella was just her roommate, but she felt a stirring of guilt anyway because she knew if Lindy wasn't in the picture, she'd be asking Ella out.

"I *was* busy for the first part of the weekend," Lindy said. "Until this happened."

She held out her thumb to show the thick bandage wrapping it.

"I thought that happened Sunday evening," Tucker said.

"Saturday," Lindy corrected. "It was so chilly I had to move the old fan to get the window to shut."

"It was pretty cold," Tucker said, but inside her mind she was scrambling to remember the order of events over the weekend. She remembered calling Lindy on Saturday around noon and Lindy saying she was busy and planned to just focus on work. She didn't hear from her again until she called late Sunday to see how she was, at which point she thought Lindy had said she hurt herself that afternoon in the kitchen.

Tucker took a few slow bites of pasta, but the flavors were going dull in her mouth.

"I thought you cut it in the kitchen," she said.

"What?"

"When I called Sunday you said you hurt your thumb in the kitchen and had to go to the campus medical center. You'd just gotten back."

Lindy looked at her for a long moment and then tore off a piece of garlic bread and held it without biting into it.

"Oh, I cut it on the fan on Saturday but I just tossed together a bandage because I didn't feel like leaving my place, but on Sunday in the kitchen I banged it good and it opened up and started bleeding again so I thought I should get it looked at. They wanted to give me stitches, but I told them to just tape it up."

"That makes sense," Tucker said, but it didn't.

It was theoretically possible. So close to possible, in fact, that it stood out as a well-crafted lie. She filed it away to think about later when she was alone and Lindy wasn't watching her face.

"Did you pick out a movie for tonight?" Tucker asked.

"I thought we could start this really great Japanese anime series from the late eighties. It's supposed to have some lesbian subtext."

"Sounds awesome, what's the premise?"

Tucker let Lindy talk about the series and its influences; she let the sound of Lindy's words wash over her without really listening to their meaning.

When they finished dinner, Tucker paid and then they walked back to Lindy's apartment. They made it through the first two episodes of the series before Lindy announced, "Vivien was surprised you didn't tell her you're not really trans."

She got up to refill their glasses of herbal iced tea. Despite the casual tone she'd used, Tucker felt angry.

"I didn't because she was a jerk about it. The minute she thought I was a trans woman she got all icy."

"She has good connections in the academic community and I really need her help to get into grad school, so please don't piss her off," Lindy said.

"I'm not trying to piss her off," Tucker said and then reconsidered the truth of that statement. "Look, if she's not cool with trans women, that's just really weird for a feminist."

"No it isn't. Some feminists think trans women are just men willing to do anything to invade women's space."

"You don't think that," Tucker said.

Silence.

"Do you?"

"Well, I agree with Germaine Greer when she says that sex change surgery is a really conservative act because it shapes people to fit the gender roles created by our culture. And I also agree that just because a guy puts on makeup and a dress, that doesn't make him a woman," Lindy said.

She put the newly filled glasses on the table and tucked herself into the corner of the couch so that she was facing Tucker directly, but she didn't look at Tucker's face as she talked. Her gaze wandered across the coffee table and to the TV and back to the table.

Lindy went on, "Being a woman happens because you get born with a female body and you get raised as a girl and you have to deal with all the shit that happens to girls—and then you grow up to be a woman and have to deal with all the shit that happens to women. Someone who was born with a male body and spent a bunch of years having male privilege and then is sick of it or whatever, they can't just turn into a woman, no matter how many surgeries they have."

"Wow, you really don't understand transsexualism," was all that Tucker could say to that.

"I can understand it without agreeing with it," Lindy said. She stretched her right arm along the back of the couch, bending her elbow enough that her hand rested near Tucker's. She started playing with the thick seam of Tucker's sweatshirt cuff.

"That sounds like what a lot of people say about gays and lesbians."

"Being a lesbian doesn't make me infringe on anyone else's space. Transsexuals want to have everything women do."

"Only if they're trans women," Tucker said. Lindy didn't get it. She didn't seem to understand that transsexual women were women and so asking to have what any other woman had wasn't an unreasonable request.

Plus, she probably wasn't even thinking about the trans men who tended to have a somewhat easier time transitioning into socially accepted male roles, probably because everyone took it for granted that some women would want to be men and couldn't figure out why some men would want to be women. It didn't occur to them that "want" wasn't the issue. But even if it was, why should that be so hard to accept?

"You think there's some army of trans women just waiting to invade your women-only space?" Tucker said.

"You're dramatizing again," Lindy responded. "I'm just trying to tell you how Vivien and a bunch of feminists see things. Don't get mad at me."

"I'm sorry, I think that's stupid."

"You're entitled to your opinion, but could you keep it out of my academic career?"

Lindy's fingers plucked harder at Tucker's sweatshirt seam and she wanted to move her arm away but was afraid she'd offend Lindy.

"But you met Emily when we went to WisCon. Are you really ready to say she's not a woman?" Tucker asked.

"She's not a woman the way you and I are."

"But by that logic lots of women aren't the same...I'm not the same kind of woman that you are. I grew up in a different place with widely divergent economic circumstances. By that measure, Emily and I are more alike than you and me since we both come from small towns and working-class families."

"You're trying to muddy the issue. You know there are elements of womanhood that cut across culture and affluence."

"Like what?" Tucker asked.

"Like being the target of male predation," Lindy said. "No matter where you grow up, men think they can have access to you whenever they want, however they want."

Her index finger wrapped itself in the fabric of Tucker's cuff and twisted tight enough to slow the blood flowing into Tucker's hand. She barely noticed the thick feeling as blood pooled in her fingers because she was so caught up in the argument.

"Really? I think I've heard of some egalitarian native cultures. Does that mean the female-bodied people in those cultures aren't women?" Tucker asked.

"Well, if they moved here, they'd face the same discrimination and harassment and predation that we do and men don't," Lindy said.

"So if instead of moving from another culture they moved to being a woman through hormones and surgery, if they're subject to all the effects of being perceived as a woman in our culture, then they're a woman?"

The heat and pressure in her fingers from the closed loop of fabric around her wrist was becoming unbearable. She reached over to move Lindy's hand away from her cuff. Lindy caught Tucker's hand in a tight grip, but she let go of the sweatshirt. The release of tension made her hand flash hot and then cold as the blood rushed up and down her arm.

"That's not right, because he wouldn't have grown up female," Lindy said.

"What about this: if a girl is born and her family makes her grow up as boy because they wanted a boy and then she finally gets away from them and starts living as woman, then is she not a woman because everyone treated her like a boy growing up?"

"She's a woman," Lindy said and dropped her grip on Tucker's hand. "But what if there's a guy who really fetishizes womanhood. What if he's really turned on by the idea of being a lesbian and he goes through everything to change his body so he can have that fantasy. Would you want to have sex with him?"

It sounded like a mean-spirited question to Tucker, but she had to stop and consider it anyway. If such a person existed and they really were male inside, would she have any interest in them? Not really. She wasn't interested in men, no matter what they looked like, and she was interested in women but it didn't matter how they'd come to be women. What mattered was how they knew themselves. She'd met a number of transsexual women during that whole Pride weekend who were very attractive to her and, just like with cisgendered women, their look figured into it, but the main part of the attraction came from what she felt they were like as people.

Heck, she'd have considered asking Emily out if she and Claire weren't an item and if Tucker hadn't been with Lindy already.

"If there really was a man in a lesbian body, I wouldn't want to have sex with him," Tucker said. "But in my experience trans women are women and some of them are damn fine, and I don't mean only physically."

"Well, why don't we go find one and see how into her you are then."

Lindy got up from the couch abruptly and walked into the kitchen. She paused when she got there and looked around like she wasn't sure what she'd gone in there to get.

"Now you're just being mean," Tucker called after her.

"Am I? Maybe that's why you've been spending less time with me. Maybe you really want a transsexual girlfriend."

"You told me not to come around this weekend," Tucker said. She got up from the couch but didn't know if she should go over to Lindy or not. Lindy was standing by the sink with a dishtowel in her hands.

"That was Saturday morning," she said. "You didn't even come check on me when I cut the shit out of my thumb."

"You didn't tell me until Sunday!"

"You could have checked on me," Lindy insisted.

"I did! That's why I was calling on Sunday. And you told me not to bother coming over, that everything was okay," Tucker reminded her.

"You sounded like you had other things on your mind anyway."

"I didn't," Tucker said.

"I don't believe you."

"Oh for fuck's sake!" Tucker grabbed her jacket from the back of the couch. She didn't even know what to say. Lindy was being impossible and she wanted to get away from her and think about everything that was said that evening. She didn't wait for Lindy to respond, she just walked quickly to the door and down the stairs.

Lindy called to her when she was nearly to the ground, but she didn't stop. They'd been together all of nine months and it was time to figure out where she really stood with this relationship.

* * *

Tucker knocked on Ella's door but got no answer. She was probably studying or playing games with Shen and Johnny. Tucker sat in her desk chair and idly twirled it left and right. She turned to her computer and opened a file she had hidden deep inside a series of directories. It was her journal and lately the last page had become a list:

Said she was working all day, then referenced a movie she watched.

Said she went out to get Chinese food and then saw a traffic accident and forgot to pick up the food, but her car hadn't moved from where she'd been parked the day before.

Accused me of messing with her research papers but they didn't look touched at all.

Has been talking to Vivien about me: has she been telling her stories?

She added:

Said she cut her thumb in the kitchen on Sunday, then that she'd cut it on the fan on Saturday. Said she was working all weekend, but she wasn't.

She needed to talk to someone. The easiest course of action would be to just walk over to the Union and see who was holding court at the table. Cal and Tesh were both great listeners, if you could get Tesh away from Summer, who liked to offer advice every few sentences. Plus if Tucker went to the Union and Lindy showed up to pound on her door and alternately apologize and yell at her, she wouldn't have to hear it. She grabbed her bag and headed for the back stairs out of the dorm.

To her surprise when she walked into the Union, Ella was at the table with Cal, Tesh and Summer. As she walked up to the table, Ella looked up and caught her eyes with that level celadon gaze that Tucker couldn't dodge.

"What's wrong?" she asked.

"Can I talk to you alone?"

"Ooh," Summer said and Tesh smacked her arm.

Ella ignored them and got up from the bench. "Our rooms?"

"Somewhere else," Tucker said.

Ella seemed to understand that meant Tucker was trying to avoid Lindy. She nodded once and said, "I know a place, but it's a little cold."

"I don't mind."

They left the Union and walked across campus to the math and science dorm. Tucker had been here once with Ella to play games in the common room, but it wasn't her scene. Ella took her up the central stairway but they didn't stop at the third floor, they went up another flight of stairs and came to a short platform in front of a door marked "Roof Access—Locked." Someone had tossed a pair of old, cracked, black vinyl beanbag chairs on the platform. Ella settled into one and patted the other.

"We might get interrupted by couples wanting to make out," she said. "But other than that, it's totally private. The acoustics are awful, so if you talk quietly people using the stairs can't hear you."

"How do you know about this place? I've been hanging around campus since last winter and I didn't know it was here."

"It's where the gamer guys bring their dates," Ella told her. "Johnny and Shen showed me, in case we play a strategy game in this dorm. They didn't want someone else getting the jump on me."

"Or *they* were trying to get the jump on *you*."

Tucker settled into the other beanbag chair and felt it try to mold itself to her backside as much as its ancient and cold vinyl allowed. Bundled into her coat, with the chair cradling her, she was warm enough. In the dead of winter it would be too cold to be comfortable, but for now it was just right for a private conversation.

"What's going on?" Ella asked.

"I don't know what to do about Lindy and I'm starting to wonder if I should break up with her," Tucker said and was surprised that her voice sounded completely steady. She watched Ella's face for a shocked response but didn't see one. Ella tipped her head a little to the right and looked thoughtful.

"I've been worried," she said. "I hear you argue a lot and you seem stressed out about her."

"I am," Tucker admitted. "I really like her and in some ways we're great together, but it's been getting weird. I don't know if it's the start of the school year and her being all stressed about writing another paper to present or if it's me saying I'm trans and…not so much what's happened to me but her fears about how it reflects on her."

Tucker filled her lungs up and blew out a big breath of air that hung in front of her face like a weak gray ghost before dispersing.

"We went out to dinner tonight to celebrate me finally getting that monster paper off for Gender Studies and I think she lied to me and it wasn't even anything important. She'd cut her thumb and she told me it happened Sunday but then she said Saturday. She's been doing that a lot lately and she acts like she doesn't even know she did it. Like she'll tell me she was working all day and then tell me about the movies she watched."

"Is she on something? Or maybe there's a medication she's supposed to be taking that she's skipping?"

"No idea. You don't think I'm crazy?"

Ella shook her head. "She seems random sometimes. Maybe that's just school and pressure or maybe there's something going on, but if it's making you unhappy or stressed out, you don't need to put up with it."

"It is really tough, especially with the crazy harassment for being the only out transsexual in the history of the world who isn't. But then I'm afraid I'm just stressed out from that and overreacting."

Tucker settled back further into the shapeless beanbag chair and then had to straighten up again so it wouldn't shift and dump her out flat on her back.

She went on, "I used to love listening to her talk theory, or talking about anything with her. Now we just get into fights about stupid stuff like whether trans women are 'real' women, whatever that is. I mean, hell, most of the time I know that Emily's more of whatever a woman is than I am. She actually likes femininity, and isn't that the basis of feminism anyway? Not just making the world safe for women but for femininity so it's seen as something powerful and not artificial. I mean, don't you ever feel like people don't take you as seriously because you look like a girlie girl?"

Ella laughed. "All the time."

"And wouldn't it be cool if looking feminine was perceived as powerful and not weak?"

"Sure."

Tucker sighed and slapped her palms against her thighs. "I'm getting all caught up in theory again and really I'm just upset about Lindy. I'm so mad she doesn't believe what I believe. But is that enough to break up over? Or do I stick with her and try to change her mind?"

"It's not just her politics," Ella offered. "What's causing her to lie to you?"

"I have no idea. I wish it could go back to the way it was last spring. I wanted to be around her all the time."

"Are you going to tell people you're not trans?" Ella asked.

"No way," Tucker said. She shifted forward in the chair and spread her hands on her thighs for balance. "I'm pissed. One way or the other, they should have to deal with that. And think about that poor girl…what if she hears about some of this shit?"

"She has," Ella said.

Tucker had her mouth open, ready to go on with her rant, but she shut it. Ella looked as serious as she'd ever seen her. In the dim glow from the one weak overhead service light, Ella's face and lips and hair all seemed to be the same honeyed-cream color. Her cheeks looked like they'd been carved in ivory.

"You know who it is? Is she okay?" Tucker tried to sound more concerned than curious, but she was burning with the desire to know who it was. Maybe it was one of the gamers and she'd come out to Ella recently, or it was someone in a class with her.

Ella tucked her hands together between her knees and lifted her chin, putting her eyes level with Tucker's.

"Tucker, it's me," Ella said.

Every muscle in Tucker's face went loose and her mouth fell open. Ella watched her, wide-eyed and waiting. Tucker worked her mouth into a grin.

"No shit?" Tucker asked.

She forced herself not to do the stupid body scan look that she'd seen too many people do to Emily when they met her: looking at her facial structure, then her chest and shoulders, then her hips and hands to see if they could spot some lingering masculine characteristic.

"Utterly devoid of shit," Ella said. "I was born with a boy's body, started hormone blockers when I was eleven and transitioned to living like I am now between fourteen and fifteen."

"That's amazing!" Tucker said and meant it. She opened her arms and leaned forward to hug Ella but the beanbag chair shimmied out from under her and dumped her butt-first onto the concrete. Ella's effort to meet the hug or catch Tucker sent her tumbling into the gap between the beanbags. She landed on top of Tucker.

Tucker wedged her back against the edge of her capricious beanbag and got her arms around Ella. With a half wriggle, Ella balanced herself sitting across Tucker's lap. She was laughing into Tucker's shoulder and holding onto Tucker's jacket to keep herself from sliding backward onto the floor. Her hair smelled like balsam, vanilla and clover honey. Tucker tightened her hold on her.

"That's why you stopped at the graffiti on my door," Tucker said.

Ella's head was under Tucker's chin and she nodded.

"Well, that's why I knew what a shitty thing it was to do to someone," Ella said quietly.

"The other day when I showed you Emily's book, I was trying to figure out what you were going to say before Lindy and Nico showed up."

"Did you figure it out?" Ella asked.

"I thought maybe you were going to come out to me as genderqueer or trans, but as female-to-male."

Ella laughed. "Been there, not going back."

Tucker tightened her hold on Ella. "All this time…" she started and trailed off, not sure what she wanted to say.

"All this time you've been making my first year at university safe for me," Ella said.

Without question, Tucker thought, this was the most righteous moment of her whole life. No matter what happened, she had a kind of invulnerability because she'd now done one thing completely right. It was noble to protect a stranger, but it felt incomparably fulfilling to protect a friend. *This is why soldiers go into battle*, she thought.

"Thank you," Ella whispered.

They sat together until the dropping temperature and hard concrete floor finally drove them apart and back to their dorm rooms.

On the way, Tucker said, "While we're doing true confessions, you should know my full legal first name is Jessamine. I went by J.T. for a while but then I liked just using my last name better."

"Wow, that's quite the secret burden. It must have taken you tremendous courage to share that," Ella told her with a smirk.

"Years of therapy," Tucker replied.

* * *

Tucker went through the next day feeling bulletproof. She was ready to have a talk with Lindy and break up with her if it came to that, but she also hoped that Lindy would be able to explain the discrepancies in her stories and actions in a way that made sense at last.

Lindy beat her to the punch and sent Tucker a text saying: *Maybe we should cool things down for a while. I'll talk to you after fall break.*

Fall break was a four-day weekend slipped into mid-October—and it was two weeks away. That was a long "break" for a relationship. Tucker wanted to run over to Lindy's apartment and demand to know what she'd done wrong. She wanted something to change, but now that it was changing, she wasn't ready.

She went to the gym to run but mostly to not do anything too stupid. Ever since the attack, she used the well-lit front door rather than the back entrance, even in the middle of the day, and she'd stopped changing in the locker room. Just walking by the door to the women's locker room made her feel sick to her stomach.

Now she wore her running shorts under a pair of sweatpants that she tossed on top of her bag next to the track before she ran. So far she hadn't seen the mean girls and she wondered about the one whose boyfriend had been kicked out of school. Was she angry at Tucker or was she on some level happy? Tucker figured the kind of guy who was willing to attack a stranger probably didn't act like a prince in his intimate relationships.

In the middle of the run, the anger and sadness about Lindy hit her. She sped up her pace and drummed her feelings into the track. They had just made it to the nine month mark, so this was Tucker's longest relationship to date, unless she counted the on-and-off again relationship that spanned her junior and part of her senior year of high school. They'd been off more than on, though, as the other girl kept trying to date guys and didn't want to be seen in public with Tucker once Tucker was out.

It wasn't that she thought she'd be with Lindy forever, or even through all of college; it just hurt to think that it meant little enough to Lindy that she was willing to chance throwing away the whole relationship via text. Of course on the other hand, this could be Lindy's attempt to get Tucker to come running back to her, which she badly wanted to do.

She finished three miles and wiped the sweat off her face, then put on sweatpants, boots and jacket. Back at the dorm she showered and tossed on clean sweatpants and a tank top. The room was usually on the hot side for her since she shared a thermostat with Ella, who was perpetually chilly.

She knocked on Ella's door.

"Come on in," Ella said and Tucker opened the door to find her sitting propped in her bed with her laptop in her lap and papers fanned out on both sides of her. Tucker wheeled the desk chair next to Ella's bed and turned it so she could sit backward and rest her arms on the back. She called up the text on her phone and handed it to Ella.

"What does it mean?" Ella asked.

Tucker shook her head. "I'm trying to stop myself from running over there to find out."

"I'm sure that's what she wants. Why doesn't she just tell you to come over instead of this reverse psychology?"

"You really didn't date much, did you?" Tucker asked with a smile.

"Everyone thought I was a boy."

"So? Boys date."

"Straight girls and gay boys aren't my type," Ella said.

"Oh yeah, so what is?"

"I don't really know yet. I thought maybe I should, like, date randomly this year. I don't even really know if I like girls or boys better, but I think maybe I just like people. When did you know?"

"What?"

"What you like?" Ella asked.

"I always liked girls. In about fourth or fifth grade, when the girls and boys started teasing each other, I thought all my friends were being really stupid and it was just obvious that the girls should stick together. I fooled around with a couple of guys when I was thirteen and fourteen and it just didn't feel like anything at all...not like being with a woman. But beyond that, I'm not sure that I know what I like either. I thought Lindy and I were really good together but the last few months it's just been more and more shit."

Her voice broke on the last word and she cleared her throat but it didn't help.

"Hey, do you have plans for fall break?" Ella asked.

"The usual," Tucker said.

"What usual? Isn't this your first fall break?"

"Oh, I thought you meant for my birthday. It's that Sunday."

"Oh my God, what are you doing for it?"

"Just hanging out with whoever's around like I do every year."

"Tucker, come home with me for break. It'll be fun, I promise. We can go shopping for your birthday."

"You've mistaken me for Lipstick Lesbian Barbie," Tucker said, but she was grinning. In the face of the shit with Lindy, the idea of getting away for a weekend and spending it with Ella, even if she had to go shopping, seemed wonderful.

"You'll like my parents," Ella went on. "They're sweet. Don't get Dad talking about sustainability, though, he'll never stop. Come on, half of the students will be gone for break, you can't just sit around here and mope."

"I don't want to get in the way," Tucker said.

"Please."

Ella's pale green stare made her breath catch in her throat. "Yes," she breathed and escaped back to her room.

How could she want to go running back to Lindy so badly and at the same time be so dazed by Ella?

CHAPTER THIRTEEN

Ella

Fall break was just Friday and Monday off from school, like a practice session for Thanksgiving. We took the bus down Friday afternoon and planned to stay until Monday afternoon. Mom picked us up because she had the day off too and drove us to the house. I had a duffel, a suitcase and my backpack. I wanted to do some of my delicate laundry at home where the washer actually had a gentle cycle. Tucker just had a big green army-style backpack.

We carried the bags into the foyer and Tucker stared up the spiral staircase that commands the middle of our house. She looked worried.

"Dad's an architect, remember," I whispered to her. "This is basically his third kid."

"Oh yeah," she said quietly.

"Mom, we're going to put all our stuff in my room for now," I called to her where she'd stopped to sort the mail onto the little table in the foyer.

I motioned to Tucker, who picked up my second suitcase and followed me up the grand staircase. My room was the second door at the top, just after the door to the master suite that ran along one whole side of the house. I went in and dropped my bags by the open door to the attached bathroom.

"It's not pink," Tucker said when she saw my bedroom.

"Really? You've seen my room at school and you thought I'd sleep in pink at home?"

A little grin cracked the startled mask of her face. "I was hoping you did so I could tease you about it."

"Foiled!"

My bedroom was a smoky blue-gray-green color with a light tan-gold trim. I didn't tell Tucker that I went through a pink phase when I was eleven, and then a bright gemstone green phase that Dad said was terrible to paint over.

"It's very...you," Tucker said. She put both bags down next to my bed.

I glanced around the room and wondered what her bedroom at home looked like. Mine was on the spare side now that I didn't live here all the time: there was a double bed with a small table on one side and a bookcase against the wall on the other side, then the closet across from the foot of the bed and a little desk by the big window. Most of the room was neat, except for the bookcase. I'd run out of room for books and notebooks and notes, so they were all piled onto the shelves on top of each other.

"Let me show you something really cool," I said and stepped back out of the room.

I went around the curving hallway, past the utility room to where the hall dead-ended in a shallow bookcase. The catch for the door was the fourth shelf and when I touched it, the bookcase swung out. Inside was a room just a little smaller than my bedroom with two walls lined with books and a small desk under the far window.

Tucker followed me into the room and walked slowly along one wall, her fingers tracing the books.

"I want one of these," she said in a thick voice.

"Secret room?" I asked.

"Library."

"If you don't mind an old air mattress, you can sleep in here. There's also Amy's room, but it's full of Mom's files right now."

She nodded and went back to looking at the titles of the books.

"I'm going to check in with Mom," I told her. "I'll be back in a few."

Mom was in the kitchen making a list on a piece of paper. She looked up when I came around the corner and smiled.

"Is your friend settling in?" she asked.

I turned one of the dining room chairs perpendicular to the table and sat. "She's in the library. Can she sleep up there? She really likes the books."

"Of course. I'm headed to the store, do you want to come?"

I shook my head.

"What do you eat for breakfast these days?"

I detailed my favorite options along with what we'd like to drink and my top picks in ice cream flavors. Then I went back upstairs. When I peeked into the library, Tucker was sitting at the desk with a book open in front of her. I tiptoed back out of the doorway and went downstairs to put in my first load of laundry.

* * *

Friday night we watched movies. My parents went to bed while we were still in the middle of one. When that one finished, Tucker said, "I'm tired but I'm not sleepy. I kind of want to watch the next one."

"Let's watch it upstairs," I suggested.

The old air mattress that Dad had inflated and put in the library easily fit two people and with all the pillows off my bed we could prop ourselves into a halfway sitting posture against the wall. I got my laptop and put it on my legs where Tucker and I could both see it.

We started up the show and then all I could think about was the warmth of Tucker next to me. She put her arm around my shoulders and I leaned into her. I felt every centimeter of her body where it touched mine but I had no idea what to do or even what I wanted. Was this friendly or more? Did I owe some kind of loyalty to Shen even though we'd only been to a movie with his cousin? I told myself that if anything I owed it to him to figure out what I liked, though I had to admit that was a pretty thin rationalization. It sort of didn't matter what else I thought then because I was very clear that I didn't want that moment with Tucker to end.

She reached across my legs under the blanket to adjust the angle of the laptop and then her hand rested on my leg and stayed there. I felt as if her fingers were moving up my thigh with microscopic slowness, but then I thought that might be wishful thinking. Her hand moved again, maybe a whole centimeter.

"Tucker," I said and turned toward her.

Her face was inches from mine. She leaned down and kissed me. Her lips were bigger than mine and so soft I melted into them.

The arm around my shoulders shifted and her hand went up the back of my neck and into my hair. I got my hands untangled from the blanket enough to slide around her back and press myself closer. She kissed me harder and all I could feel was her lips and tongue and how hot her skin was through the material of her T-shirt.

Her right hand traveled farther up my leg. It sent a jolt of wanting her and an equal surge of fear into my gut. I pulled away from the kiss.

"What's wrong?"

"Too fast," I said and my voice came out squeaky because I was breathing so quickly.

"Okay," she said with a wide smile. "It's okay. We can just kiss if you like that."

"I do," I admitted. "I just never…"

"I thought you'd kissed girls before," she said.

"Kissing is all I've ever done. With anyone."

She took her hand off my leg and hugged me. I realized I was shaking.

"It's okay, baby," she said and to my horror, I started crying into the side of her neck.

I had to stop after a minute and go find a tissue to blow my nose. When I came back from the bathroom, Tucker had moved the laptop off to one side. The screensaver was playing. That and the dim light from the windows was the only illumination in the room, giving everything a ghostly look. Tucker ran a hand through her hair, settling it all to the right, and patted the mattress next to her.

I wasn't sure how close to sit now. Most of my previous makeout sessions ended with someone saying they had to get home or get back to studying, not with me bursting into tears. I sat close enough that we could touch, but not so close that we actually were.

"What are you afraid of?" she asked.

"Everything."

"Even kissing?"

"Well, no. I like that part," I admitted.

"Touching?" she asked.

"No. I mean, not the general kind."

"There's a specific kind?" she asked and then said, "Oh. There is, isn't there?"

I nodded.

"If I promise no specific touching, can I kiss you again?"

I nodded again and she closed the distance between us.

* * *

On Saturday, Tucker was a lot more talkative and I was a lot more tired. We'd been up just kissing until about two a.m. and then I lay awake in my bed for at least another hour thinking about it. And just so nothing would look suspicious, I got up early with Mom to chat and help make breakfast, so by noon my eyeballs felt gritty.

We went out shopping with Mom. She and Tucker had a lively conversation about the nutritional value of organic produce, while I mostly smiled from my seat on the passenger's side.

My parents know better than to have a drawn-out conversation with me about genetically modified food, but Tucker didn't. It's one of those topics that I've read about a lot but actually haven't formed a strong opinion on yet—at least not until I've had some time in a lab and can understand that level of the science. Not having a strong opinion means I can get pretty silly in an argument and it took Tucker a while to realize I was winding her up.

She caught on while we were at the big farmers' market. It's a huge building that fills up with vendors every weekend and Mom likes it because she can find weird spices there—most of which she never uses. I think seeing them on her shelves makes her happy. The most arcane and esoteric of the spices aren't found in the nice heated building, though; they're outside in the back parking lot where people are selling out of their cars.

It wasn't quite freezing, but it was a damp, chilly day and I shifted from foot to foot trying to warm up.

"How many languages does your mom know?" Tucker asked as Mom switched from English to Hindi to barter about a price.

"She's only fluent in three," I said. "But she has a smattering of a few others and I think she's been working on her Farsi."

"Wow. What's that like?"

"I suck at languages," I said.

"I mean having educated parents?"

I tried to see the expression on her face without turning my head noticeably. Her eyes stared at something far away. I moved a step closer to her so that our shoulders touched.

"It's great," I admitted. She would know if I lied about it. "I mean, it's tough to win an argument with them, but I wouldn't trade it. I think if Mom didn't know so much about other cultures…coming out would have been so much harder. But your mom—"

"Dropped out of high school because she was pregnant with the twins," Tucker said flatly.

She didn't talk about her family much so I just kept quiet to see if she'd say more.

"And then when she got pregnant with me, my dad just split." She paused for a long time before she added, "Mari's dad isn't the same as mine, but she's my favorite sister. I tell her that all the time and that she looks like me, only prettier. She'll be fourteen soon and I worry about her so much. I think seeing our mother's life scared her—she says she's sworn off boys until she's graduated and got a job."

"We kind of lucked out," I said and Tucker gave me a questioning look. "Neither of us is going to accidentally get pregnant."

She laughed and pressed her shoulder closer to mine. "You're shivering," she said.

"I should've worn my winter coat."

She unzipped the front of her heavy army surplus-style jacket and held it open. I didn't move but I smiled a little. She stepped behind me and wrapped her jacket around both of us.

"Put your hands in my pockets," she said.

I did and she put her hands over mine. They were like generators throwing off heat.

"Do you wish you could get pregnant?" she asked.

"Not yet," I said and tried to keep my voice light. It was hard to voice what I actually wished, even to myself, because that part was all so complicated.

"Me either," she said.

"Will you someday? Do you think?"

"I have no idea. Maybe when I'm older and if I have money. I don't want to have a kid if I don't have money," Tucker said. "Any kid of mine, I want to be able to give her everything."

Mom had moved on from the open hatchback of the Honda to another car where a wizened-looking woman was selling plastic baggies of who knows what ground powders. Even though Mom wasn't wearing a hat and had on only her fall coat, she didn't seem to feel the cold the way I did.

I lowered my voice to a near whisper. "Before…Mom wanted me to freeze some of my, you know, guy genetic stuff. Just in case someday I wanted to have kids of my own."

"Damn," Tucker said.

"I wouldn't do it. I don't want to be someone's worthless Y chromosome," I said and had to stop talking because I was a lot closer to crying than I expected.

Tucker hugged me hard and didn't say anything.

* * *

Saturday night I was exhausted, but that didn't prevent another, shorter span of kissing Tucker. I felt like it brought up more questions than it answered, but I wasn't in any mood to argue since she was a great kisser. It was hard for me to tell if I liked it so much because of how much I liked her, or if she had a lot of natural talent, or if this was some clue about liking girls or boys or both.

On Sunday we took her out to a fancy brunch for her birthday and then Mom dropped us off at the mall and I took her shopping. She got herself a new pair of jeans with a gift card her aunt sent her, and I insisted she let me buy her an HD eReader.

"You'll really like how you can save your highlights, trust me," I told her.

We ended the day reading and Tucker surprised me by saying she was going to head to bed early. My parents did the same and then I went up and got into bed to do more reading since I wasn't tired. After about a half hour, I heard a quiet knock on my door. Tucker grinned at me and I smiled back and motioned her into the room.

She climbed into my bed. We kissed for a while and then she tugged at my shirt.

"Can we take this off?" she asked.

"You first," I said.

She stripped her shirt off in one quick motion. In the moonlight her normally tan skin looked golden, as if she were a painting of herself, with her broad shoulders and her large breasts perfectly balancing each other.

I pulled my shirt off and only tangled it on my elbow for a moment due to nerves. I felt extra self-conscious because everything about me was smaller than Tucker. Had the hormones done everything they needed to do to make me enough of a woman for her?

She put her hands on my waist, both of us kneeling on the bed, and kissed me again as she pulled our bodies together. My fear cracked like ice and started floating apart as soon as her skin met mine.

Later when we were lying down and stopping to catch our breath, she said, "We should take these off," and gestured at her boxer briefs and my pajama bottoms.

"I think I'd like that," I said. "But I'm not ready to…I mean, would we be girlfriends and stuff?"

"Mostly stuff," she said with a little laugh. "Do you want to be girlfriends?"

"Would it be okay if I didn't?"

"Yes," Tucker answered in a long sigh. "I might still be with Lindy when we get back."

"I don't like her," I whispered.

"But you like me," Tucker said.

"Oh yes, I just don't know—" She cut me off with a kiss.

I didn't know how many women Tucker had been with, but it was plenty more than my zero.

She leaned on one elbow and traced fingertips down my collarbones and around my chest. It tickled and felt great and strange all at the same time because she was looking at me and the expression on her face was really happy. I tried to just lie still but I couldn't stop touching her also.

Her hands cupped my breasts and then she bent down to kiss all over them. I felt the velvet of her lips, moments of quick suction, and the heavy press of her breasts against my ribs.

She scooted down and put her fingers on the waistband of my pajama bottoms, then looked at me.

"Is this okay?"

"I don't know." The fear was surfacing again, iceberg-style, with more underneath.

She put her hands on my thighs and electric currents shot up and down my legs, but mostly up.

"I want you," she said. "Do you…?"

I slid my pajama bottoms over my hips and kicked them off under the sheets. I wanted this with Tucker and I also wanted to get it over with.

"Do you have any idea how beautiful you are?" Tucker whispered.

"As beautiful as science can make me?" I offered and immediately regretted it. I shouldn't be reminding her that I was different. Not now. What if she decided she didn't want this?

She laughed. "I love science." Her fingers started touching me so gently I almost couldn't feel them at first. "You have to tell me if I do something you don't like," she said. "Or something you really do. Okay?"

I nodded but I was too scared and keyed up to be able to say anything. She crawled back up the bed and held me and kissed me again until I started to relax, and then made her way back down.

Her fingers were too light still; I could barely feel them and it brought the edge of panic into my gut. After the surgery, for months I was afraid to touch myself. I mean not just touch but try to orgasm. I knew there could be nerve damage. Not so much these days, but it can happen—and I tried to be brave and tell myself it would be okay, but I didn't want a sex life that was just okay.

And I could, that was the great thing, but could I have an orgasm with another person? Was I like the other girls Tucker had been with? How stupid was I to pick a lesbian for my first— at least with a guy he wouldn't pay that much attention, but then that had its own issues. I mean, what if he plain didn't fit?

Tucker's fingers shifted, pressed harder and I gasped. She stopped.

"Good or bad?" she asked.

"Good," I breathed.

She grinned and kept changing the angle and pressure of her touch until my brain stopped its crazy spinning. I held onto her shoulders and gave in to the sensations she created for me.

CHAPTER FOURTEEN

Tucker

On the bus ride back to campus, Tucker watched Ella doze. They'd been up most of the night and she felt weightless with happiness and lack of sleep. This wasn't the first time that Tucker was another girl's first, and she knew it took some trial and error to find out what someone liked when they didn't know themselves. She'd been afraid that she wasn't going to do it right—that the techniques she'd learned with the other women in her life wouldn't apply to Ella. But they did.

Ella was the fifth woman she'd been with and even in that small sampling there was considerable variation in what each liked. And although, as Ella said, she'd been surgically constructed...well, Tucker thought she'd like to send that surgeon a huge thank-you card. The most impressive part for her was how much it wasn't really any different from the other women she'd had sex with. Actually the most different experience she'd had was with a cisgender woman who was just really big down there in every dimension and got even bigger when she was turned on; Tucker never quite knew how to navigate around all that enlarged geography. Compared to that,

Tucker felt really grateful that they lived in a time and a place where someone had the resources and expertise to help Ella fully grow into herself.

Now Ella's bottom lip still looked redder than usual from where she'd bit it to keep from making noise and Tucker wanted to brush it with her own lips, but instead she just settled back in her seat.

Ella was amazing and compelling and by far the most enticing girl Tucker had met since school started, but that didn't erase her history with Lindy. She'd told Lindy things she'd never told anyone before and felt closer to her than most members of her family. This weekend was a blessed vacation from her complicated life, but when she got back to school it was going to be time to talk.

On top of that, she had the feeling that Ella wasn't ready to settle into a relationship. Maybe she would be soon. Maybe she had to try a few options. It was easy to mistake her coolness for self-assurance, but she was a year younger and in terms of relationships, much younger than that. Tucker had been sleeping with women since she was fifteen, and Ella...well she'd made a darned fine start but it was just a start.

Tucker had thoroughly enjoyed herself. She adored Ella's sweetness and innocence, but she also ached for the electricity she had with Lindy. Being with Ella was still in many ways like being with a friend.

She remembered the time last spring when she and Lindy had sex halfway up the stairs to her apartment because they just couldn't make it to the door. And then they'd staggered, laughing in their half undone clothing, into the apartment and fallen together on the couch where they snuggled and talked about Wittig and Winterson for hours.

Lindy always listened to her ideas and she didn't always agree with them, but she'd say when she thought Tucker had a great idea and encourage her to pursue it.

"What are you thinking?" Ella asked. She was still slumped in the seat the way she'd been as she slept, but her eyes were open and clear.

"Just stuff," Tucker told her.

"What are you going to tell Lindy?"

"Nothing," she said. "But I'm going to talk to her about everything and see. I'm not telling her about this weekend."

"Good," Ella said. She turned away and looked out the window.

"Are you upset?" Tucker asked.

Ella shook her head. "I don't want to complicate things."

Tucker didn't know what that meant, but maybe Ella felt like she did: that their night together should exist apart from day-to-day reality and talking about it would only drag it into the middle of Tucker's messy life.

The bus pulled into the campus stop in the midafternoon and she and Ella carried their bags back to the dorm. In her room, Tucker unpacked her bag and then, with a mix of regret and anticipation, turned on her cell phone. There were four texts from Lindy, increasingly apologetic in nature.

The last one said: *Come over when you get back, no matter how late. I want to see you. I have something for you.*

Tucker texted back: *Just got in. Sorry, had my phone off. Needed a break.*

She wondered if Lindy knew she'd spent the weekend at Ella's house. If no one else from the LGBTQIA group mentioned it, Lindy would probably think she'd just stayed at her mom's house and worked at the hardware store as usual when she wasn't on campus for a weekend. She wasn't going to say anything to change that assumption.

Can you come over or are you busy? Lindy texted back. It was unusually polite and respectful compared to the last month. Did this mean things were changing? Would she get the old Lindy back? The one who was wickedly funny and fascinating?

I'm on my way, Tucker responded.

* * *

"Do you love it?" Lindy asked. She was holding up a thick gray sweatshirt with the word "DYKE" in a college font across the front.

Tucker thought it was adorable. She unbuttoned her overshirt and shrugged out of it, then pulled the sweatshirt on over her head. It fit perfectly. The material was heavy and warm but super soft on the inside.

"This is great," she said.

"The best thing is that there actually used to be Dyke College in Cleveland," Lindy said. "They changed the name like twenty years ago, but for about fifty years it was called Dyke College and for a while it was women-only."

She rubbed the thumb of one hand across the palm of the other and bounced on her heels like it was too hard to stay still, but her eyes held Tucker's evenly with her old humor in them.

"Wow, I'd love to see that," Tucker said.

"Yeah, too bad they renamed it, huh? That looks really great on you."

Tucker grinned and Lindy leaned in and kissed her in a way that was intricate but soft. When she pulled away, Tucker wanted more.

"I'm sorry about the last few weeks," Lindy said. "I just had to get some space and clear my head. It's just, last spring I felt like I was on top of the world with that presentation and then, you don't really know how academia is until there's all this pressure. It's like: what have you done for me lately? The semester started and nobody cared what I'd done last year, they just wanted the next big thing from me and I didn't have anything and I freaked out. It was like I couldn't catch my breath but it went on for weeks and weeks."

She paused and reached out to stroke her finger gently along Tucker's cheek. "I'm really sorry I pushed you away like that."

Tucker didn't know what to say so she curled forward into Lindy's lap and wrapped her arms around Lindy's waist. Lindy laughed and bent down and kissed the side of Tucker's face. She planted little kisses from Tucker's ear down the side of her jaw.

"You missed me," Lindy said.

"Yeah. It was like you were there but you weren't."

"I'm here now," she said.

Tucker wanted to relax completely into Lindy as she had in the spring and summer, but something inside of her wouldn't unwind. It must be the weekend with Ella and how clear their night together remained in her memory. She forced herself to set it aside and settle back into her relationship with Lindy.

* * *

It was smooth sailing for about three days. Then Tucker found herself blinking at the message in her student email account, sure that she was reading it wrong:

Subject: Low Grade Warning

This email is to inform you that you have a grade D or below in your course: Women's & Gender Studies. At the midpoint of the semester it is time to take action to raise your grade. If you cannot think of ways to raise your grade, please talk to your instructor.

D or below? How? It was still before her first class of the day and she threw on clothes and ran across the campus to her physical mailbox in the Student Union. There was the copy of her paper for Women's & Gender Studies with a resounding D on the cover page. The comments said, "Lacks analysis, originality and depth."

"What the fuck!"

She pulled out her phone and logged into her student email so she could send Vivien a message.

"A D?" she wrote. "Why?"

The response pinged back into her phone just after her history class. It said, "The subject was extremely lopsided and lacked analysis, as I noted. You have two weeks until the deadline to drop a class has passed."

She stomped from the history building across the corner of the quad to the Union. It was a cloudy day but the slight wind that moved between the buildings held a touch of warmth and didn't cool the sweat on her skin.

Summer and Cal were at The Table in the back of the Union. She showed them the message and the writing on her paper.

"She's trying to force you out of the class," Summer said.

"Can she do that?"

They looked at each other and Cal shook his head.

"Don't know," he said. "Never had it happen to me. Seems wrong. You should talk to the professor."

"That class is the prereq for all the Gender Studies classes," Tucker said. Her words snarled together. "I can't get a degree in it if I don't take the foundational course."

"You want me to talk to Viv about it?" Summer asked.

Tucker stared at her trying to imagine something more embarrassing. "I thought you two were over. And no, I don't."

"We hooked up again last week, but then she was gone all weekend again. It's just weird. Speaking of weird, what's up with you and Ella? Ever since you and Lindy called a time out, she's been super touchy with you."

"We're just friends," Tucker said.

"Really good friends," Cal said.

"Really *really* good friends," Summer added. "You'd make a cute couple."

"We're not a couple," Tucker said. The anger from the low-grade warning spilled over and made the statement come out more harshly than she intended. She took a slow breath and said, "I'm with Lindy. We talked and I get what's been going on and it's cool. And Ella's into Shen, so just focus on the crisis."

"Talk to the prof," Cal said.

Summer turned to him. "What if she already saw the grades? What if she's in on it? I think you should go outside the department and complain."

"To who?" Tucker asked.

Summer shrugged. "I don't know, look it up?"

Tucker texted Ella and asked where she was. With a professor mom, Ella had to know the right course of action.

"Texting Lindy?" Summer asked.

"Ella," Tucker said.

"Uh-huh."

Tucker rolled her eyes at Summer. "Her mom's a professor. And Lindy is friends with Vivien so that would be as weird as asking you for help."

"Right..." Summer elongated the word.

Ella wrote back: *Lunch with Shen at the sandwich place, join us.*

"I'm out," Tucker told Summer and Cal.

As she walked away from the table she heard Cal mutter, "No kidding," and laugh.

The sandwich place had to be the restaurant where Ella picked up the bánh mì to bring over to Lindy's that one night. That seemed years ago now. Tucker walked over. The place was crowded and Ella and Shen were finishing as she came in. They stood up and Shen said a quick goodbye to both of them before excusing himself.

"What's wrong?" Ella asked when they were out on the street.

Tucker showed her the paper and the email.

"Summer thinks she's trying to force me out of the class but I need it for my major. Cal said I should talk to the prof, but what if she already knows about it and agrees with Vivien? Can you ask your mom who I should complain to?"

"Sure," Ella said. "She'll only know how to complain at OSU, but that should give us a place to start."

The fact that Ella said "us" and not "you" made Tucker smile. It wasn't intrusive like Summer offering to talk to Vivien, it was just this assumption that they were naturally in it together, on the same side.

"Do you have anything to show that this is because of her anti-trans position?" Ella asked.

"Just the material in the paper," Tucker said. "And how cold Vivien got when she thought I was trans, Cal saw that too and I'm sure he'd say it was weird to anyone we need to tell."

CHAPTER FIFTEEN

Ella

I called Mom right away about Tucker's low grade and she said going to the professor was a good choice, or to the dean of the department. But when I looked it up, Women's & Gender Studies didn't have a dean because it combined professors from English, History, Sociology and Psychology. The representative of the department who took general questions was Professor Callander, the same professor who taught the Intro course that Tucker was in.

While I tried to figure out who to talk to, Tucker was loaded for bear. She moved up to the front row of the Gender Studies class and made sure that on the days when Professor Callander was lecturing, she answered questions and participated. But at the same time, I could see that she was worrying. She'd worked her butt off for that paper and to be told it was poor quality, when she wasn't busy being pissed, started to eat away at her self-assurance.

Still looking for another option, I went over to the administration building. One side of it was under construction with scaffolds and workers crawling over the brickwork doing restoration. Dad would know exactly what they were doing. I just glanced up at it and went inside.

The inside had already been restored. It gleamed with warm, honey-brown wood above a slate floor. Dad would love it. There was even a little plaque by the door saying they'd used eighty percent locally-sourced building materials. I went up to the work-study student at the desk.

"Hi, who do I talk to in order to find out more about contesting a grade?" I asked.

He looked up and smiled at me. "I'm sorry to hear you're having trouble."

"It's for a friend."

"Well then, you're a good friend to have. You can go talk to the assistant provost. Do you want me to buzz him for you?"

"Would you?"

He was chatty for an administrative guy. Or maybe it was me. If I'd been a boy, would he have answered me in monosyllables? He certainly wouldn't have flashed that smile at me.

"He'll be out in just a minute," the student said. "Can I get you a cup of water or anything?"

"Thank you, I'm fine."

I sat in the row of chairs arranged along the wall facing his desk.

"What's your major?" he asked.

"I haven't declared, but I'm thinking biology."

"Oh cool. Nursing?"

"Microbiology, maybe genetic engineering," I said.

"Holy shit."

"Basically."

Yes, it was one of those days where I felt like I'd become the lightning rod for gender perception. Nursing? Really. Did I look like someone who goes into nursing? Oh right, I have breasts and that's really all you need, isn't it? Pun intended.

I managed not to say that out loud and his phone rang so I was relieved of small talk duty. While I was sitting there getting good and annoyed, a trim man with his brown hair in an unfortunate bowl cut came down the hall and gestured to me. I followed him into a heavily oaked-out office. There was so much wood in there I expected to see him using wooden pens. He introduced himself as Assistant Provost Gordon Dack and I gave my name but explained that I was just there to find out some things for a friend.

"I wanted to know the process for contesting a grade or complaining about a TA," I asked, sitting in one of the chairs in front of his big oak desk.

He didn't take the seat behind the desk, just leaned back against the edge of it so that he loomed over me.

"You can complain about the TA to the professor," he said. "Usually grade complaints are done at the end of term. It's on the website."

"I looked at the website. My friend just got her low-grade warning and it seems like it would be better to contest it now. Plus her professor's out of town all the time and it's like the TAs are running the class. It doesn't seem fair."

"She does have half a term to get the grade up."

"What if she can't because the TA is opposed to her point of view?"

"We encourage everyone to keep an open mind here," Dack said and leaned forward a few inches, which made me crane my neck worse just to keep eye contact with him. "I'm sure if her grades are low it's because of the quality of her work."

I stood up and put one hand on the back of the chair. I knew how to take up space when I had to. He leaned away from me.

"Let's just assume that's not the case," I said. "Is there any way to contest a grade mid-semester?"

"There's still a week for her to drop the course," he said. "Sometimes new students get in over their heads, especially in the first semester. She can drop it and still have enough credits to graduate."

"So what you're saying is there's no way to contest a grade until after the semester ends?"

"That's right," he said as if he'd finally gotten through to me.

"Who handles complaints against TAs if the professor isn't available?"

He paced to his window, then back to his desk. "Complaints are a serious matter," he said.

"I understand that."

"You can talk to the dean of the department," he said.

"It's a small department. There isn't a dean."

"The representative," he suggested.

"That's the same person as the professor," I told him.

"Then that's the right person to talk to."

I wasn't going to get anything more helpful from him. I said, "Thank you for your time," and left quickly.

Outside the front door of the building I heard a wolf whistle from above. I looked up at the worker on the scaffold.

"Did you seriously just whistle at me?" I called up.

"Oh sorry, I couldn't see from up here that you were a bitch," he replied.

That did it. If the patriarchy picked today to mess with me, then I was going to mess with it right back. I let all the frustration about Tucker and her situation and the stupid responses I was getting rise to the surface of my mind. By the time I was back down the hall to the assistant provost's office, I had tears in my eyes.

"He whistled at me and then he called me a bitch," I said, swiping a tissue from the box on the desk and sniffling loudly into it.

"Josh at the front desk?"

"No, the worker out front up on the...the ladder thingy, what's that called?"

"Scaffold?"

"Yes. He made one of those dirty-sounding whistles and then he called me a bitch."

"I'll take care of it," Dack said sternly. "Wait here." He put a protective hand on my shoulder on the way out and I managed not to shrug it off.

He was back five minutes later.

"He won't be working on this campus anymore. I'm sorry that happened to you."

"I'll be okay," I said, and then added with genuine feeling. "Thank you for taking care of that, I really appreciate it."

I walked out of the building without further incident and made it all the way across campus to the Union without being flirted with, condescended to or aggressively sexualized by strangers (as far as I could tell). Tesh and Summer were at The Table with Cal and a woman I didn't know. They introduced her as Alisa Foss, a junior who hadn't been around nearly enough lately, according to Cal. She seemed nice in a quiet, mousy way; she had a lot of medium brown hair that she liked to hide behind. I understood the feeling.

"I'm having a ridiculous day," I told them.

Cal struck a chin-in-hands storytime pose.

"I went over to admin to talk to someone about the thing with Tucker's TA and the provost guy was so condescending— like a first-year student doesn't know harassment when it's happening."

"Was that G-Dack?" Summer asked. "He's kind of a prick."

"I noticed. I go to leave and the guy on the scaffold wolf whistles at me and when I call him on it, he calls me a bitch. So I turned around and ran right back into G-Dack's office and did the crying girl thing."

"You did not!" Tesh gasped.

"Complete with real tears. He lit right out of there and 'handled' it for me."

"Isn't that sort of hypocritical?" Alisa asked quietly. "I mean if you don't like being condescended to but then you're going to act all helpless."

I thought about that. On the one hand, she was right, but on the other hand, why should I have to be the well-behaved one? Did I have to be perfectly good until the long future day when guys like G-Dack got a clue and stopped treating women like airheads? Audre Lorde said you couldn't dismantle the master's house with the master's tools, but she didn't say you couldn't just screw around with the master's tools until you break them.

"If people want to treat me like a girl, then I'm going to weaponize girl," I said.

The Table cracked up.

"I want a T-shirt," Summer said. "Weaponize 'Girl.'"

"I'm not sure it translates into that medium, but you're welcome to print some up. Just don't ever wear them to an airport."

"No kidding. I don't want to be on the receiving end of that strip search," Summer said.

* * *

I told Tucker a shorter version of the day that boiled down to the fact that we couldn't contest the grade and we should make an appointment with Professor Callander. I was at my desk, turned toward the room's inner door where she leaned against the frame.

Tucker sighed. "I guess we should do that. Something in me rebels against the idea of going after another feminist. There aren't enough of us to go around already."

"Vivien went after you first," I pointed out, but I felt the same. "Professor Callander will probably want Vivien in there too—do you want me to come with you so the sides are even? I'm good with academic types."

"That would be cool. I'll make us an appointment during her office hours and text you."

I closed the cover on my tablet and asked, "I'm headed over to the dining hall, want to come?"

"I'm going to Lindy's. She's making something."

Guilt flashed through me at the mention of Lindy's name, followed by a kind of sad regret. When we got back from fall break, I hadn't known what I wanted—and Tucker seemed to crave being in a relationship—so even though I wanted to get into bed with her again, I didn't bring it up, afraid to find myself in a capital-R "Relationship." But it felt like Lindy had swooped in vulture-style and carried her off.

"Did things get better?" I asked.

"Yeah, a lot, sort of," she said. She came a few steps into the room and sat down on the bed, slouched forward so her elbows rested on her legs and her fingers knit together between her open knees. "I kind of figured you didn't want to hear about that."

I put a hand on hers but I didn't really know what to say. If everything with her could be as simple and straightforward as having sex had been, I'd want to be with her all the time. But even on the ride back to campus, she was back in the drama in her mind.

She didn't have to tell me what was going on. Lindy was over in her room all the time if she wasn't over at Lindy's, and I didn't need to hear the details through the wall to know that the last week had included plenty of laughter and a strong dose of sex.

That had even driven me out of the room once and over to the gaming room to destroy an unusual number of opponents in *Halo*. I wasn't jealous exactly. My feelings for Lindy had gone from low neutral to active distaste and I didn't want her with Tucker—anyone else but not her. But I couldn't tell Tucker that. What would I say: *I don't want a relationship with you but I want you to stay broken up with your girlfriend anyway?*

It wasn't fair and there was nothing to do but suck it up and support Tucker.

"We're friends," I told her. "I didn't want anything serious. It was perfect."

Tucker grinned. "I like perfect."

"You can tell me about you and Lindy, I'm not going to freak out," I told her, gritting my teeth and promising myself that was true.

She looked into my eyes for a moment and then shrugged. "It's been pretty nice," she said. "She apologized and explained about all the stress she's been under and I guess it made sense to me. And then, you know…" A blush crept over her cheeks and I tried not to wonder what Lindy had come up with that would make Tucker blush.

"Did she explain to you why she lied so much?"

"I think she was just really distracted," Tucker said, but her words didn't hold conviction.

Tucker seemed like the one who was distracted, but I couldn't accuse Lindy of using sex to distract her, even if it was true. Maybe I'd get lucky and Lindy would call for another "break" or Tucker would get fed up again and go find someone better for her. Maybe by then I'd be ready.

Right now I really wanted comfortable and light, not dark and dramatic. Shen was so much easier to be around. He made me laugh and not overthink things and around him I could just experience whatever we were doing together. Was it wrong to want that?

Tucker squeezed my fingers in hers, then got up and went back to her room. I didn't feel like walking into the dining hall by myself so I packed up my laptop and headed for the library.

Shen was in the usual spot at the big table in the nook behind the vending machines. I sat in the chair next to him.

"Your eyebrows are unhappy," he said.

"Tucker and Lindy," I told him. "I keep thinking they're going to split up and Tucker just stays with her."

"I don't understand," he said.

"Neither do I. It's like now Lindy's being nice again and Tucker just forgets how upset she was. I'm worried Tucker thinks some of it was her fault or feels like Lindy needs her around to fix things."

"Perhaps she likes chaos," Shen said. "Not every person desires peace in the same amount."

"I'm glad you do," I said. "You do, right?"

"Peace in the real world," he replied with a grin. "Winning in the game worlds. Now, maybe I can make you smile. I found a little something."

He reached into his backpack and pulled out a flat, square box with a ribbon around it. He set it on the table and pushed it a few inches toward me.

"What this for?" I asked.

"I think you'll like it, that's what it's for."

I slipped the ribbon off the box and opened it. Nestled on a piece of white tissue paper was a silver charm bracelet with six old rectangular computer RAM chips dangling from it. In the context of jewelry, the small black, green and silver chips looked gem-like.

I laughed. He smiled at me and lifted it out of the box. His fingers opened the clasp and I held out my left wrist. He fastened the bracelet onto it and I lifted it and jingled the charms lightly.

"I love it," I told him. "How much RAM do you think this is?"

"Much less than your phone," he said.

Still smiling, he opened his textbook. I set up my laptop, but I watched him out of my peripheral vision. What did the bracelet mean? Were we dating? We'd been spending more and more time together, especially this last week and a half since fall break. He walked me from Machine Learning to my next class three days a week and most days we met up in the library or the dining hall, but he hadn't asked me out.

"Cal's big Halloween party is in a week," I said. "Do you want to go with me?"

"I'd like that," he said. "But Johnny will be upset if he and I aren't at the same party."

"He can come too," I said, but I felt disappointed. It definitely wouldn't be a date if Johnny was coming with us and I was no closer to understanding how he really felt.

"Do you know there is that movie opening Friday, *Cloud Atlas*? I'm fairly certain Johnny has no interest in it. He believes it will be too long and artsy," Shen said.

"Oh, do you want to go? I totally want to see that."

"Yes," he said. "Just you and me, on Friday, we'll go."

Then he turned back to his book.

"Shen, are you asking me on a date?"

His laughing eyes met my questioning look. "Ella Ramsey, will you accompany me on a date this Friday during which, at no point, will my cousin trouble us?"

"I'd love to," I said.

I wanted to scoot around the table and kiss him right there, but that seemed too forward so I pretended to look at my laptop and wondered if he was only pretending too. He was so hard to read that I found it almost infuriating and yet it was one of my favorite things about him—maybe not that he was hard to read, but the sense of calm good humor that he projected most of the time. Even when Johnny beat him in a game, he wouldn't yell or shake his fist at the screen like other guys, he just shrugged and said "Good game" and went on.

* * *

Halloween was midweek but that didn't stop Cal from planning a blow-out house party. The upstairs renters were having a party too and from what I'd heard from Cal the whole house was covered in orange Halloween lights and fake spiderwebs.

Tucker and I had our meeting with Professor Callander and Vivien the day before and as we walked across the campus I asked her about her plans for the party.

"Are you going in costume?" I asked.

"I hadn't decided," she said. "I'm tempted to go as a girl."

I laughed. "Does that include a dress?"

"Do you have one to lend me?"

"You're like two sizes bigger than me, I'm not letting you get your hands on any of my dresses. Though I do have a stretchy skirt that would look cute on you. It would even go with your boots."

"What about you?"

"I was thinking of going as a very white Nicki Minaj. I have the perfect shoes for it and I found a huge pink wig. I've got to figure out how she does her eye makeup, though. That's way beyond my skill level."

"I thought you were good at that," Tucker said.

"You haven't noticed that I always wear the same look?"

"Well, it always looks good. And no, I don't know how to tell one look from another," Tucker admitted.

"If I get the Nicki Minaj look down, you'll see the difference, I promise."

We'd reached the English Department and I squeezed Tucker's hand. She flashed me a worried smile.

Professor Callander sat behind her desk and Vivien was in one of the chairs in front of it—the one farthest from the door. I'd never actually seen Professor Callander before. She looked younger than I expected—her hair was more black than gray and pulled back in a neat braid. She also looked tired. Having grown up with a professor mom I knew that professors had stuff come up in their lives just like anyone and sometimes that made it hard for them to keep up with their teaching schedules. I wondered what was going on in her life that made her look exhausted and haunted.

I offered my hand and introduced myself.

"You're not in this department?" she asked.

"Biology," I said.

"Ah, it's good to see more women in science."

"Totally," I told her and grinned.

Once Tucker and I were sitting in the other two empty chairs, me in the middle between Tucker and Vivien, she continued, "I understand that you have an issue with the grade you received for your midterm paper."

"I worked hard on that," Tucker said. "It didn't deserve a D. It was at the high end of the length range and had multiple sources. I feel like I got that grade just because Vivien doesn't agree with me."

Callander looked at Vivien who was sitting with her arms crossed and her pale hands in fists tucked into her elbows. Her red hair was tied back and up so it fanned behind her head and would have been pretty if she wasn't scowling.

"There was no critical thinking in it," Vivien said. "That's a hotly contested issue with strong works representing the other side and you didn't cite any of them. It was a single viewpoint stated as if it was a fact."

"Which you know because you disagree with me on it," Tucker said. "When you thought I was trans, you were dismissive and said I shouldn't be in a women's locker room. My paper can't be the only one with a single viewpoint. Did you give all the others a D or only the ones you don't like?"

Callander held up her hand before Vivien could respond. "I missed something," she said. She pinched the bridge of her nose with her thumb and forefinger, like she had a headache, and motioned to Tucker to continue.

"I told everyone I was transsexual even though I'm not," Tucker said. "Because some girls were being horrible about there being a trans woman student at the school this year."

Tucker didn't look at me as she said that and I was grateful. Vivien was high on my list of people I didn't want to come out to, her name right under Lindy.

Callander's thick, dark eyebrows rose high on her forehead. "That's an interesting approach," she said.

"It's not just that I disagree with you," Vivien said. "Most of your citations were from sources that are feminist-bashing. How can I give that a good grade in a Women's Studies course?"

"It's not feminist bashing to let trans women use the women's bathroom," Tucker's voice gained volume as she said it.

"Have you looked at how some of the sources you used attack feminists for daring to suggest that women-born-women should have the right to a protected safe space away from men?" Vivien asked at an equally loud volume.

"Gender's not as clear-cut as that," I said, much more quietly, into the silence that followed her remark. "I mean, there's still a lot more research to do, but it's likely that it's made up of many biological and social elements—and let me tell you the biological elements aren't particularly clear-cut. There's all sorts of craziness with the hormones and genetic receptors for hormones."

Vivien said, "But the patriarchy has had a lock on defining womanhood for so long, women need to be able to define what it means to be a woman."

"I get that. It makes sense," I said. "But don't all women get to figure out what being a woman is?"

"Of course they do, but you said, 'all women.'"

"Even the ones born with male bodies," I added. I glanced over at Callander, who was rubbing the back of her neck. She saw me and gave me a half smile, but it still looked like she was in pain.

"Shouldn't being born a woman also count for something?" Vivien demanded.

"If the body is the issue, where do you draw the line?" I asked. "What if someone's born with ambiguous genitals—are you going to describe the exact measurements they have to meet to be considered a woman? What happens if someone has a hysterectomy, is she no longer a woman or maybe just half a woman?"

"Are you sure you're not in our department?" Callander asked me. She waved a hand at Vivien in a gentling motion because it looked like Vivien might come out of her seat at me. Vivien sat back with a loud sigh and folded her arms tighter.

"We had a biology of gender course in my high school," I said. "It was pretty progressive." I didn't add that I co-taught the course.

Vivien looked at Callander. "Don't you think it's critical for women to have safe spaces away from men?"

"It's important for any group to have safe spaces," she said. "I suspect there are times when it's very important for trans women to be in places that are just for them and address their concerns. But it becomes a different matter when you're talking about shared public spaces."

"But trans women benefit from male privilege and then they think they gave it up but their insistence on being in women's spaces shows that they didn't," Vivien said.

I bit my tongue. Vivien was getting under my skin and this wasn't about getting into a fight with her.

Tucker picked up our side of the argument. "Maybe some of the people in the world who know the most about being women are the ones who gave up male privilege or whatever to be women. It's not privilege to ask for the same rights as other people."

"This is a very rich discussion," Callander remarked. "And I can see some of the factors that went into your paper, Tucker, and your thinking behind the grade, Vivien. Let's focus on resolving this. Vivien, what do you think would raise the grade of the paper?"

"Include sources in support of bathrooms and locker rooms being for women-born-women only," she said. "At least two."

"You know 'women-born-women' is offensive and misleading, right?" Tucker said.

"She's not saying you have to use that term," Callander interjected. "I don't see harm in including the other side of the issue. You're free to refute it. We want to encourage students to see all sides of an issue."

"But only some issues," Tucker said. "You wouldn't ask a student to refute feminism."

"Probably not in a Women's Studies class, no," Callander said with a faint smile. "Nevertheless, those terms seem fair to me. I'll read the rewritten paper and Ms. Yarwood and I will determine the grade together."

Tucker opened her mouth but I kicked her in the ankle behind the desk where Callander couldn't see it, though she probably gathered what had happened since Tucker let out a cough of surprise and glared at me.

"It's fair," I said to her.

Tucker rolled her eyes at me. "If you say so." Then she straightened up and spoke to Callander. "Thanks for taking the time to meet with me."

We walked out of the office and down the hall to the door leading outside.

"Women-born-women," Tucker said with a growl.

"Well, I guess no one wanted to say 'making large gametes' or maybe they just didn't want to have to check that."

"Large gametes?" Tucker raised an eyebrow at me.

"Hey, if you want to get really biological about it."

"How do you even check that?"

"It's complicated."

"Thanks for coming with me. Professor Callander seems pretty cool about all this, but if she hadn't been…"

She trailed off because Vivien was coming down the hall toward us.

"Lindy told you I wasn't trans," Tucker said and the words came out half statement and half question.

"She told me you'd said you were out of some noble and probably wasted gesture and you were riding it out for attention."

"What? Are you serious?"

Vivien turned so that she faced Tucker completely. "Why wouldn't I be? What you want to tell people is your own deal, though there are a lot better ways to spend your energy. People do a lot of crazy stuff to get noticed."

"Lindy said that? She fucking said that?"

"Ask her yourself," Vivien replied. She pushed open the door next to us and walked out onto the quad.

"That is such bullshit."

"Maybe Vivien is lying," I offered.

"I doubt it," Tucker spat the words out. "Fuck, now I'm going to feel like a moron every time I'm in her class. I wonder what else Lindy said to her. It's like one minute she's all supportive and cool and then she's coming after me about trans politics or doing this kind of shit."

"Maybe she's threatened because you're smarter," I suggested.

"I'm not."

"Um, yeah, you are."

Tucker gave a single, sharp laugh and opened the door. Outside it was crisp and the air smelled like decomposing leaves. Tucker walked steadily away from the building and I hurried to keep pace with her.

"Fuck Lindy," Tucker said. "I'm going to run off some of this anger and then I'm going to break up with her for good."

Thank God, I said, but not out loud.

* * *

After watching a few YouTube tutorials on Halloween morning, I did pull off a reasonable facsimile of the Nicki Minaj eye makeup. My pink wig looked fantastic and after that I just put on some tight black pants, boots and a hot pink, lacy mesh, silver-sparkles shirt that I picked up for two dollars in a secondhand store.

We got Tucker into my black skirt and did the black bra under semi-transparent white shirt look for her. I applied her eye makeup and she surprised me by coming up with a pair of dangling rhinestone earrings, saying she "borrowed" them from her mother.

"Look, I'm a girl," she said and twirled in the skirt. "For some reason this is so much easier to wear on Halloween than on any other day."

"We can't all, and some of us don't. That's all there is to it," I said, not mentioning that it was a line of Eeyore's from *Winnie the Pooh*.

"That's exactly right. Let's go to a party."

"Did you break up with Lindy last night?" I asked. "What are you going to do if she's at the party?"

"It was weird," Tucker said. "I went over there so pissed off and she just shrank in on herself and listened to everything and said if that's what I really wanted then there was nothing she could do. And then she locked herself in her bathroom and started crying, so I left. It didn't feel like a real breakup, but I didn't know what else to do."

I texted Shen and he and Johnny met us on the corner of the North Quad to walk over together. Johnny was dressed as a character from some game I'd never played, with his hair spiked up and a mismatched ninja/samurai outfit. Shen wore a Starfleet uniform and had on an exceptionally lifelike pair of pointed ears.

"Generic Vulcan science officer or Spock?" I asked.

He and Johnny turned as if they were conjoined twins. "Spock," they said in unison.

"Of course."

"Who are you?" Johnny asked.

I sighed. "You're serious, aren't you?"

"Some kind of Barbie?"

"Nicki Minaj, she's a hip-hop star."

"Is she good?" Shen asked.

"If you like obscenity and mild gender play."

"One out of two's not bad," he said and didn't elaborate. I wanted to ask, but it didn't seem like the right time.

The house was decorated with a mishmash of Halloween lights and decorations on the first floor, and blue and white holiday lights on the second floor. I guessed they figured if they got them up this early they could just leave them up through the new year. We could hear the music a few doors away, but hopefully no one would call the cops to come tell us to turn it down for at least a few hours. Students already spilled over the porch and into the yard. But they made way for Nicki Minaj, her backup singer, ninja bodyguard and Spock.

Shen and Johnny went to get us cups of barely chilled beer and I considered the dancing area in the hastily cleared living room. We could probably fit in there if no one in the group danced too wildly. When Shen and Johnny returned, Tucker wasn't with them.

"She knows everyone," Johnny told me over the loud music. "She can't go three feet without stopping to talk."

We stood around sipping the beer for a few minutes and occasionally yelling a comment to each other.

"Do you dance?" I asked them. Now that Shen and I had a real date, I didn't mind having Johnny around as much as I had in the past two weeks.

"You can dance in those heels?" Johnny asked.

"Watch me," I said. I put down my cup and pushed into the dancers with the two of them behind me.

CHAPTER SIXTEEN

Tucker

Tucker was a lightweight and she knew it, so after her second beer, when her skin started to tingle and buzz, she went out on the back porch to stand in the cold. The air smelled like ice and pine needles, and maybe snow was on the way. She wouldn't mind a few cooling flakes on her skin just now.

Ella seemed to be having a great time with Shen. Tucker had danced a few songs with the two of them and Johnny but then wandered away because she wasn't in a party mood. Watching Ella and Shen flashing little smiles at each other, and finding excuses to touch, made her feel lonely. She didn't think it had been a mistake to break up with Lindy, but she wanted to have someone with her tonight.

"Tucker?"

She turned and saw Lindy staring at her, light brown eyes burning like candle flames in the dusk. Lindy was dressed as an artist, with a big smock covered in smears of paint. She even had paint on her cheek and she held a full cup of beer in each hand.

"You're in a skirt," Lindy said with a shallow smile.

"I borrowed it from Ella so I could dress up like a girl."

"It looks good on you. Look, I wanted to talk to you more about yesterday."

Tucker opened her mouth to protest or make some excuse to go back into the party, but Lindy put the beers on the porch railing and held up her hand.

"Please, hear me out. I know you were really upset because you thought I told Vivien you only came out as trans for attention, but that's not what really happened."

Tucker waited and Lindy leaned back against the porch railing, looking sideways at her.

"That's not what I told her," Lindy said. "I told her I was worried about the kind of attention it was attracting. She must have misheard me. Look, I'm really sorry. It must have been so hard for you to even go talk to her and then to hear that…well, I'm sorry."

Lindy picked up one of the cups of beer and held it out to her. Tucker took it even though she thought she shouldn't drink it. She wanted something to hold onto and the cold cup against her palm added to the overall weight of numbness in her body.

"I know you want to split up, and I don't blame you," Lindy said. "I'm not going to crowd you if you want to date Ella or whatever."

"Ella's interested in Spock," Tucker told her.

"What?"

"I mean Shen, he's the one dressed up like Spock."

"Then I'm sure he's perfect for her. Anyway, I'm sorry about everything and that we're not going to work out. I thought we had a really good thing going."

"Me too," Tucker said.

"What went wrong?" Lindy asked. She was still turned sideways from Tucker, drinking her beer, deliberately not looking at her. Tucker wondered if Lindy was afraid of what she'd see in her face or if she was trying to give Tucker room.

Tucker took a sip of the beer. It was flat and bitter. She said, "You being so stressed out the last few months is tough with everything else going on."

"But the last couple of weeks have been good, haven't they? Other than the Vivien remark, which was just a misunderstanding. And we're good together in bed."

Tucker smiled. "Yeah, really good."

"You know, just for the sake of closure, you could come back to my place tonight. I bet you've never had sex wearing a skirt."

"That's true," Tucker said.

"Think about it," Lindy told her and walked away, into the body of the party.

Tucker drank more of the beer and thought about it. She didn't trust the "misunderstanding" line about Vivien, but there was no way to check it.

And she really was done with Lindy, but their sexual chemistry had been one of the best things about their relationship. Would one more night hurt anything?

She felt buoyant inside: her feet numbing with the cold, her head expanding from the alcohol. More than anything right now, she wanted to be warm and to be touched, to be lifted out of her life and carried along on a wave of good feelings. She didn't want to be alone. She went back into the party.

"All right," she told Lindy. "Let me tell Ella I'm going."

Lindy grinned back at her, eyes still bright, almost feverish. "I'll meet you out front."

Tucker shoved her way around people until she found Ella and Shen dancing by the fireplace. The heat and sound of the room pressed on her, but inside her head still felt light and cold.

"Hey," she shouted into Ella's ear. "I'm going with Lindy."

"No way," Ella shouted back.

"Last time."

"Tucker, don't."

"Closure," Tucker yelled and pushed through the crowd to the front door.

They walked down the sidewalk together, away from the noise, down the six blocks to Lindy's apartment. Along the way, Lindy took her hand and wrapped it in her strong fingers and Tucker started to feel warm again.

When they got inside, Lindy opened a bottle of wine and poured glasses while Tucker got out of her boots and coat.

"I've had enough," Tucker said.

"You'll like it. It's sweet."

Tucker took a sip. Lindy was right. She determined to drink it slowly. Lindy set out a bowl of rice and seaweed chips and Tucker grabbed a few to get something in her stomach.

"Do you think we could make it work?" Lindy asked.

So that was her agenda: to get Tucker back to her apartment and try to keep them together. The breaking up talk yesterday had lasted all of fifteen minutes, so maybe Lindy thought they still had a chance.

"It's just too much pressure to have something serious going on right now," Tucker said.

"I can back off some, make it easier on you."

"You don't deserve that. You should find someone who wants the same level of commitment you do."

"I don't want someone else," Lindy said. "I want you."

She leaned in and kissed Tucker. Lindy was a great kisser and even now it was easy to get lost in the feel of her nimble lips. But another part of Tucker's brain was knocking on the door of her awareness and waving a sign that said: *This is a bad idea!*

She pulled away.

"Hang on," Lindy said. "Let me just slip into the bathroom and get this paint off my face."

She fairly skipped across the room and into the little bathroom. Tucker stood up and looked around the apartment. Maybe she should leave right now without saying anything, but that felt too abrupt, too rude an end to their relationship.

Her gaze fell on Lindy's computer. If it was on, maybe she could just lean over it and look at Lindy's email. Maybe there would be an incriminating message to Vivien and then she'd know for sure that Lindy was lying to her.

But she didn't need to look for evidence. The fact that she was considering it meant that she didn't believe Lindy, and she didn't want to stick around someone she couldn't trust.

Lindy came out of the bathroom and saw her standing by the couch. She pulled Tucker back down to sitting so they were side by side again. Putting a hand on Tucker's thigh, she moved it upward.

"I like the feel of these," she said as she stroked the pantyhose.

"Lindy, I should go."

"No, you should stay. Just for tonight. One last time."

She kissed Tucker hard and leaned against her so that Tucker was pinned between her and the couch. It felt good and bad at the same time, but as the kiss lingered the bad outweighed the good. Tucker turned her face away.

"I don't want this," she said.

"It doesn't have to be like this," Lindy told her. "Just tell me how you want it."

"I want to go," Tucker said.

"No you don't."

She didn't know what to say to that and while her brain was trying to crank out a reply, Lindy moved with surprising speed. The weight of her body pressed Tucker into the couch, and her hand pushed up under Tucker's skirt.

"Stop," Tucker managed, but if Lindy heard her, she gave no sign. "Lindy, please stop." The words came out in a near whisper.

"No," Lindy said. "You need this."

Tucker's eyes focused on the barely-consumed glass of wine on the coffee table. She didn't think there was anything in it other than wine, but her body felt numb and frozen. In the dim light, the wine looked like fake blood, like a movie prop, as if the whole room and everything in it wasn't real.

She didn't want to be awake for what happened next, but she was.

* * *

The sky still refused to snow as Tucker walked back to her room, but the air was cold enough that it should have. She held her boots in her hand for the first block and then realized that was stupid and jammed her freezing feet into them. Her fingers shook too hard to get the laces tied, but the fit was close enough to keep them on the rest of the way. She couldn't remember if she'd had a jacket. She must have, but she had no idea where it went.

Wherever it was, that had to be where her keys were. She got to the front door of the dorm and rang the buzzer for the RA on duty. A sleepy-looking guy came to let her in.

"Too much party?" he asked.

She nodded.

"You have some ID or something so I can let you into your room?"

"Roommate," she said. "She'll let me in."

"Okay."

She took the elevator two floors up, leaning against the wall as it lifted her. On the third floor, she paused at Ella's door and then knocked. There was rustling and a mumbled "Sec." Then Ella opened the door.

Tucker held up a hand and shook her head. She couldn't talk. Ella stepped back and let her in. She went through the bathroom and into her room.

"I'll be right here if you need something," Ella called after her.

She shut the door behind her and locked it. She kicked off her boots and stood looking at the bed but she couldn't touch it like this. Stripping out of her clothes, she went into the bathroom and started the shower. It took her a long time to get warm and an even longer time to feel clean. Then she crawled into her bed and curled on her side until the sleep she craved finally came over her.

In the morning her head pounded with jackhammers trying to beat their way from the inside out. Any shivering now was purely the effect of fever. When she went to pee, she left the door to the bathroom unlocked and at some point in the morning Ella tapped on it.

"Come in," Tucker called, but it sounded more like a wounded goose call.

"You sound awful," Ella told her.

"Feel worse."

"Flu?"

"Uh-huh."

"I'll get you some soup and tea, do you need anything else?"

"NyQuil or something."

"Are you okay? Last night…"

"Feel like shit," Tucker said.

"All right, I'll be back soon with some cold medicine."

Tucker stared at the ceiling after she was gone and tried not to think about anything. It was easier than she expected.

CHAPTER SEVENTEEN

Ella

The first two days of Tucker's flu, I didn't worry overmuch; I took my vitamins and hoped I didn't catch it. By the fourth day, I was worried. It wasn't her stuffy nose or pasty gray complexion that bothered me so much as the fact that she just wasn't doing anything—not even reading a fun, not-required-for-class novel. I wasn't sure if she was eating either.

I'd left the door from the bathroom to my room unlocked so when I wasn't there she could help herself to my microwave and fridge, but whenever I went into the fridge myself, I could see that nothing was gone.

"Go to the health center," I told her. I'd pulled her desk chair up to the side of the bed figuring that if I was going to catch something from her, I would have already.

She sat propped up on pillows, the area around her littered with crumpled tissues and books that I had yet to see her open. Each time I visited her, there was another book on her bed, and yet she didn't seem to be reading any of them. A blue Freytag U mug steamed on the table next to her. At least she was using my electric kettle.

"It's just the flu," she said. "I feel a little better today. I can probably go to class in a day or two."

"Are you working on the new paper for Gender Studies?" I asked. "I can read it over for you if you want."

Tucker shrugged. "I'm thinking about dropping the class. Maybe I'll do another major, something useful like Communications."

"You're still running a fever, aren't you?" I asked because that didn't sound like her at all.

"I'm sick of all the shit with Vivien," she said. She didn't add "and Lindy" but I heard it in the silent pause before she went on. "I just want to get my degree and move on."

Her rounded shoulders and the darkness in the skin under her eyes signaled defeat. Until this week, Tucker had always seemed larger than life to me—so outgoing with her opinions and her affections, and now I was looking at a shadow of her.

I had no idea how to respond, so I said, "Shen's coming over to watch a movie on the laptop. You're welcome to join us."

She shook her head. "I'm going back to sleep."

Either this was one hell of a flu or something else was going on. I wanted to push the issue, but I knew what it was like to have to give out information before you were ready, so I went back to my room.

Shen showed up with a brown carryout bag that smelled of garlic and peanuts. "There is no good Chinese food here, so I got Thai. It's not good Thai either, but at least I'm not personally offended by it."

I laughed. "That's important."

We settled onto my bed, sitting against the wall at the head of the bed with my laptop on his shins and our takeout boxes in our laps. I rested my shoulder against his and he leaned over to kiss the side of my face high up on my cheek. I grinned and opened the white cardboard carton in my lap. It was pad thai with tofu.

"Not spicy," he said. His palate could take a lot more heat than mine and Johnny beat both of us, though I think some of that was bravado and not personal preference.

Shen reached into my lap and picked up my right hand, pulling the chopsticks I was holding forward until my hand was up near the base of them. I wasn't bad at chopsticks, Mom taught me as a kid, but I'd asked him for help weeks ago because it was a good excuse to touch and now I was in the habit of holding them wrong to get his attention. I snapped the sticks at him and he laughed.

"You're almost ready to compete in chopstick relay," he said.

"Is that a real thing?"

"If by 'real' you mean a party game Johnny invented to pick up girls, then yes, very real."

"Does it work?"

"Not to my knowledge."

"Have *you* ever used it to pick up girls?"

His smile was confident and reticent at the same time. "I never needed to," he said.

"How many girlfriends have you had?"

He paused and looked up at the ceiling, counting under his breath, "…eighteen, nineteen, twenty-two…" Then he chuckled and looked at me. "Four, counting you."

"Who were they?"

"When I was nine, Meirong brought me a flower and asked if she could tell the older boys that I was her boyfriend. She was very forward. I didn't disagree so I was her boyfriend for the rest of the year, but I don't think that meant anything. Then in high school I was with Yanmei for the last two years but we both knew we would go far away from each other for college. And last year I went around with Laura for the second semester, but we weren't well suited."

"What happened?"

"She found another boy, less thoughtful."

"I like that you're thoughtful," I said.

He smiled and didn't say anything, but I knew he was curious and too polite to ask the same question of me.

"I dated Nico for a while," I told him. "Off and on for over a year. And I kissed some boys. And…um…I kind of hooked up with Tucker over fall break, but then she was with Lindy again."

The phrase "hooked up" wasn't at all fair to describe what had happened between me and Tucker, but I thought it was a safe place to start to see if Shen was going to have objections.

"Would you rather date her?" he asked.

Sometimes I thought that if there could be two of me, like me and a clone, then one of me could be with Tucker and the other with Shen. But right now I'd still want to be the one who was with Shen. I felt a lot for Tucker, but some of it was so complicated I didn't even know where to start thinking about it.

"No," I snuggled closer into his shoulder, "I really like spending time with you."

"Good," he said.

"But I'm worried about Tucker. She's a really good friend and something's bothering her and I don't know how to get her to talk about it. I don't want to blaze in there with questions because sometimes it's important to have secrets."

"Yes," he agreed. "I will never tell you that I'm secretly drawn to Japanese flower arranging. Oh, rats."

After a moment of silence where we both ate a little, he added, "If she is going to tell anyone, it will be you. And you'll be the right person for her to tell."

"Thanks."

We didn't say anything more on the topic of Tucker or other people we'd dated, but I felt better. Being around Shen had a calming effect, whether we were watching a movie or studying or playing games.

We'd only kissed a few times, and already I wanted it to go further—but I didn't want to come across like a tease. It wasn't like he was pressuring me, it was the opposite, but my mind couldn't help racing into the future. What would it be like when we'd been together three months or six? The only threats to the relationship that I saw came from my end. First, that part of me was also interested in Tucker, and second, that I was probably the most virgin kind of virgin ever when it came to guys.

Not only had I never had sex with a guy, but I'd only had a vagina for just over a year. How many eighteen-year-old girls could say that? I could tell him, "I'm sorry, it's new and they didn't give me instructions," but actually it did come with instructions. These instructions involved dilating it daily with a series of glass rods so that the newly rearranged tissue would develop adequate depth and width. For that I was really glad I had my own room.

Judging by the size of the glass rods and the size of the bulge I once saw in Shen's jeans when we were kissing, someday we could have a problem. There could be internal tearing if we had sex, especially if it was too soon after surgery. I kept looking online to see when people said was too soon but it varied from a few months to over a year.

And I was afraid it wouldn't feel right to him. I was afraid of a million ways of doing it wrong. I think at least a half million of those were shared by all women the first time they seriously considered having sex. Another quarter million had to do with being trans and the last quarter million were just me personally.

I wanted to talk to him about it, but it seemed too early to bring up. And I wanted to talk to Tucker about it, but she was in no shape for that. That left Mom and that was too weird a conversation. Did anyone really *want* to talk to their mom about sex after the age of six and the "boys have pee-pees, girls have hoo-hoos" conversation? With my mom it was lingams and yonis, but still.

This was really the first time I was dating a guy I actually wanted to be sexual with. I could put it off for a while—wait until I turned nineteen as if that was going to make a difference—I knew he would understand. But at the same time, we'd come to that place in the relationship where I wanted him to know even more about me. Even if sex wasn't on the table (or the narrow dorm room bed), at what point did I tell him about my unusual life journey just because it was information worth sharing?

It was an important part of my life—like growing up in another country. Shen grew up in China and I grew up in Boy; was it really that different? Well, he could go back to China and he seemed a lot more proud of coming from there than I did about my country of origin.

* * *

Tucker went back to class at the end of that week, but she wasn't recovered. She walked as if something in her body hurt when she moved, and she spent all her time either at class or in her room. I invited her to the Union, but she declined. I suggested she go to the gym, but she said she didn't feel strong enough yet. Finally I told her she had to get out and insisted, gently, that she come over to the gaming room. To my surprise, she agreed.

She turned out to be a natural at the racing games and as soon as she learned the courses, she gave the old pros a run for their money. We stayed longer than she planned and I was glad to see her laughing again. Dusk brushed across the campus as we left, turning the buildings into low gray hills with lit windows like distant signal fires.

"Thanks," she said on the way back. "I needed that."

"I'm glad you came. You totally smoked Johnny on—" I stopped because she froze and was staring in the direction of our dorm.

"Is that her? That's her isn't it?" she said.

I looked in the direction she faced and saw a tall figure with Lindy's distinctive long, tight stride, walking with another woman.

"Yes," I said, but Tucker was already moving into the cover of the nearest building. I tried to follow, but I lost her in the shadows. She had too much of a head start and was jogging. I thought she had to be going back to our dorm rooms, so I headed there.

When I opened the connecting door to her room, I found her sitting on her bed, crammed into the corner with the cover wrapped around her.

"Cold," she said when she saw me. Her teeth clicked against each other, body shaking, her face white as paper.

I went to a high school with a lot of delicate, artsy kids and I knew a panic attack when I saw one. I sat on the edge of the bed.

"Just breathe, you're okay."

"It's stupid," she said. "It's stupid."

"Keep breathing. Is it okay to touch you?"

She nodded, but when I reached for her she jerked back. "No!"

"Okay." I got up and walked to her desk where I pulled the chair around to face the bed. "I'm just going to sit over here, but I'm not going anywhere."

"I'm sorry, it's not you," she said breathily, nearly panting.

"You don't have to apologize. Have you had this happen before?"

She shook her head.

"I think you're having a panic attack," I told her.

That got a nod, but she repeated the word, "Stupid."

"What's stupid? The panic attack?"

"Yes." A ghost of a smile crossed her lips and then faded. "And me. I was stupid."

"I doubt that," I said.

Talking seemed to be having a beneficial effect on the panic. Her hands were relaxing their white-knuckled grip on the blankets and her breathing was slowing down from the effort and distraction of making words.

"I tried to say no," she said. "I think I said it. I don't remember. I wanted to say no. I think I said no."

I didn't say anything right away because conclusions snapped together in my brain too quickly to express. Trying to say no, coming home in the middle of the night looking a mess after the party at Cal's, having a panic attack—they all added up in a way I really didn't like. I tried to remember all the people at the party. Hadn't she left with Lindy? Was there a man who paid too much attention to her? Could it have been one of the boyfriends of the mean girls?

"Do you want to tell me what happened?" I asked finally because I just couldn't add it up in my head. If it had been any of the guys at the party or someone's boyfriend, she'd have reported it days ago.

"I remember," she said. "I told her to stop. I said I didn't want it. She didn't stop."

"Oh God." The words slipped out of my mouth.

Tucker bent forward, curling in on herself, and covered her face with her hands. She was crying with deep, gasping breaths and I wanted to go hold her so badly that I had to put my arms around the back of the chair to keep myself in place.

After a while she turned her tear-streaked face up to me and held out her hand. I climbed onto the bed and took her hand in both of mine. I was careful not to touch her more than she wanted me to. She rubbed the back of her other hand across her face but fresh tears started down her damp cheeks after she'd wiped the others away.

"When I got to her apartment, I knew I should leave," Tucker said. "And she kept pushing herself on me and trying to persuade me to stay and at first I thought I could but then when I realized I couldn't…" The words choked off.

"She raped you," I said because someone had to get the word out into the grief-soaked air of the room and it wasn't going to be Tucker.

"No!" the word came out fast and hard, but then she whispered, "I guess…yes."

"It's not your fault," I told her.

She shook her head. "How can it even happen? I was there and I still don't understand it. How can a woman rape another woman?"

"You told her to stop and she kept going, that's how."

"I told her to stop," Tucker repeated. "She acted like she didn't hear me but she had to hear me. She was right on top of me. I pushed against her, but she just acted like that was part of it. She said I wanted it. No, she said I needed it."

"You don't have to tell me," I said.

"But can I?"

"Of course."

Tucker settled herself against the wall a little straighter and looked across the room. Focusing on the stacks of books on her dresser, she spoke haltingly, barely above a whisper.

"She had me pushed into the couch and at first I couldn't figure out what was going on because I'd told her to stop and she was still moving on top of me. I asked her to stop more than once, but she didn't. She was touching me and she got my hands pinned under me. I thought I could bite her, but I didn't want to hurt her. It's like part of me was freaking out and this other part was thinking she's someone I cared about, I couldn't hurt her like that. I kept trying to sit up and just move away, but she had one hand on the back of the couch and her whole weight on me so the only way I could get up would be to hurt her. I kept looking at her ear and thinking I should bite her and hating her, but I couldn't hurt her. And then she—"

Tucker broke off and lowered her face, covering it with her hand. She cried silently and then started talking again without lifting her head from her hand.

"She put her fingers inside me and it hurt and I couldn't believe it. I wanted to tell her stop again but all the pain was jammed up in my throat and I couldn't talk. I think I finally said something and she changed position and pulled my hand out from under me. I was frozen. I couldn't believe she was doing this. She got herself off using my hand and then she curled up on me and went to sleep like it was all okay.

"I got up after a while and went into the bathroom and when I came out she was still asleep so I took my boots and I left."

I squeezed hard on Tucker's hand where it was clasped between mine.

"I'm so sorry," I told her.

"Thanks." The word sounded hollow, but she tried to smile. The gesture was more of a grimace, her face splotched with red and her eyes bloodshot.

"Do you think you should talk to a counselor?"

"I don't know. I just want to forget it but I can't, and then I saw her and my whole body freaked out. I didn't even realize it was happening and all of sudden I was freezing cold and shaking and dizzy."

"Panic attack," I said.

"That's just great."

"It's normal for what you went through."

"Maybe I should just drop this semester and try again later, or somewhere else."

"Tucker! You could report this to student services."

"And tell them what? They're going to think I'm crazy after I reported the attack outside the gym. I don't want to be a victim and I don't want them to throw her out of school."

"Are you listening to yourself?"

She paused and the grim, ghostly smile came back. "Go on," she said.

"Report her," I said. "Let student services get you help; that's one of the things your tuition is paying for. Stay here, with me, and I'll help you get through the rest of the semester. You protected me for the first half of it, now let me take care of you."

Now the smile on her lips was real. Even if it was small and didn't take away the lines of pain around her eyes.

* * *

After our conversation, Tucker went to take a long, hot bath and I settled into my room to call Mom.

"I thought you'd be out with that boy," she said when she picked up her phone.

"Mom, I have a question and I need you to not freak out, okay? This isn't about me."

"Go on," she said and all the humor was gone from her voice.

"If a student reports a rape to student services, they have to keep it confidential, don't they?"

"That depends on your campus policy and whether the student agrees to have the police involved—assuming the campus is one that regularly gets the police involved. Sweetie, what happened?"

I paused because I never lie to my mom. I figure it's the best gift I can give her since she trusted me when I came out to her as a girl. However, never lying to your mom can get really tricky, so I decided a year ago that I could obfuscate from time to time.

"A friend, one of the girls in the LGBTQIA student group, was raped about a week ago but she's afraid to report it."

Mom let out a long, pained sigh. "I understand that."

"Really?"

"Some campuses are more advanced than others. Some have a real zero tolerance policy and others just want to sweep it under the rug. I can find out about yours. Does she know the guy who raped her?"

"It was another woman," I said.

Silence and then, "Oh. I don't know if that makes it better or worse—in terms of prosecution, that is—I'm sure it was horrible for your friend."

"She's pretty freaked out."

"Can she talk to her parents about it?" Mom asked.

"I don't think so, but she has some older friends. Maybe if she talked to them that would help."

I was thinking of Claire and Emily. Tucker talked about them often and seemed to view them with a respect bordering on worship. Surely they'd also tell her to report it and help her through the emotional minefield.

"Do you want me to make some calls?" Mom asked.

"Yes. Thank you."

"Sweetie, promise me you'll stay safe."

"You didn't raise a fool," I told her.

I hung up and went into Tucker's room to check on her and suggest she call Claire and Emily for support. I didn't give her the details of my conversation with Mom because I didn't want her to know there were campuses that didn't do much in the way of reported rape.

Mom called back an hour later, which was shocking since it was getting late on a Saturday night and I figured she couldn't make her calls until Monday. My mom isn't the loud-and-in-your-face type. She prefers listening to talking, and takes time to think through problems. Dad says she has a reputation as the "meeting-breaker" because she can summarize an issue so clearly that it breaks up deadlocked committee meetings.

"I don't like these statistics," she said. "Your campus only has a few rapes reported each year of the last five. With ten thousand students that means serious underreporting. Only one went to a criminal proceeding and in that case the rapist wasn't a student. Your friend might have better leverage if she goes directly to the police."

"She won't do that," I said.

"She could call the Women's Center in Canton and see if they can send an advocate to go with her."

"That could work." And if they didn't have an advocate to send or if Tucker didn't want to call them, I could offer to go with her. "What happens after she reports it?"

"They'll take statements and any evidence and then they convene a student conduct board to look into it. It's possible they'll consider this student misconduct and not sexual violence."

"Will they expel the woman who raped her?"

Breath hissed through her teeth. "Maybe," she said and I knew even that answer was her effort to make the situation sound better than it was.

"So she could end up having to walk to class every day on the same campus as her rapist."

"Once she's reported it, I can talk to your Dean of Students."

"Let me think about this," I said. "We might need that."

"I'll do anything I can and please tell your friend I'm very sorry."

"I will," I said.

We talked about my classes for a while and the latest date Shen and I had, just to lighten the mood. When I hung up, I peeked into the bathroom and saw that Tucker left the door to her room cracked open. I leaned through it. She was asleep, curled on her side in the bed with a pillow clutched to her chest. I wanted to kiss her cheek and tuck the blanket up around her, but I was afraid the touch would startle her, so I just turned off her light and went back to my room.

I picked up Erasmus, the stuffed tortoise, and ran my hand along the soft fabric of his shell over and over. How could Lindy…? How could anyone do that to someone they loved? To anyone? There had to be something wrong with Lindy.

But underneath the metal-edged fear and anger in my chest was a feeling of sick dread. Was it possible that by coming out as trans, even though she wasn't, Tucker had changed how Lindy saw her? Did it make her seem less human to Lindy? Or did Lindy think that somehow she was reinforcing Tucker's cisgender womanhood through what she'd done?

Did she see it as the act of violence it was or did she really think she was doing something Tucker needed? The idea made me feel like puking. I curled up with Erasmus between my knees and my chest and pulled the top blanket of my bed over him, up to my shoulders. How could any woman do something that awful to another?

CHAPTER EIGHTEEN

Tucker

Tucker went in with Ella on Monday morning, gave a statement at the student health center and let the nurse examine her. It was actually gentler than an annual exam from her gynecologist but Tucker had to hold on to the edge of the table to keep from flinching over and over again. She didn't want anyone to touch her there again for a really long time.

The stout, chestnut-haired woman who took her statement was a mix of sympathetic and baffled. Much as Tucker had been until a week-and-a-half ago, she clearly had no idea that lesbian date rape could happen.

Tucker kept a tight grip on Ella's hand and walked through the facts. Her brain kept flopping around like a landed fish desperate to get back to safety. She couldn't deny what had happened, but she kept flipping between feeling that it had been her fault somehow or that she was a bad person for reporting it. What if Lindy really thought they'd been having consensual sex? But how could she when she was basically holding Tucker down? And she remembered Lindy saying, "You need this."

In a way that was the worst part—that Lindy could have been serious, that she didn't know Tucker well enough to know how awful that would be for her.

She'd gone over it a thousand times wondering if she should have bitten Lindy just hard enough to let her know she was serious about stopping, or if she should have given her a good shove before her hands got pinned. She could have thrashed around or tried to kick free, except that she'd been paralyzed by the shock of it. She'd kept thinking in just a few more seconds Lindy would register that she'd said "No," that Lindy would stop.

The student center woman offered counseling, but it was clear from her expression that the counselors wouldn't be any more help so Tucker declined. She told Ella she was okay and went to her history class to have something to do, but she skipped Gender Studies because she was too likely to run into Lindy in that building, plus the idea of having to deal with Vivien was way too much. She was used to feeling thick-skinned and powerful, but now she felt that if someone tried to tell her which bathroom she could or couldn't use, or lecture her about woman-born-woman crap, she'd start crying.

She wanted to call Claire, but she didn't know what to say. Not wanting to tell the story of what happened again, she just sent Claire a message asking if she was available later in the week.

She spent the next few days in a numb stasis. From the safety of her room, she caught up on her remaining three classes and emailed Prof. Callander of the Women's & Gender Studies class to say she was still recovering from a bad flu and wouldn't be in class that week. And she researched majors other than Women's & Gender Studies that she could take. Journalism or Public Relations both looked possible—not exciting, but doable, and she'd have better job prospects.

Every evening, Ella invited her to come watch shows on her computer or play games on the Xbox her Mom had driven up to deliver from their house. Sometimes Shen was there too.

"What did you tell him?" Tucker asked Ella after the first night the three of them spent playing a racing robot game together, jammed into Ella's small room.

"Bad breakup," she said.

"Oh, that makes sense. Thank you."

Ella smiled, "I like having my best guy and my best girl in the same room. I hope you don't mind."

"It's cool," Tucker said, and she meant it.

She just wanted to be around friends right now. The idea of dating or hooking up with anyone felt so far away, like a postcard of a foreign place she wasn't sure she wanted to visit.

* * *

A week after she'd reported the incident, she got the first response from the Student Conduct Committee. It was fast, but it wasn't good. They wanted her to come in for another interview in a few weeks because allegations of misconduct had been brought against her by another student.

Tucker put her head down on her desk. She should have the energy to yell and to fight it, but she didn't. If it had been someone else, she'd stand up for them in a minute. If it had been some guy shoving her down at a party and trying to rape her, she'd have beat the crap out of him.

But she and Lindy had been lovers and friends. They'd been as close as she was to anyone, and she could still remember the late-night conversations, the sweet gestures, falling in love with Lindy's quick mind and wild ideas. The only part she had trouble remembering now was the sex. Every time she tried to remember the good nights they had together, she remembered that last night and her mind shied away from all of it.

Lindy's complete disregard for her that night got into her like acid, dissolving everything it touched, all the feelings, all the memories, all the dreams. She felt hollow except for a numb echo of pain where her life used to be.

Tucker knocked on the door to Ella's room. She was glad to see that Shen wasn't there, so she didn't have to worry about what he might hear. Ella brought the textbook she'd been reading, holding it like a shield, and came through the bathroom to sit at the foot of Tucker's bed.

"The conduct committee wants me to do another interview," Tucker told her. "They say I've been accused of misconduct."

"That is such shit," Ella said. "Lindy?"

"It has to be."

Ella's eyes narrowed and she didn't say anything for a minute but her body thrummed with tense energy, like a cat about to pounce. She lowered the textbook to her lap, spread her hands on it and stared down at them. Tucker wondered if she was contemplating which video game weapon she wanted right now to blow Lindy away with, because that's what it looked like. Then Ella shook herself, blinked a few times and looked at Tucker.

"Come home with me for Thanksgiving, please? You can just forget about all of this."

That was exactly what Tucker wanted to do. She wanted to get on a bus headed away from campus and never have to come back again.

"When are you going?" she asked.

"Wednesday after class. I'll get you a ticket."

"All right," Tucker said and managed not to add: could you make it one-way?

She didn't want to go stay in Ella's big house and listen to her clever family, but she didn't want to stay here. Here she could run into Lindy. Here the tight bars of muscles across her back and sides never released and she felt like her body was turning to stone.

She'd ruled out going to her mother's house for the holiday because her sisters would know something had happened. They'd get the story out of her and then they'd be horrified but have nothing they could say to her because they didn't even understand her being queer, let alone this. And if she went to her mother's house, she'd go to the hardware store to have something to do. But that was her sanctuary and she couldn't go there now and dirty it with these hands that had failed to push Lindy away.

If she had the energy, she'd get a bus ticket going west and just ride until she found a place that looked like no other place she'd ever been. Maybe she'd go to Minneapolis and see if Claire and Emily could help her get a job and start again. Could she go far enough and fast enough to outrun herself?

Easier to go with Ella for now. At least Ella's home wasn't a place she could mess up just by being there. She could get some rest away from here and away from Lindy.

CHAPTER NINETEEN

Ella

Tucker showed me the email from the Student Conduct Committee asking her for more information because she was the subject of another student's complaint. I'm not the sort of person who has a hot temper and even then I didn't rage or yell, I just read it through a few times and studied Tucker's face. She looked as bad as she had the night she told me what happened, maybe worse. At least then she was crying. Now her face was gray.

One very clear thought rose to the front of my mind as I looked at the oh-so-official signature at the bottom of the message: Whether you wanted a fight or not, Lindy, you got one.

I went back to my room and texted Tesh: *where are you?*
Union.
Come meet me in the library alone please
10 min, she replied.

I met her in the entryway and took her up to the second-floor study nook by the vending machines where Shen and I usually studied. It was still early, dinnertime for most students, so it was empty. I didn't worry about Shen showing up. He'd understand if I told him I needed privacy.

"What's wrong?" she asked when we were sitting at the big table on the far side of the small space.

"I need this conversation to be secret," I told her.

Tesh nodded and ran a hand roughly through her short hair.

She didn't gossip as far as I could tell, but just to make sure, I added, "So secret that you and I never had it, okay?"

"I promise," she said.

"Tucker got an email from the conduct committee because another student has accused her of misconduct. We think it's Lindy. Have you heard anything?"

Tesh looked around the room. Even though it was empty, she moved her chair closer and lowered her voice. "Lindy told Vivien that Tucker followed her home from the Halloween party and tried to get her to have sex and it got rough. She's saying she broke up with Tucker and Tucker can't handle it and is coming after her."

"Tucker broke up with her," I said.

"I know that. Lindy's a horrible liar. I mean, horrible because she lies all the time, not that she's bad at it."

"She's pretty good at it from what I've seen. But if you know that…?"

"It's not my story to tell," Tesh said.

I wanted to pry, but her eyes held a stony resolve. The same confidence I had that she'd keep Tucker's secrets and mine meant she wouldn't tell me anyone else's. I had to honor that.

"What else is Lindy saying?" I asked.

"Just a lot of bullshit. That Tucker's failing in women's studies because she can't hack it and she's taking it out on Lindy. And what kind of crazy says she's trans and sticks to that story even after she gets beat up for it. That Tucker likes violence and attention and…you get the gist."

"She says all this to Vivien?"

"And Summer when she'll sit still long enough to listen, but Summer kind of hates her right now because she's pretty sure she's hooking up with Vivien and that's why Vivien isn't into Summer anymore."

"What?" That wasn't a question, more an expression of shock. Tesh just looked at me and shrugged while shaking her head. "Does Tucker know?" I asked.

"Nobody *knows* anything," Tesh said. "Summer is just suspicious and the rest of us don't want to get close enough to Lindy's bullshit to try to figure it out."

If Lindy was hooking up with Vivien on the side, that explained some of Vivien's dislike of Tucker. Of course it could be the case that Vivien was just one of those radically anti-trans-women feminists—there were such people, though I'd never met one in real life. Still, if she had a bad impression of trans women, thought Tucker was one, and then found out she wasn't but still saw Tucker as a rival for Lindy's attention, that would be a pretty nasty blend and would go a long way to explaining why she'd given Tucker a terrible grade on a good paper and then tried to justify it.

"Who's on Tucker's side?" I asked.

Tesh blinked at me in surprise. "We all are," she said. "Tucker's amazing and Lindy's a lying jerk."

"I'm not sure Tucker knows you feel that way."

"Summer told her she'd beat the crap out of Lindy for her, but she just looked uncomfortable," Tesh said. "She doesn't seem to want to talk about it. I don't know what else to do."

"Keep letting her know you're there for her and that you believe her," I told her.

I didn't want to say that last part, about belief, but it was important. There are a lot of things where you shouldn't have to say, "I believe you," because it shouldn't even be a question, but where it's so important for the other person to hear.

When I first looked up at Mom and said, "I'm a girl," and she worked it through in her head and said that she understood, that she believed me, it was like someone lifted a ten-ton weight off my shoulders. Nobody was treating me like a girl and that invalidation just kept heaping up on me until she believed me and started treating me differently.

I had to imagine it was similar for Tucker now, with Lindy lying and invalidating what had happened. Not that our situations were similar, but the pain of knowing something and having people deny it to your face—I knew that pain. And no way was I going to let Tucker suffer with it.

Tesh's comment made a lot of sense to me. She didn't know what to do, and Summer and Cal probably didn't either. Neither did I, but I'd come up with a plan somehow.

"Tell Summer and Cal we've got to find a way to show Tucker we believe her, that we're one hundred percent for her," I said.

* * *

We hopped the bus Wednesday afternoon. I was glad Tucker didn't have to spend another evening cooped up in her room worrying that Lindy was out there in the spaces they'd shared, waiting for her to come out. We got to my house in time for dinner and then a movie and off to our respective beds.

I knew Tucker wouldn't come knock on my door in the middle of the night and climb into my bed, and in terms of my relationship with Shen I was relieved I didn't have to make a choice, but at the same time I felt sad because I knew Tucker also didn't feel like she had any choice in the matter—since Halloween, she'd rarely wanted to be touched in any way by anyone.

The next day, I focused on keeping everything lighthearted, which was easy because Thanksgiving at my parents' house is a huge social event so there are always too many people around for any serious conversation to happen. Every year, Mom invited Nico's family, plus a few graduate students from OSU with their significant others and kids. Because she was in anthro, she always ended up with a crazy blend of cultures.

This year we got Nico's parents, Nico and per two younger sisters, plus a Native American woman and a Canadian guy, both grad students, and a visiting professor from a town somewhere in Eastern Europe that I couldn't pronounce. He had the kind of accent that you hear in spy films when someone mangles a Russian accent. He brought his wife and their three children, so there were five little people between the ages of six and twelve romping through the house. Amy came back from school and brought her boyfriend. Mom spent the whole day cooking and we all took shifts helping in the kitchen and then the eighteen of us jammed ourselves around a series of tables that started in the dining room and spilled into the den.

I listened half-heartedly to a lot of high-volume conversations about the global political scene. Tucker hardly said two words during dinner and I saw Nico watching her with an uncharacteristically somber expression on per face.

After dessert, the party broke up into groups based on interest. The political conversation continued in the kitchen, the kids went into the basement rec room to watch TV and play games, and sports fans collected on the couch in the den in front of the other TV. Nico and Tucker vanished.

I helped Mom get the first load of dishes started and then wandered around the house looking for them. At the top of the stairs, I heard their voices coming from the library. The bookcase-door stood open and from outside of it, I could see them sitting on Tucker's inflated mattress.

Tucker had her back to me and Nico was sitting sideways on the mattress with per back against one of the bookcases. Nico had toned down per outfit to a brown, buttoned shirt with a mandarin collar and burgundy jeans, but compensated with a touch more makeup and long, dangling earrings made from tiny coins. Next to Nico, Tucker's flannel shirt and worn jeans looked very classic butch.

"Is it hard staying between genders?" she was asking Nico.

"It feels very natural to me, but I think it would be hard for a lot of people. It's always hard to be what you aren't, but there are so many ways to be, it's difficult to tell, you know?"

"You mean how do I know until I try it?" Tucker asked.

"Do you want to try it?"

Nico grinned sideways at her, but per eyes ranged up for a moment and saw me. Per gave me a quick shake of per head that

Tucker didn't notice because she was staring down at the knee of her jeans where her fingers idly toyed with a loose thread.

"I don't know," Tucker said after a while. "I like being a woman, well, a lesbian specifically, which is kind of like another gender half the time anyway. Mostly when I was a kid I didn't feel like a girl or a boy, not until I was old enough to be interested in other girls, and then it all made sense."

"Maybe you're not strongly gendered," Nico said. "Or you like to do woman in a way that isn't traditional. It's cool."

Nico was two inches taller than me, closer to Tucker's height than I was, and per darker skin and black hair contrasted beautifully with Tucker's midwestern tan and bleached hair. They would be a striking couple and the jealousy hit me with a wave of nausea. I leaned against the wall and didn't make a move to go into the room.

"Hey, I'm going to get something to drink, you want a pop or whatever?" Nico asked Tucker.

"Sure, thanks."

Nico came through the doorway and took my hand in one fluid movement, drawing me down the hall and away from Tucker.

"You look like you're sucking a lemon," Nico said.

"I might be jealous."

"You might be silly," Nico said. "I'm just easy to talk to 'cause I'm outside of it all."

"Thanks for—"

Nico waved a hand dismissively. "Silly," per repeated. "Go enjoy the party. I've got this."

We'd walked down to the kitchen while talking, and Nico got two glasses and filled them with pop. When per walked back down the hall toward the stairs, I didn't follow.

* * *

Black Friday we went shopping. Who can resist being jammed into crowds of maddened bargain seekers? Okay, just about anyone. Our tradition was to get a front table at a restaurant overlooking the mall so we could view the madness from a safe distance. Then, after lunch when the most insane six a.m. shoppers went home for their naps, we slowly browsed the scraps they'd left. Tucker came with us for that and also for the hike Dad and I took on Saturday. Between the two, I think she liked the hike a lot better.

She'd started to smile again, though it looked strained. She and Mom talked for a while about what you could do with an anthropology degree. When they finished and Tucker went to read in the other room, I pulled Mom into her home office.

"I'm starting to come up with a plan," I said. "But I don't know how to pull it off without drawing too much attention to Tucker. How do I get the Student Conduct people to realize she's the victim without letting the whole campus know what happened?"

"You need to protect her confidentiality," Mom said. She walked over to her desk and moved a few papers around without really looking at them.

"I know. She's been so great about not talking about me, even after she was the one who took all that shit for coming out for me. Oh…"

An idea peered up over the horizon of my mind. I looked at the parts of it I could see, willing it to clarify. It had to do with Tucker coming out for me and becoming a target because of it.

Mom waited. I think she was watching the cogwheels of my brain click together and turn. Tucker was already a target. I didn't need to tell anyone about the rape for them to understand that she did something brave and got hurt because of it. I could say that a number of things had happened to her because she came out for me and now she needed help. I didn't need to detail all the things. And maybe Lindy's willingness to do violence to Tucker had something to do with her pseudo-coming out too. Though it sounded to me more like Lindy wanted to get her way and was willing to ignore other people's feelings to get it.

"I can ask people to come to her defense because she was willing to come out to protect me," I said and I realized what it meant as I said it.

"That could work," Mom said.

"I have to come out."

Her eyebrows quirked up and she brushed her hair back behind her ear while she watched me, waiting for me to keep talking.

"If I'm going to ask a bunch of people who don't know Tucker to come to her defense, they should know she was hurt protecting me. Plus it'll take the pressure off her. You know as soon as I come out, *that's* going to be the big deal."

It had happened often enough in my high school—the minute the word "transsexual" came up in conversation, all the other topics were swept off the table.

"Sweetie, think about this," Mom said.

I was thinking about it. The cogwheels whirred so fast they blurred into each other.

Was it stupid to come out at a school where some of the students and at least one professor were clearly anti-trans? Of course. But it meant that as soon as I did, all eyes would be on me. I didn't want to be the center of attention, but if I was, I could use that attention to help Tucker. And if she was willing to come out for me, I couldn't do any less for her.

"What's the worst that could happen?" I asked Mom. "If it gets really bad, I can just transfer to OSU. Tucker's family doesn't have money. She could barely afford school and I'm afraid if she drops out she's going to see it as a huge waste and maybe not try another school. I know you'll make sure I get a degree. Tucker doesn't have that."

"And you have a group of people who will look out for you and Tucker?" she asked.

"I have an army," I said.

* * *

My next stop was my sister Amy's room. Technically now it was just the guest room, but I still thought of it as hers. Her boyfriend was downstairs with Dad and Tucker watching sports on TV and she was trying to decide if there was anything else in the closet full of her stuff that she should take back to school with her.

I shut the door behind me and sat on the bed. "Can I talk to you about sex?" I asked.

She flashed me a lopsided grin like Dad's. "You didn't want the 'sexual mores from around the world' chat from Mom again?"

On the scale of sisters, Amy was pretty cool. She didn't hit the top of the scale only because we ended up having nothing in common. She was tall and aristocratic-looking with an interest in world economics and international trade. I was short and with the right eye makeup could look like an anime cartoon of myself, and other than allowing me to buy cool stuff, I didn't really care about money. But she'd handled the part where her brother turned into her sister with reasonable grace. She started out worried that the kids in her high school would tease her about it and ended up concerned that I was turning out prettier than her. Actually I'd always been prettier than her, it's just no one felt comfortable remarking on it when they saw me as a boy.

"I think I've memorized that chat," I said. "But I'd prefer talking to someone who might actually remember the first time they had sex."

"You're thinking about having sex with Shen!" she blurted.

She'd already heard all about him the first night we were both home. In the past few days, I had showed her a ridiculous number of pictures of him, especially my favorite where he's wearing a bright turquoise knit wool cap and a scarf with about eight colors in it and smiling more with his eyes than with his mouth.

"Not right away," I said. "It's only been like a month, but I have started to wonder what it would be like and, you know, if it's going to be okay."

"Well, the first time can hurt," she said. "I don't know if it's the same for you."

"Probably worse," I admitted.

She turned so that she faced me completely and really looked at me. Her eyes had the same dark, open quality as Dad's when a problem got his attention.

"You have to take it really slow, and I mean really, like six times slower than you think slow means. And he probably won't last that long anyway, so get ready to try to have sex a few times before you manage it. My first time mainly felt awkward, lots of fumbling and I kept worrying because it didn't feel good, just uncomfortable. But he liked it okay."

"It got better, right? Even with the hurting and all."

She laughed and sat down on the bed next to me. "Oh yeah, it got a lot better. He and I talked about it a bunch and did it again when I'd relaxed and it was completely different. But what's great about it isn't the intercourse only, it's the whole thing. You know there's a lot of stuff you can do that isn't just intercourse, right?"

"It does seem like the big deal part," I admitted.

"That might be because people don't know any better," she said. "They see the whole tab A into slot B mechanism and figure that's about it, but it really isn't."

I took a deep breath and gave voice to my underlying fear, "What if I can't have regular sex?"

"First off," she said, "there's no such thing as regular sex."

"I'm pretty sure there is."

"Do you want me to go get Mom to tell you how many different human cultural views on sex there are?" she asked.

"Don't you dare."

"Secondly, lots of women are worried that they're not doing it right or they're not going to be able to orgasm or whatever. Having good sex is about communication more than the parts. If you care about him and he feels the same way, you just try stuff until you find what you both like."

"Try stuff?"

"Trust me," she said. "Have you told him you were built in a lab?"

"No, that didn't come up."

She gave me a hug. "Well, I hope when it does that he's really cool about it. You'll probably turn out to be his best ever 'cause it's better when you have to talk about sex stuff anyway."

I rolled my eyes at her and watched her go back to sorting through her closet. I didn't want to have to talk to Shen about sex. I wanted it to be like it was in movies where it all just flowed smoothly and everyone seemed to be having a really good time doing tab A into slot B. But with Tucker we had talked and that hadn't felt weird at all. Maybe I could do this…when I was ready. Someday. Maybe.

* * *

The hardest part of my whole plan to come out and rally support for Tucker, in my mind at least, was telling Shen. I thought about it all Sunday morning and during the bus ride back to campus. I wanted to tell him before anyone else so that he had time to absorb it and to react.

I texted him from the bus and asked if he'd come over to my room that evening. He replied that he was so sick of Johnny he was moving his bed into one of the study cubicles of the library, but once he finished that, he'd be right over.

I had leftovers from Thanksgiving dinner that I brought back with me, so we ate those in my room while telling silly stories from our holiday events. He'd spent the weekend with Johnny's family, which apparently drove Johnny crazy because Shen spoke fluent Mandarin with Johnny's parents the whole time and Johnny couldn't follow most of it.

"I was actually saying what a clever student he is," Shen said. "But he thought I was making a dog out of him."

"Dogging him?" I offered.

"Yes, that. He's very funny because I offer to teach him Mandarin about every month. He says he only wants to learn the insults and pickup lines."

"I want to learn the pickup lines," I said.

"One Chinese boy isn't enough?"

"It's so I can pick you up over and over again," I said.

"Then I will most absolutely teach you."

When we finished eating, I sat in the middle of the bed cross-legged against the wall and told him, "I have something serious to talk about."

He nodded. "About Tucker?"

"No, about me." I breathed in quickly before he could say anything and went on. "I want to share something with you about me that's very…oh heck, I don't know how to start this."

"At the start?" he suggested.

"I'm a girl who was born with the body of a boy," I said in a rush. "I felt like a girl but the wires got crossed or whatever and I had this body that didn't match that. I started transitioning when I was eleven and now I'm completely female, but I thought you should know."

I looked at him and down at my lap and at him again. His face was tipped down. He said, "I am ashamed."

Tears came to my eyes but he held up a hand and continued. "Ashamed that I gave you the idea that I would be upset about this."

It seemed to take an eon for the words to get through my ears and into my brain. And then I had to play them back a few times just to make sure I understood what he'd said. That wasn't the direction I'd expected at all.

"Oh," I managed to say. "You didn't. It's just Americans are so weird about it and I thought Chinese culture was pretty conservative." I was so surprised that I went back to rambling, or at least it felt like I was.

"China is bigger than America," he said. "There is no one way we are. I come from the south, near Thailand. I spent vacations in Thailand and I have friends who are kathoey. They're wonderful people."

"Kathoey" was a Thai word that could refer generally to transgender women, very effeminate gay men who lived as women, and sometimes to transsexual women, though as I understood it they had other words for that too. It could be loosely translated as "girlie-boy" or "lady-boy." I wasn't sure if Shen thought I belonged in that category too now or if he was just saying that he had transgender friends so he wasn't totally ignorant about the subject. I thought I'd better clarify.

"I'm not a lady-boy," I said. "I'm a woman."

"I know that, but why are you making it so clear for me? Will I be making medical decisions for you?" His eyes sparkled with humor. "Ah no, I see, we must have this talk because you've decided you will have sex with me. Now this is the best conversation ever."

I punched him in the shoulder. He chuckled.

"I'm not ready for sex," I said.

"I was teasing. It's too soon. I like this dating and spending time. It's only that when I'm with my Thai friends, with kathoeys, it's always 'Hey, what do you have down there?' from strangers. I find it distasteful. I don't want to be one of those people."

I lunged across the bed and hugged him hard. He smelled like warm cedar, sunlight, and black pepper. I nuzzled the side of his neck and that turned into a kiss. He pulled me further into his lap and we made out for a while until I had to push him away so I could catch my breath.

"I really like you," I told him, leaning against his chest with his arm around my back and my arms around his waist.

"Same," he said.

"I wanted to tell you that because it's part of who I am and I want you to be able to get to know me completely—but also because I think I'm going to have to come out to a bunch of people soon."

"Oh?"

I moved off his lap and back onto the bed as I told him my plan and asked for his help in setting it up. When I finished, he said, "You are more clever even than Johnny."

"Not bad for a girl," I quipped.

He rolled his eyes at me. "You know I didn't say that."

"Sorry, I'm too used to it, or maybe I'm not used to it enough. It's very strange sometimes. I lived as a boy until I was fourteen because my parents thought it would be safer. And sometimes it's really weird to go from one to the other."

"I can't imagine it," he said.

"I used to compete in the Central Ohio Science Fair every year. They had it in the late fall and when I was a junior, after I was able to start living as a girl all the time, I was at this science fair with my project and one of the judges came up to me and looked at my project and asked, 'Is your brother here this year?'"

"You don't have a brother," Shen said and then he got it. "Oh, he thinks you are the sister to the boy he met last year."

"Exactly. I didn't know what to say, but before I had to say anything, he went on talking about how great my brother's project was and how much promise it had for solar energy use in the future and would I please convey that to my brother because he really hoped this promising young man would continue in the field of science."

"No," Shen said in disbelief.

"Absolutely. So I said this project was the continuation of my brother's work and what did he think. He said the ideas were all great but there were some obvious flaws in the execution, but I should keep up the good work."

"But you were the same person."

"Not to him. Suddenly I was just a pretty girl trying to do something obviously too hard for her instead of a promising young man. It was the same work, though, and it was really good. I took third place for it and I didn't even place the year before, but that was probably because all the Chinese kids graduated."

"Assuredly," he said. "Ah wait, is this all a distraction to keep me out of the science fair?"

Grinning at him, I said "Assuredly." I held out my hand and, when he took it, dragged him over to my part of the bed and kissed him with all the distracting power I could muster.

* * *

I set the Monday night meeting in the Student Union because I figured we'd get twenty or thirty students and that's a lot for any common room. But when I got there, the big room was packed with people. My first impulse was to turn and run, but Shen came up and took my hand.

"We sent the invitation to our list and some members forwarded it," he said. "That's okay, right?"

"It's great." My voice squeaked with anxiety.

"Some are from other schools. Will we still have roles for them?" he asked.

"We can make them up."

Johnny came up next to Shen. "Hey, this is a crazy turnout. You want me to warm them up for you?"

"Would you? I'd love that."

He winked and bounded up onto the raised divider between the seating area and the serving area.

"Hey! Hey!" he shouted a few times until a general silence fell over the room. "I'm Johnny Han, welcome to the biggest, baddest real-world game ever played in the state of Ohio and maybe the world. I think you all saw the email, but if you're here for some other reason you can either stay and join in or go eat on the second floor 'cause we're taking over this place. Right?"

The crowd gave a terrifyingly loud cheer.

"Now we called this game Kind 2 B Cruel because we're just not that creative. How many of you played our Cruel 2 B Kind game earlier this year or the one last year?"

A bunch of hands went up.

"Great, I need you to forget all those rules. This is nothing like that."

They all laughed.

"For those of you who didn't see it, I'm going to read the invitation and then introduce you to your Game Mastermind."

He pulled a folded paper out of the back pocket of his jeans and opened it. He was great at this; no one in the room made a sound. A few of them shifted but all eyes stayed focused on him.

"Kind 2 B Cruel is a multiday, multilocation game of fierce protection and protest," he read loudly. "We have a student who has been attacked more than once by other students and teachers for standing up for the rights of transsexual students. Now the Student Conduct Committee is not paying attention to her complaints and failing to protect her on our campus. If you choose to play, you will be divided into teams with specific missions to protect this student and raise awareness of the rights of transsexual women to be treated fairly—plus a number of other women's rights issues. If you're not cool with feminism or trans rights, you're encouraged not to play. Please, no trolls or haters."

Johnny added that last bit. Trolls were members of online communities who came into games just to rile up the people trying to play. As he read that part, I saw a group of kids at a table to the side get up and walk toward the door. A few other people saw them go and were emboldened to follow: two got up by themselves and another whole table stood up and went toward the nearest door.

About ten people total walked out. I didn't know how to feel about that. I was glad they didn't stay and heckle or act shitty, but at the same time it hurt see them go. They were willing to come out for a social justice game, but not one that was about transsexual women.

"We clear?" Johnny yelled.

"Clear!" the crowd shouted.

"Then let me present your Game Mastermind, Ella Ramsey!"

I was afraid that if I tried to bound up onto the platform the way Johnny had, I'd fall and land right on my head, so I walked up slowly and let him give me a hand up.

"Hi everyone," I said and saw people in the back making the thumbs-up "more volume" gesture.

"Hi everyone!" I yelled and braced myself for having to come out at top volume. "Let me tell you what's been happening." I pointed to where Tucker was standing, leaning against one of the big room's pillars. "That's Tucker. At the start of the school year she heard some girls being mean about a new transsexual student at the school. Tucker thought it was unfair for this student to show up and immediately be the focus of a witch hunt of harassment—so she told them she was the transsexual student."

Every head in the room turned toward Tucker.

"The thing is, she's not trans," I yelled and the heads turned back toward me. "But once she said that she was, she started getting shit from other students and a TA. She got her dorm door spray-painted, she was beat up and threatened, got a crappy grade from a class that she did good work for, and more. All that because she was willing to stand up for a scared, vulnerable transsexual woman student."

Johnny was still next to me on the platform and he yelled, "Is that fair?"

"No!" the crowd bellowed.

"Is that right?" he yelled.

"No!" they yelled back with greater volume.

"We gonna let that stand?"

"No!" they screamed.

The sound vibrated in my chest. I looked down at Shen, who stood next to the raised area, and he nodded. Then I glanced over at Tucker, her arms folded hard across her chest, her jaw tight. I could do this. It was just like any other time I came out, only a hundred times bigger and louder.

When the sound of the crowd dropped enough, I raised my voice and said, "Tucker needs our help. And I need your help. I'm the student she came out to protect. I'm a transsexual woman."

A hundred different expressions of surprise came from the crowd and next to me Johnny said, "No way."

I held up my hands and the crowd settled a bit.

"I transitioned in high school," I yelled. It was a talk that felt familiar, just not on this scale. "And there are more and more women in the world like me. If you want more information on transsexualism, we have a flier with the basics and some good websites. It has my email on it so you can also ask me questions."

Shen was already moving through the crowd passing out stacks of the flier. I tried to channel some of Johnny's bombast and yelled, "Tucker put herself on the line for me, now I need an army of kindness. Will you put yourself on the line for her and for me?"

A cheer started in the back corner of the room near The Table. It wasn't a whooping-style cheer, but a chant accompanied by clapping hands and stomping feet. In seconds the room was roaring: "Ella! Ella! Ella!"

"Oh my God," I said to Johnny.

He grinned. "You're doing great."

The cheer crested and as it started to fall, he raised his arms again. "Rules!" he shouted. "You will receive assignments. If you cannot perform these, you must email us right away. The flier you got also has a web address for a site we tossed up last night, so no dogging on the graphics. Please register with your game moniker. We will be tracking every act of kindness daily on our site. You may form teams of up to four individuals or you can play solo. We need escort details and a whole lot of people willing to protest the university's bathroom and locker room policy. We will meet back here in a few weeks for pizza and awards."

He paused and drew himself up taller. "My friends, this is the most ambitious game we have ever played and the most impactful. I am proud to stand with all of you. Check in with Shen if you live on campus. Shen, wave. Check in with me if you live off campus. Let's go change the world!"

The group broke into chaos. Shen and Johnny sat at two tables next to each other and people lined up to register teams and get assignments.

Tucker came over to me. "I think you might be out of your mind," she said.

"You're welcome," I told her.

The denizens of The Table descended on us.

"That was so cool," Summer said. "You're trans, I had no idea."

"That's just because you haven't seen my collection of trans rights T-shirts," I joked.

"I still wouldn't know," Cal put in. "But that's not really a compliment, is it?"

"No."

"You know we have a ton of really annoying questions," Tesh said. "Do you want to just answer them all at once or tell us to stuff it and go do our own research?"

I laughed. "I can answer questions. That's usually what happens right after I come out."

I ended up sitting on top of The Table and answering questions for a group of about thirty-five students until the Union closed. Tucker and I walked back to our room together. She didn't say much and I didn't know what to ask her, but when we got to her door, she pulled me into a hug.

"That was cool," she said, her voice a little rough. She let go and went into her room before I could say anything.

CHAPTER TWENTY

Tucker

Tucker thought the rally in the Student Union was a great gesture and one of the best rallies, she'd ever seen, but she didn't have faith in it doing much of anything. The LGBTQIA students had rallied a few times last year when Cal was the victim of someone painting "faggot" on his car door repeatedly. Nothing came of it.

She loved that so many people showed up and seemed so into it. And when Ella came out, it was amazing to see the surprised looks on people's faces and then to watch how many of them smiled or nodded, or quietly asked their friends a question and then nodded. At least a lot of students learned a few things about trans people.

Tuesday morning when she opened her door to walk to history class, she was startled to see three students, one man and two women, waiting there. They were all wearing Freytag university shirts under their jackets with the university logo in white on dark blue.

"Oh, hi," she said.

The guy stood up straight and gave her a light salute. "We're your escort," he said. He had Irish-style freckles and a lot of shaggy brown hair.

She remembered Ella mentioning that, but it was buried under the general loudness of the evening.

"Thanks," she told him. "I'm just going over to history."

"It's our pleasure to accompany you," he said and he actually sounded sincere.

He fell in next to her as they walked down the narrow hall and the other two trailed behind. He introduced himself as Kieran and gave the names of the other two, which she promptly forgot. Once they came out of the building onto the quad, the three students flanked her. She felt a little silly but also grateful.

"I heard your team almost won the last game," Kieran said.

"That was mostly Ella," Tucker told him. "I was just the cannon fodder."

"Not anymore," he said.

When they reached her history class she thanked them.

"We're not done," Kieran replied. "We're going to wait here for you. We're your escort until noon."

"You three are going to follow me around for an hour after this class?"

"Yes, unless you don't want us to," he said. "I hope that's okay. We get a ton of points for it, plus it's kind of awesome and secret agent-like."

She thanked him again and went in to her seat. It was mind-boggling and yet she kind of liked it. This morning was the first time she'd walked across campus in almost three weeks without feeling afraid.

After class they were waiting for her in the hall. Kieran handed her a hot cup of coffee.

"I texted Ella to get your preference because Sue wanted to make a Starbucks run," he said. "It's an Americano with cream."

"Okay, I could get used to this," Tucker admitted.

"Sweet, extra points," he said and high-fived one of the women.

Tucker gave Kieran a questioning look. He grinned sheepishly and told her. "We score more points if we can do favors for you."

They walked her to the cafeteria and sat a discreet distance away while she had lunch with Tesh and Summer. At noon a pair of people in dark blue university shirts came and spoke to the first group for a minute before taking over for them.

"I'm Meryl," said a woman on the new team with short hair dyed indigo and intense blue eyes. "How was your experience this morning?"

"Actually kind of fun," Tucker said.

"Perfect. We're your escort for this afternoon."

It went like that for a few days. Tucker met more of the team leads. There were nine escort teams of two or three students each and she was told other teams would be on call for the weekend if she needed them. Some of the students weren't even from Freytag. Some were from a nearby community college and she heard that a few were from a local high school's Gay-Straight Alliance. They brought her coffee and pop and silly toys until the whole thing really did feel like a game, but an unnecessary one except that it did get her going to all her classes again.

* * *

It took two days for her to realize how much she needed them. On Wednesday afternoon when she was coming out of gender studies, she heard Lindy call her name. She froze and her heart raced ahead of her down the hallway. She took a few steps in that away direction, but her knees felt like they weren't connected to her body and she had to put a hand out and touch the wall to make sure she knew how to keep standing upright.

Behind her, she heard Lindy say, "What the fuck, get out of my way!"

Tucker turned. Her escort team stood with their arms crossed, facing Lindy. The three of them blocked the hall. The one on the end uncrossed her arms long enough to pull out her phone and type a message.

"I need to talk to you," Lindy said to Tucker over Kieran's shoulder.

"No," Tucker told her.

"You people get the fuck out of my way," Lindy said to the three blue-shirted guards.

They didn't respond. Lindy put her hands on two shoulders and tried to force them apart. Kieran and the woman next to him linked arms.

"Please don't touch us," Kieran said.

"Then get out of my way."

"She doesn't want to talk to you. Please leave." His voice was even.

"Fuck you," she said, but the commotion was drawing a crowd and Lindy turned on her heel and left.

"We have backup at the north exit," the woman who'd texted the message said. "Let's move."

Tucker felt like she was playing the role of the president in a spy movie, but compared to the panic attack, it was a pretty fine feeling. They met two other blue-clad guys at the north door.

"She left headed northwest," one said.

"Good," Kieran told him. To Tucker he said, "Did we do all right?"

"You did great. Thank you. That really was so much better than what could have happened."

They all grinned and insisted on walking her to the Union for a plate of garlic cheese bread.

* * *

That night Lindy came to her dorm room door and knocked on it, saying, "Please, Tucker, talk to me. We can resolve this."

Tucker's gut told her that wasn't what Lindy meant at all. With a sickening lurch in her belly, she wondered if Lindy wanted to get her alone to threaten her and then, if that didn't work, to fire off more lies and accusations about Tucker attacking her.

Tucker went into the bathroom and knocked on the door to Ella's room. Ella opened it with her phone in her other hand.

"I'm calling the cavalry," she said.

"You heard that?"

"She's not quiet."

A few minutes later they heard voices in the hall. Tucker recognized Lindy's angry tones and then the calm but firm sound of the RA from the second floor.

"She's on a team?" Tucker asked.

"Yes. Have you seen your scoreboard?"

"I have a scoreboard?"

Ella woke up her laptop and called up a website. It was rudimentary, but the biggest feature across the top was a scoreboard with a bunch of numbers. The measures were:

Acts of kindness: 14

Acts of protest: 6

Acts of defense: 2

Hours served: 57

Letters written: 98

Tucker pointed to "letters written."

"That's the number of people who have themselves written or have caused to be written letters protesting the bathroom policy or asking the Dean of Students to take your complaints seriously and proceed quickly on them."

Below the scoring dashboard was a list of teams and individual nicknames that showed the top ten in each category in descending order. Down the right side were photographs of players. She saw teams and individuals posing in their university blue shirts. One in particular caught her eye: a person of indeterminate gender, dressed up in super femme attire, standing in a campus parking garage, holding a sign that said "Women Protect Women."

"What's that?"

"We let people design their own challenges and this is a senior in the Social Science department who's choosing to protest at Vivien's car every evening."

"How's that going?"

"Vivien pretends to ignore it, but I think it's a pretty amazing statement. Plus it's started to go viral."

"Do you think this will actually make anything happen?" Tucker asked. Then she thought about it and corrected herself. "Wait, that's not the right question because things are already happening. I feel better. All the attention is kind of weird, but it feels awesome to be part of something big."

"And we just educated a lot of people about trans issues and they're having a great time doing it. I'm about to add two online modules about transsexualism and feminism that players can study and take tests on for more points."

"I hope I pass!" Tucker said.

Ella laughed. "You should help me design them. I'm glad you're smiling again."

"Me too."

"What are you doing for the winter holiday break?" Ella asked. "Want to come down and stay with me for a bit?"

"Emily and Claire invited me up to Minneapolis for a week or two," Tucker said.

She'd been texting and emailing with Claire almost every day since she told Claire everything that had happened, and Claire insisted that she should get away and come stay with them. It was exactly what she wanted to do. She just wasn't sure she wanted to come back when the break was over.

"You should totally visit them," Ella said.

Tucker looked at Ella, who had turned back to the computer screen. Ella would be the person she missed most if she didn't come back, though maybe Ella wouldn't feel the same now that she was spending so much time with Shen. If there was one aspect of her time at Freytag she wasn't ready to let go of, that was Ella.

"If it's cool with Emily and Claire, do you want to come with me? If we left on that Sunday after classes end, you could bus up with me and stay a few days and still get back in time for Christmas."

Ella smiled. "I'll ask Mom. Does it have to be the bus, though? Flying is so much faster."

Tucker shrugged because she had no idea what a one-way plane ticket cost and she didn't want to commit to coming back.

* * *

In the end, Ella talked her into plane tickets. She said her mother had a bunch of frequent flier miles and she could get a ticket for free so she'd split Tucker's and they could both fly for the cost of taking the bus. Tucker didn't tell Ella that this was the first time she'd been in an airplane. Her mom had always said she thought flying would be too frightening, though Tucker figured she couldn't imagine spending that much cash to get from one place to another.

The takeoff was fun. Tucker liked feeling weightless and buoyant as the plane gained altitude. Ella chatted about the sights they could see in Minneapolis, particularly the huge mall and the science museum. Tucker was more interested in seeing Emily's place and the University of Minnesota. It was a much bigger school than Freytag and Tucker wondered if she could disappear into it. She'd have to live in Minnesota for a year first to get the residency rate, but then she might be able to afford it if she had a job at the same time.

Ella caught her staring out the window thoughtfully and she tried to remember what part of the conversation they'd been in. Without her at Freytag, Ella would be okay. The gamers would stick up for her and protect her from the mean girls, right?

"What are you thinking?" Ella asked.

"How cool it's going to be for you to meet Claire and Emily. It's cool, right? Not weird?"

Ella smiled. "You mean the whole 'Hey, meet my other trans friend' thing?"

"Yeah."

"If that was the only thing we had in common, that would be weird. But I kind of feel like I already know them, you know?"

They landed and rolled up to the gate, and then Tucker had to wrestle Ella's insanely heavy bag down from the overhead bin, followed by her lighter backpack. They were headed to the baggage claim, even though they had nothing to claim, because

Claire said it was the best place to meet a ride. The Minneapolis airport was bigger, cleaner and brighter than Columbus, and Tucker hoped the whole city was the same way.

In the baggage claim area, two women waved as soon as they saw Tucker. One was short, in a knee-length skirt with calf boots and a red sweater. Black hair spilled over her shoulders and her dark eyeliner made her eyes stand out starkly in her pale face. The other woman was tall with swimmer's shoulders and a chin-length bob of brown curls. She had on jeans and a sapphire jacket over a cream-colored shell. They swept down on Tucker and folded her into a hug.

"Claire, Emily, this is Ella," Tucker said when they finally let her go. They both hugged her as well.

"We're so glad to meet you," Claire said. "I feel like we know you already. Come on, you have so much to tell us."

"I want to hear about this game you set up," Emily told Ella as they started walking.

The four of them wove through the labyrinth of escalators and tunnels between the baggage claim and the parking garage to Emily's gleaming silver Volvo station wagon that somehow looked old and new at the same time.

"Our new place is so cool, it's got a writing loft and everything," Claire said as they drove. "And it's just off a park, but this city has so many parks that's not unusual."

They had the top of a duplex that included both the second and third floors of a house. The second-floor area held a living room and dining room joined by an archway, a kitchen and bath, and two bedrooms. The third floor was a large room with a desk for each of them and another, smaller bathroom.

"We were going to put the master bedroom up there," Emily explained. "But then we realized this way one of us can be working and the other one can watch TV without disturbing her."

"It's not crucial yet," Claire said. "But when I graduate this spring, I'll be living here all the time and Em shouldn't have to put up with my crazy hours."

"You're already up here most weekends and all the holidays," Emily pointed out.

Claire slipped an arm around her waist and Emily put an arm over her shoulders in a sideways hug. Tucker felt the sharp burn of envy at their easy closeness and it made her wonder if there was any place that would be far enough to run away from her memories of Lindy and the ruin of their relationship.

"Where are we staying?" she asked to pull herself back to the present.

"There's only one bed in the guest room, but we also have an air mattress so you don't have to share," Claire said.

After putting their bags in the guest room, Tucker and Ella came out to sit in the living room in front of the Christmas tree that brushed the ceiling. A little black cat slept on the tree skirt between two wrapped boxes.

"If you don't mind my saying, you two would make a cute couple," Claire said.

"Don't pressure them," Emily scolded her.

Tucker looked over at Ella, feeling the heat in her cheeks.

"I know," Ella said. "But I'm seeing this really sweet guy right now and I'm not sure where I'm going to fall on the orientation spectrum. Did you always know?" That last was directed at Emily.

"I always liked girls," she said. "That can make it harder to transition, but I think the world needs more lesbians." She laughed. "Actually the two things just aren't related for me. And who knows, it could turn out that I'm just Claire-sexual. I dated a few women in college, but nobody really compares to her."

"Oh hush," Claire said. "You know I'm fickle and bitchy and temperamental and you only stick with me because I edit your writing and co-mother your cat."

"Some people aren't as certain about their sexual orientation, trans or cis," Emily said, grinning at Claire. "And I hear that occasionally in the woods if you sit really quietly you can spot a bisexual."

Ella laughed. "That sounds like me, except for the quiet part. I like everyone. But Tucker was taken for a while and Shen's great."

"You should start at the beginning and tell the whole story,"

Claire said. "And let me get a notepad in case I want to take notes. This has the makings of a great novel, since no one would believe it as nonfiction."

Tucker started the story, Ella filled in details when she faltered, and the telling of it kept everyone up well past midnight.

CHAPTER TWENTY-ONE

Ella

Emily and Claire had planned a solstice housewarming on that Saturday so people could have their own family Christmas celebrations. They set up a buffet table on the side of the dining room but no formal table because there simply wasn't room. Tucker ran to the store with Emily for a list of last-minute items while Claire and I set up the living room and dining room with a bunch of folding chairs.

I'd been watching Tucker, how her shoulders were more relaxed, how she'd stopped walking around like someone who'd been punched in the gut, how eager she was to go out shopping with Emily and see the city—and it scared me. I wanted her to be happy, but I didn't want to go back to a university where I'd just come out at the top of my lungs and not have her there with me. I didn't know how to stop her from just running away from Lindy and everything.

The event started in the late afternoon and Emily's parents were the first to arrive, having driven in from Liberty with her brother Mike. They seemed so normal midwestern that I felt like I must have seen them on a TV show at some point. Emily's dad was a hair shorter than she was but her brother was already her height and looked like he wasn't done growing. He was at that awkward mid-teens stage where his efforts to grow facial hair gave him a faint, patchy goatee. They brought two casseroles and Emily's mom went into the kitchen with her to help enact the reheating and serving plan.

Claire's mother and her boyfriend arrived next. In her mother, I could see what a middle-aged Claire would look like without the heavy eye makeup. She had fine crow's feet around her eyes and reddish brown hair. The boyfriend was a little heavy, looked friendly, and seemed very relieved that he could go stand next to Emily's dad and talk about sports.

Two friends from around town arrived: a well-dressed guy named Gabe and his even more fashionable friend Paige. They brought drinks and once those were settled in the kitchen, Gabe set about plugging his iPod into the stereo speakers to play a funky, retro rock holiday mix. I wandered over to him.

"How do you know Claire and Emily?" I asked.

"Emily and I went to the same group for a bit," he said. "You?"

"I came with Tucker, she's been friends with them for a while. Is it weird being the straight guy in the group?" I asked.

He gave me a considering look. "Not with so many pretty girls around," he said. Then he added, "I met Emily in a trans youth group, you know."

"Oh, I thought it was like a writing group or something."

"Nah, can't write to save my life. I'm a DJ."

"That's cool. I am too."

"A DJ?" he looked dubious.

"Trans," I said.

"Huh."

We stared at each other. I thought about Nico and all the people who couldn't or didn't want to pass as one gender or the other. What a strange world where half the time we couldn't pick each other out in a crowd and yet so many people I met still thought trans folks were only the stereotypes they saw on TV.

The bell rang again and Emily and Claire's friend Natalie arrived with her mother and older sister and a huge turkey under foil that had to be immediately transported into the kitchen and fussed over by Emily's mother. By then Emily and Tucker were back from the store and the apartment was packed with people talking and pushing past each other with table settings and dishes.

* * *

After we filled our plates and sat down around the dining room and living room, Claire said a simple, elegant grace and everyone got to eating. I wished Vivien could see this. I wondered what she was doing for Thanksgiving. Was she in the bosom of the anti-trans feminist sisterhood? What did that look like? A bunch of angry women sitting around a table saying a grace that began with "Fuck the patriarchy?"

That wasn't fair of me. She was probably with a group of good friends and family spanning two or three generations, not unlike this one. Hers probably had fewer trans women, but who could say. Maybe she had a cousin or a relative's partner who just wasn't out to her.

I sat on a folding chair between Tucker and Natalie, who spent most of the meal having an animated discussion of employment law, bathrooms and transgender rights. Natalie was pre-law and Tucker now knew a surprising amount about the legal issues surrounding bathrooms.

"What do you think?" Natalie asked me mid-conversation. She caught me off guard as I was listening to the tunes from Gabe's mix.

"I'm pretty sure Tucker knows more about being a transsexual woman than I do," I said and they both laughed.

Claire and Emily were at the short end of the dining room, what would have been the head of the table if there was one, with Emily's mother on her other side and Natalie's mother next to her. I'd read Emily's book and they sort of looked like they could be those parents, but her mother smiled a lot more than I expected; she and Natalie's mother seemed to have lots to talk about and when I caught snippets of their conversation I was surprised that it was about house remodeling and not about their daughters.

Gabe was on the couch, with Paige on one side of him and Emily's brother Mike on the other side. Mike clearly had a huge crush on Paige and was trying to impress her by saying something smart about music; he was totally out of his depth with Gabe. Emily's father had pulled his chair up to the side by Mike and was eating silently until the song playing from Gabe's iPod switched over and then his head came up and he looked at Gabe.

"That Paul Simon?" he asked. "'Loves Me Like a Rock?'"

"It is." Gabe's face was momentarily wary until Emily's dad's mouth twisted up into an appreciative grin.

"I was nine years old when that came out," he said. "My favorite damned song that whole year and most of the next."

"What replaced it?" Gabe asked and then they were off and talking about songs of the '70s with a speed and passion that I couldn't follow.

All the conversations reminded me of holidays at my house. I was eager to get home again and to have Shen with me and have him meet everyone. He seemed to like being the quiet one in the eye of the conversational storm, so I hoped it wouldn't be too intimidating.

When everyone was done eating, I helped with the dishes and then wandered back through the living room, looking for a conversation to drop into. I ended up gazing at the ornaments on the tree and staring out the front window at the snowy park across the street.

"You're standing under the mistletoe," Tucker said from beside me.

I turned, put my hands on her cheeks and kissed her quickly.

"Come back to school with me," I said.

"My flight's not for a week," she reminded me.

"Next semester. Please, tell me you'll still be there."

"Ella," she said, and sighed.

"I know you're thinking about staying here," I told her.

"It's that obvious, huh? The game has been great and the rallying, but I just don't want to spend every day wondering if I'm going to run into Lindy, or trying to avoid any class that Vivien TAs."

"What would you do?" I asked.

"Move up here and get a job fixing snowblowers," she said. "Just get away from everything. Apply to some other schools."

I saw the doubt in her eyes. We were still standing together under the mistletoe, so I pulled her close and hugged her for a long time. I didn't know what to tell her to make it all right again. What I really wanted to say was: "I don't want to be there without you," but that didn't seem fair. How could I kiss her and ask her to come back into a shitty environment just for me when I was seeing someone else? What did I have to offer now?

* * *

I left Tucker in Minneapolis and flew back to Ohio two days before Christmas. I hoped that more time away would do Tucker good, but I was ready to get home and see my family. I love the holidays with them. Dad gets sillier than usual, Amy comes home from school and we usually sit around watching sappy movies and talking about cool stuff. Although I'd invited Shen, all the way back from Minneapolis I worried about what it would be like to have him there. Would he think my family was crazy? Would they find his quiet manner off-putting? Would Amy ask us some really embarrassing question about whether we were having sex yet or not and if so how it went? Okay, not that last one because she had a pretty fair sense of decorum, but still I could imagine so many things going wrong.

Shen caught the bus down from Cleveland and Dad and I went to pick him up because Mom was cleaning for company, which always seemed futile to me because we were just going to mess the place up again. He looked darling standing on the bus platform with his suitcase, his bright knit cap and his long, dark, winter coat. He introduced himself quite formally to Dad, which was the only sign that he felt as nervous as I did.

When we got home, Mom toured him around the house and showed him the air mattress in the library where he'd sleep. She apologized for it a few times, but with Amy and me both home, there weren't any extra bedrooms and Mom wasn't about to let him sleep in my room.

We usually did a big meal for Christmas Eve and each opened a present from someone else, then had a smaller family meal of leftovers on Christmas and sat around watching a movie together. As usual, Mom brought home anyone from the university who didn't have somewhere else to go. We had Nico's family again and this time she invited a few Chinese grad students. I suspected that was for Shen's benefit.

Dinner table conversation was wide-ranging. At one point, Nico's mom asked Shen what was the current state of the one-child per family policy in China.

"It's still enforced in many cities," he said. "It's not an ideal solution, but I understand its implementation. When I was young, I badly wanted a brother, but now that I live with Johnny, I see that my childish wishes were misplaced."

I laughed but at least half of the table didn't understand that he was joking.

"Brothers are overrated," Amy said. "Now if you got to have a sister, that would be something."

"Yes, then Ella would not have to teach me how to dress so late in life," Shen replied.

"If we really want effective population control, we're going to have to educate more of the world's women," Mom said. "That and improved healthcare are two of the factors that have the most impact in birth rates."

"Educating more women would take care of most of the world's ills, as I understand it," Dad said. "I think men should just take a backseat for the next two thousand years."

"I don't know, Dad, you're talking about billions of men who'd suddenly have to become comfortable with a new way of doing things. They'd have to deal with communication and alliance-building and prettier civic spaces."

"I'm in for that last one!" he said.

"The gate of the mystic female is called the root of Heaven and Earth," Shen said, then added, "The Tao Te Ching."

Dad raised his wineglass. "To the mystic female," he said. "I couldn't have put it better myself."

We all toasted and fell into small side conversations. Later, cuddling with Shen on the couch in the den, I asked him, "Are you just trying to get access to my gate of the mystic female?"

"Without a doubt," he said. Then he chuckled and kissed me. "But it's not what you think I think it is."

I had to ponder that for a long time.

* * *

Tucker didn't have to say anything more for me to know she still didn't want to come back to Ohio. Her texts got farther apart the closer we got to her flight home. I made sure that I was forwarding all of the new scores for the Kind 2 B Cruel game and the creative ways players were coming up with to get points for their teams. I wanted her to see that the campus she came back to could be a welcoming place, even though I couldn't get rid of Vivien or Lindy for her.

I sent her photos from a campaign that one team did to change the gender signs on the bathrooms all over campus. One set of signs now said "innies" and "outies." Another said: "danglers" and "hot pockets."

Yet another set changed it to "skirts" and "pants." And in that same building there was a set of restrooms that replaced the stock image of a person in a skirt with an exact copy of that icon that looked like C3PO from *Star Wars* and the distinction was "humans" and "AIs."

Up one more floor the icons had been replaced with pictures of Spock and Captain Kirk in which Kirk was yelling and Spock looked as cool as always. The signs read: "logic" and "emotion." I suspected Johnny and Shen did that one.

The administration and probably some of the mean girls were tearing down the signs as fast as they went up, but the players were great about taking photos of the signs and posting them on the game site so that everyone involved could enjoy their creativity.

Tucker responded to my photo messages with a few of her own. She sent me a pic of a fresh snowfall in the park across from Claire and Emily's apartment, and one of a waterfall surrounded by icy branches. They looked cold but beautiful.

When are you coming back to campus? I texted her.

Sunday night. I fly in Thurs., work at the shop all weekend.

I had trouble believing a small hardware store had that much work to do the weekend after New Year's. I texted back, *Still worried about Lindy? I'll make sure we have a team available if you want to come back earlier.*

Yeah, of course, but the shop's putting two snowblowers aside for me. You don't need to have folks to watch over me. Unless they need the points.

Lol, everyone wants more points.

I tried to stay lighthearted in the texts and other updates, but the fact that she'd already talked to the shop where she worked on weekends and asked them to let her work on snowblowers felt like a very bad sign.

CHAPTER TWENTY-TWO

Tucker

Tucker made it back to the school late Sunday night with just enough time to catch up with Ella before they both wandered off to bed. She was glad to have an escort to her classes that first week. As soon as she'd set foot on Freytag again, she'd started looking over her shoulder for Lindy. But now the escort also felt claustrophobic. She didn't want to be the student everyone was looking at and talking about, at least not for this reason.

She thought about what Vivien had said in class, about wasting resources, and she was starting to feel some truth in that. These players in the Kind 2 B Cruel game could be spending their time on something more important than walking her around campus.

A week into the new semester, the Dean of Students called Tucker and Ella in for a meeting. They were shown into her office as soon as they arrived. Dean Chilvers invited them to sit and closed the door. She was a stocky woman with rust-brown hair kept short and curling randomly. Tucker was surprised to see her office shelves crammed with sports memorabilia and trophies from Freytag and other schools, for team sports and a few that looked like solo events. She couldn't tell if they were the dean's or from her kids or maybe students she knew.

The dean sat behind her desk and let them introduce themselves before she said, "Help me understand what's going on. I've got a real mess here. I'm seeing groups of students in university logo gear moving around the campus, staging small protests. I have two complaints here from Ms. Tucker, but as I understand it the protests are about anti-transsexual sentiments and the student who is transsexual is Ms. Ramsey?"

"Yes," Ella said. "Tucker only said she was in order to protect me."

"Protect you from what?" she asked. "Nothing ever happened to you."

"I didn't share information about myself until late November," Ella said. "I consider it to be rather personal."

"And no one would guess," the dean said. "You look very natural."

"I am the product of millions of years of evolution," Ella said.

Tucker thought the dean should have looked at least a little embarrassed about the "natural" comment, but she didn't. Breaking into the conversation, Tucker explained, "It all started because a student working in admissions saw a memo about a transsexual student in the dorms. She was talking about it with her friends in the Union."

Now a ruddy color rose in the dean's cheeks, and she jotted a quick note before asking, "Do you know this student's name? That information should be confidential."

"I could point them out to you."

"I presume the student they were talking about is Ms. Ramsey," the dean said.

"Yes, but I didn't know that, I just wanted them to stop being so prejudiced so I said that it was me. And then I got harassed in the women's locker room and beat up and the university came out with this bogus policy saying that trans people can only use the facilities corresponding to their birth certificate."

"What's the problem there?" the dean asked.

"You can't change your birth certificate in Ohio," Ella said. "Mine still says I'm male."

"Well shit," the dean said. Tucker saw Ella's head jerk back in surprise and suppressed a smile. She'd heard the hint of rural Ohio farm country in the dean's words and it made her feel a little more at home.

"Yeah, basically you told Ella she's supposed to use the men's room," Tucker said.

"Plus it's offensive," Ella added. "Even if we were in a state where I could change it, I might be asked to prove I had sex reassignment surgery and I don't know a lot of eighteen-year-olds with families who can afford that and college. I'm lucky, but what about some other girl who just wants to get along with her life and the school is basically telling her she has to out herself and put herself in danger?"

"We'll take a serious look at that policy and convene a diversity committee," the dean said. "But now I have to talk to you about this other complaint against Lindy Heaton."

The dean paused and looked from Tucker to Ella and back to Tucker again. She shifted the files on her desk in order to pull one to the top, though she didn't open it. Resting her hand on it for a moment, she pushed up from her chair and walked over to the window that looked across the big quad.

"I'm not unsympathetic," she said. "But let me explain one of my many problems with this situation to you. I understand that Ms. Tucker and Ms. Heaton were dating and now I have a report from each of you saying that the other assaulted her. It is essentially your word against hers because as far as I can tell the only evidence collected simply verifies that the two of you had a sexual relationship, which neither of you deny."

She turned from the window back to them. Under her navy blazer, her shoulders looked thick with muscle and Tucker wondered what sports she'd been in. She wanted to get up from her chair too and move around the room, maybe look at the trophies, because now that the dean was talking about her and Lindy, it felt like the walls were pressing in on her. The air grew heavy and sickening.

"I know that young romance can be painful and breakups terrible," the dean said. "How do you intend me to determine if there was wrongdoing and who did it to whom? I'm not a court. If you feel strongly about this, I recommend that you go to the police."

"There must be something you can do," Ella said. To Tucker she sounded amazingly calm because Tucker felt ready to hurl.

"I can invoke a campus order for protection against both parties stating that you may not come within one hundred feet of each other."

"Yeah okay," Tucker said because she wanted to get out of the chair and the room and maybe the campus.

"I don't trust Lindy to follow that order," Ella said.

"If Ms. Heaton does break the order I expect you to report it immediately. That will be cause for disciplinary action."

Tucker got out of her chair and walked over to the bookcase by the door, breathing quickly through her mouth. She felt the dean watching her, but she didn't say anything. Soccer, that's what these trophies were for—1990 and 1991. She made herself calculate how many years ago that was while her heart slowed and the sick feeling slid down her lungs and settled in her gut.

Tucker wasn't sure if the dean had stopped talking for a minute or if she'd missed what was said, but now the dean had moved on to another topic and she didn't seem to expect Tucker to respond.

"We need to talk about these other protests," she was saying. "I can't have students staking out a TA's car or home; that's stalking and if it keeps up there's going to be hell to pay. That group playing card games in the administration office is costing everyone time and money, plus no one has been able to get into the admin building bathrooms all week because someone superglued them shut—and that is vandalism."

"We'll stop it," Ella said. "But it would be good to have some news come out about the diversity committee and the bathroom ruling."

The dean made a sound of agreement. "I understand you want students to feel a sense of agency in this. I must say, this is the most well-organized protest we've ever seen."

"That's because it's a game," Ella told her.

"What kind?" she asked.

"Technically, alternative reality."

There was a long enough silence that Tucker turned around to look. The dean had stepped back to her desk and was writing something down. Tucker hoped it was: *alternative reality game protest—what the hell?*

When they got out to the quad Tucker said, "Well, that was fun while it lasted."

She didn't know how to put her feelings into words because there were too many of them. Topmost was a thick blanket of disappointment. Probably the dean didn't have the power to just change the university's bathroom policy. Tucker loved that all these students had rallied for her, but the dean was just going to make them stop with promises of committees and a restraining order that Lindy was too smart to publicly violate.

"At least they'll look into the facilities policy," Ella said. "And if Lindy tries anything, she'll hang herself. But I really wish we had something else we could do there."

"You've done a lot," Tucker told her.

She didn't want Ella to worry about her anymore. It didn't seem fair to let Ella go on trying to make Freytag safe for her when she was planning to move to Minneapolis as soon as she could.

* * *

Dusk came early in January and when Tucker and Ella left the Student Union a light snow was falling but melting as it hit the ground. Tucker lifted her face to feel the tiny wet flakes hit her cheeks. In the two weeks since they'd talked to the Dean of Students, it seemed like almost nothing changed.

She wasn't being escorted around campus by other students anymore, and that was a relief. When Johnny and Shen officially ended the game in the Union and handed out prizes, she wanted to be proud or happy, but she felt disappointed. The players congratulated each other and compared scores and then they moved on, maybe a lot more educated about trans issues and feminism at least, but ready to get into the next big thing.

"Let's go the long way around," she told Ella and waved toward the long side of the quad. It turned a one-block walk into six, but she hoped it would give her enough time to talk to Ella about leaving the university. If she dropped out now she could still get most of her tuition, room and board refunded. That would be enough to move to Minneapolis and find a place.

"Can we walk along Main?" Ella asked. "I want to pick up another pint from the creamery."

They went around the Union to the street that was the eastern border of campus. Tucker stretched her legs into long, slow strides and let the cold air clean out her lungs and her brain. Beside her, Ella also seemed thoughtful. For the hundredth time, she wondered if Ella wasn't seeing Shen, would it be enough to motivate Tucker to stay at Freytag? Probably not. The problem was Vivien and Lindy and the possibility that at any time on any day she could run into either one of them—and even if she didn't, always looking over her shoulder for them was wearing her out.

They walked down by the athletic fields where a few die-hards were running and the big lights made the snowflakes look like falling diamonds. Then they crossed to the side of the street with all the businesses. They had another block to go, but Tucker didn't feel the right combination of confidence and heartlessness to tell Ella she was planning to leave.

They stopped at the corner and waited for the light to change. Across the street was the creamery and, through the plate glass windows, it looked warm and golden inside. Maybe if they stopped and had ice cream, then Tucker could tell her. The traffic light clicked to yellow and then to red for the cross traffic while she looked at the students clustered around the tables inside the ice cream shop.

The walk symbol lit, but Tucker didn't move. At the corner table in the back was Lindy and some girl she didn't recognize. Lindy was telling a story that involved big gestures with her hands and the girl kept giggling. Tucker knew that moment.

She'd been inside the glowing circle of Lindy's conversation often enough. She knew how the girl felt: caught up in Lindy's quick mind and flattered by her attention.

"Tucker?" Ella asked.

"It's Lindy," Tucker said. "Back corner on the right."

"Who's that with her?"

"I don't know, I've never seen her before."

They stood in silence as the light went through its green-yellow-red cycle a few more times. The snow turned from a pretty addition to the walk to a nuisance, making pinpricks on Tucker's icy skin. The girl sitting across from Lindy got up to get a napkin.

"Oh no," Ella said. "I know her."

"How?"

"She was in the game. She's a high school senior, but I don't remember her name."

The cold was all the way through Tucker now and it hadn't only come from the outside. Yes, she knew exactly how this girl felt—how she'd felt as a senior when an important upper-class college student showered her with attention. She felt as if she were standing outside herself watching the girl and being the girl at the same time.

And then her perspective shifted again as she watched herself watching Lindy. A memory rose into view: sitting in the Student Union with Lindy and looking up at the second-story mezzanine to see Alisa Foss watching her. Back then, she thought that the look of anger and fear on Alisa's face was directed at her. She believed Alisa was jealous. No, wait, that's what Lindy told her. She'd constructed a lattice of stories about what a bitch Alisa was and how she drove Lindy away by wanting to control her. She'd been so complete in her trashing of Alisa that Tucker had never given her the time of day back then.

But now she realized Alisa hadn't been angry at Tucker or jealous or afraid of her. She'd been looking at Lindy. She was afraid of Lindy.

While Tucker worked this through, Lindy and the girl finished eating and threw away their plastic bowls. They came out of the front door. Tucker stayed frozen in place.

Lindy saw her standing across the street and her eyes narrowed. She put her arm around the girl and steered her down the sidewalk away from Tucker and Ella. Their heads bent together and Tucker knew what Lindy was saying without needing to hear it. She was telling this girl how terrible Tucker was—so bad that Lindy had to take out a restraining order, no doubt. For a minute she had a sickening double vision in which she saw herself as the person Lindy described and remembered how she'd seen Alisa when she'd first been with Lindy and Lindy told her all the terrible things Alisa had done to her.

"They're gone," Ella said.

"Alisa Foss, I need to find her," Tucker told her.

"Where does she live?"

Tucker shook her head. She pulled out her phone and called Tesh.

"She doesn't give out her address," Tesh said when Tucker told her what she wanted.

"Do you have her number?"

"She said not to give it to you, but that was back when you were with Lindy. Do you want me to call her for you and ask if it's okay?"

"Please. Tell her, I'm sorry. I owe her an apology. And tell her that I understand now."

Tesh said she would and ended the call.

"Can we go back to the rooms, I'm freezing," Ella said. "And I'm not in the mood for ice cream anymore."

They walked up the street toward their dorm. Ella didn't ask, but Tucker could tell she was curious and just waiting to give her time to talk so Tucker told her about Alisa.

When she was done, Ella asked, "Did Alisa try to warn you?"

"I think she would have if she could ever get to me without Lindy being there, but those first few months we were together all the time."

Ella nodded.

"I wouldn't have listened anyway," Tucker said in the elevator to their dorm floor and then once they were safely in her room and away from prying ears, she added, "I was so into Lindy at the time I wouldn't have believed anything like that."

"I'm going to try to figure out the name of that girl she was with," Ella said.

She went into her room and Tucker stood in the doorway watching her flash through web pages, looking at photos of teams and players from Kind 2 B Cruel.

How had Lindy convinced a girl who was part of a game to protect Tucker from her to go out with her? Probably the girl had been invited after the first meeting and didn't have the whole story. And it was likely that Lindy had been sniffing around the more distant players to try to find someone who would give her an inside scoop on the game. It wasn't too much of a stretch to imagine she'd seen this girl hanging around campus with other players and then found an excuse to talk to her alone.

A knock sounded on her door. Tucker stepped back into her room and called through the door. "Yeah?"

"It's us," Tesh said from the other side.

Tucker opened the door. Tesh was standing in front of Alisa and Tucker waved them into the room. Alisa had her face down so that her long, brown hair hid most of it and her hands were clenched around the straps of her backpack so hard that her knuckles were white.

"Thank you for coming," Tucker told Alisa.

She nodded in reply and asked, "Is Ella here?"

Tucker called into the other room and in a moment Ella appeared in the doorway.

"I'm really glad you came," she said.

Alisa stepped away from Tucker, toward Ella, and looked up at Ella's clear eyes.

"Can you protect me?" Alisa asked. "The way you protected her." She pointed at Tucker.

Ella paused, thinking. "Protect you like we did with the game?" she asked.

Alisa nodded.

"Yes," Ella said. "But it would take me some time to set it up."

"I just needed to know," Alisa told her.

Ella touched Alisa's shoulder gently and when she didn't pull away from the contact, Ella guided her to sit next to her on the edge of Tucker's bed. Tucker had never realized how small Alisa was. She lurked at the back of Tucker's mind like some menacing creature, but she was the same size as Ella, who only came to just under Tucker's chin.

"What happened to you?" Ella asked quietly.

"You protected Tucker from Lindy, didn't you? That's why she had people walking her to class, even though you didn't say that. And then Tesh said you went with her to the dean and got a restraining order against Lindy."

Ella nodded.

"I saw Lindy trying to get to her and she couldn't," Alisa said. Her expression was half-grin and half-sneer: her upper lip raised to show small, even, white teeth, her dark eyes narrow.

"They did a good job," Tucker said. She had to clear her throat to get the words out but she added, "I'm sorry. Really sorry. I thought...the whole time I thought you were angry at me."

Alisa said, "No. Mostly at myself for not saying anything."

"Should've been angry at her," Tesh said in a low voice.

Alisa smiled at her and then said, "Ella, can I ask you something personal?"

"Sure."

"Is it scarier before you come out to people or after?"

"Before," Ella said. "I always think it's going to be worse than it is."

"Even though they know personal stuff about you?"

"People tend to think they can ask me all sorts of things and talk about my business like it's a carburetor or something, but at least their thoughts are out in the open and I can choose my reaction to it. And for the most part once people know me as a person, they start to see me as a person and not some Discovery Channel special."

"That's really brave," she said.

"It's not brave to be who you are," Ella told her. "It's necessary."

"But it's brave to be who you are in public," she said. "It's brave to speak up about something, isn't it? Even if you had no choice about it happening to you in the first place."

"That's for sure true," Ella said and waited.

Alisa sighed and slipped her arms out of the straps of her backpack so she could pull it around to her lap and hug it.

"Lindy took something of mine," she said. "And when I confronted her about it, she hit me. And it wasn't the last time. She hit me and did other things. I didn't know if I could talk to anyone about it but then I saw those students around Tucker and I thought maybe I could finally be safe from her."

"We'll protect you," Tucker said.

"Do you want to talk to someone about it?" Ella asked. "You don't have to."

Alisa unzipped the top of her backpack and put her hand inside. "I kept proof," she said. She pulled out a thin binder and handed it to Ella. "In case I got brave enough to go to the police. I have photos and dates and I have proof that I wrote the article she stole, the one she presented under her name at that conference, that she got the grant for."

Tucker stepped around them so she could stand at Ella's shoulder and watch as she turned the pages of the binder. There were printouts from her campus email showing that she'd emailed a draft of the paper to a friend asking for feedback a month before she emailed it to Lindy, also asking for feedback. Then there were photographs of bruises on her chest and ribs, but never on her face. Tucker saw dates spanning two months and descriptions of what had happened. She bent down and put her fingers on one page so that Ella couldn't turn it. There was a picture of a bruise on Alisa's ribs as dark as the one she'd received being thrown into the wall outside of the gym. It had a sharp edge to it and Tucker winced as she recognized the edge of Lindy's coffee table in its dark shape.

She sat down hard on the side of her bed and put her head in her hands to try to fend off the sick feeling overtaking her.

"Do I go to the police or the campus security?" Alisa asked.

"Let's start with the Dean of Students," Ella said. "She'll know what to do."

"I'll call over tomorrow morning," Tucker offered. She had to do something.

She lifted her head and looked at Alisa's stricken face. Around the sickness in her gut she felt a boiling anger and the first stirring of the strength that had been gone since Halloween. It was so much harder to feel that way about herself, but seeing it in someone else turned all the fear she'd had for Lindy into rage.

* * *

Tucker set the binder on the desk in front of Dean Chilvers and watched as she flipped through the pages. The muscles at the sides of her jaw clenched and she looked like she wanted to spit.

When she'd gone through it, she stood up suddenly, grabbed the back of her chair and dragged it around the desk. She sat down in it again on the same side of the desk as Alisa, Tucker and Ella.

She said, "This is very damning, Ms. Foss. And I want to say both as a dean and as a person that I am so sorry this happened to you."

"Thanks," Alisa said in a small voice.

"I also apologize that you didn't feel safe to come forward with this information," she said.

"What happens next?" Tucker asked.

"I'll call the police," she said. "Ms. Heaton will be banned from campus and we'll have to inform the grant donors that the presentation they funded was not authored by her."

Speaking directly to Alisa, she continued: "I hope you'll consider talking to one of our counselors. I imagine this has been very hard for you. When you've had more time to recover, if it's all right I'd like to have a conversation about what we, as a school, could have done better."

"Yes," she said in a small voice.

She reached out as if she was going to touch Alisa but rested her hand on the edge of her desk instead. "Thank you for sharing this," she said.

Tucker felt like she had a question she wanted to ask, but she didn't know what it was. She and Ella sat in chairs to either side of Alisa as she told the dean more of her story. She'd gotten used to the idea of leaving school and going to Minneapolis, but now she was back in a fight she could win. The dean looked genuinely upset by everything Alisa was saying and Tucker would bet there'd be more than a few committee meetings coming out of this.

* * *

Tucker spent most of that week with Alisa, talking about what had happened to her and eventually sharing some of the details of her own assault. She thought she'd never want to speak about it again, but Alisa understood what it was like to have someone you loved turn on you so thoroughly and bafflingly.

"I thought she must be some kind of mentally screwed up," Alisa said. "I couldn't settle on a diagnosis but it has to be one of those deep sorts of disorders that a person can have without knowing they have it. I think in her heart she really wants to be a good person and that's what made us love her."

"I hope someone figures it out, but it sure as hell isn't going to be me," Tucker said.

She was starting to feel like her old self again, or perhaps some new and improved self, now that the threat of Lindy was gone from campus. Spring semester looked like it would be fun with Ella around, and the cousins, plus Alisa back in The Table crew. She thought she'd take courses for a Communication Studies major or something in Journalism or New Media.

"Come with me to Professor Callander's brunch tomorrow," Alisa said suddenly while they were sitting at the table in the Union with Cal, Tesh and Summer.

"What?" Tucker asked.

"She used to have these brunches all the time last year, but then her partner got sick over the summer. She's doing better so brunch is on this month. It's Saturday at her house. You should come."

"I don't know."

Alisa met her eyes with a soft but unavoidable look. "Trust me," she said. "She's what kept me here after all that stuff, you know. I didn't tell her what happened, but she knew I was struggling and she just, you know, checked on me and gave me other stuff to think about. Besides, Tesh and Cal are going, aren't you?"

"Yep," Tesh said.

"Sure." Cal's tone hinted that this was the first time he'd heard of it, but he was game.

"And we'll invite Ella," Alisa said.

"It'll be like a practice party for the Valentine's bash," Cal added.

"Oh no, you're not doing that again." Summer looked at him with a combination of genuine and mock alarm.

"Absolutely, when else do I get to bust out all my pink decorations?"

"I nearly came down with diabetes just looking at your house, it was such a sappy eyesore."

"Oh please."

"Are you coming to the brunch tomorrow?" Alisa asked Summer. "I think we need two cars."

"Hell no, I can live without seeing Vivien this semester."

"So I shouldn't invite her to the Valentine's event?" Cal asked.

"Not if you want to see me there," Summer said. She got up from the table and sauntered out of the Union.

Watching Summer go, Tucker saw two students veer sharply away from her, pause and stare in the direction of The Table. She recognized them as two of the three girls she'd heard trash talking in the line at the start of the year: Skinny Face and Round Face. The one she'd dubbed Mean Face wasn't there.

Now that she'd thought about it, she hadn't seen her at all this semester. Looking through the student yearbooks, she'd identified all three of them to Dean Chilvers. Mean Face must have been the one who leaked the information from admissions. Had she decided to leave the school after losing her work-study job or been asked to leave?

The two remaining girls put their heads together talking and then turned and hurried out of the Union. They weren't going to become allies any time soon, but at least they were no longer a threat.

"I've got ten dollars on Summer hooking up with someone by the time of the party," Tesh said and Tucker brought her attention back to The Table.

"Yeah, no way she shows up alone," Cal agreed. He looked at Tucker. "What about you? You going to bring anyone?"

She shook her head at him, but his question did call up an answer inside her. After a minute of consideration, she said, "Maybe I'll see if Nico wants to drive up."

"For real?" Tesh asked.

"Are you sweet on Nico?" that came from Cal.

Tucker shrugged. "Yo's easy to talk to, that's all."

"Oh, so it's 'yo' now and not 'per' you two have been texting," Cal said.

"A little." Tucker didn't add that they'd been talking on the phone some too. Nico gave Tucker yos number during the Thanksgiving break, but Tucker hadn't really used it until she was back at school in January. Something about Nico being a friend of Ella's and close, but not too close, to the school, made it easy for Tucker to talk to yo about all her fears and frustration with school, about Lindy, about the options in life she had and didn't have. In a way Ella was too close and Tucker didn't want to scare her as she worked through her own stuff.

"Invite yo on up," Cal said. "I'll try to keep folks from doing the guess-the-gender game this time."

"That's a thing?" Alisa asked. "Why? What gender is Nico?"

"You'll see," Cal told her.

Tucker grinned at him. She was looking forward to seeing Nico again. Something about being in the presence of someone who wasn't being one thing or another made Tucker feel like she had more choices in the world, and she really liked that feeling.

* * *

Professor Callander's house was four miles from the university. Alisa picked Tucker up, but Cal said he and Tesh would come in his car because Alisa's little two-door coupe was too small.

"She used to do this every month?" Tucker asked while they drove.

"Last year she hosted it every other month and then Professor Greenhill from the community college hosted on the off months. I think they had a few last fall at Greenhill's, but I didn't go. It's for anyone in Women's & Gender Studies and also sometimes folks in English or Philosophy who seem cool."

The house sat on a big plot of land, about an acre as far as Tucker could tell, with the back half of it thickly wooded. The long driveway was full of cars and there were more along the road where Alisa pulled over to park. As they got out of the car, two midsized, shaggy black-and-white dogs ran up with their tails wagging. On their heels came a fuzzy, white mini-poodle.

"Hey, Mr. Bennet," Alisa said and picked him up. He licked her chin as she carried him up to the house.

The house had an open floor plan and from inside the front door Tucker could see the whole living room, dining room, sunroom and part of the kitchen. There were about thirty people in the house, including a few other professors from Freytag, a variety of middle-aged women not from Freytag, and about fifteen students. The spread on the dining room table looked very potluck style: none of the dishes matched and their contents were haphazard.

Alisa put down Mr. Bennet and took Tucker through the dining room and into the kitchen. Everyone was in conversation, though Professor Callander looked up from the people she was talking to long enough to wave to them as they passed into the dining room. She stood in the living room next to a thin woman in an armchair with a half-inch growth of new hair sticking out all over her head.

"Get food," Alisa said. "The good stuff goes fast."

She led Tucker around the table pointing out the dishes that would be best. Tucker got a pop from a bin filled with ice and cans that was resting on the island between the kitchen and dining room, and looked around for a place to stand that wasn't too close to a group of people locked in intense discussion. She and Alisa ended up in the sunroom, their drinks balanced on the deep window ledges, eating the quiche and fruit salad and pastries they'd snagged.

The front door opened again and Tesh fell into the room, Cal on her heels. She scanned the guests and headed straight for Tucker and Alisa.

"You will not believe," she said as she reached them. Her light cheeks were flushed red and she was trying to catch her breath. Behind her, Cal shook his head.

Tucker offered her the pop can and she took a quick sip while Cal started the story.

"You know how Tesh's place is just down the street from Lindy's..."

"Oh no," Alisa said.

"Oh yeah," Cal responded.

Tesh handed the can back to Tucker with a nod of thanks. "I came out a little early to sit on the step, you know, the sun," she said. "And there was this big car in front of her place with a U-Haul trailer, and this yelling from the back. Lindy comes around the side and this man is dragging her by the arm and they're both yelling. And this man, he's older and he's saying 'How could you do this to me?' and Lindy is shouting 'She's lying! She's lying!' and the man says 'They have photos, they have proof, why couldn't you be a normal person?'"

"That's so mean," Alisa said.

"I know, and he says worse and Lindy is crying but also yelling. That's her father and she's yelling about how it's all his fault and he doesn't understand. Then a woman comes out, short and kind of heavy in the middle, I think probably her mother, and she says something I couldn't hear, but they stop yelling. The woman puts Lindy in the backseat of the car and she just sits there for a few minutes and watches them bring boxes and put them in the trailer.

"Then Lindy gets out, while they're in the house, and gets a box out of the back and throws it into the street so it breaks open and spills out books and papers and she starts kicking them farther into the street so papers are flying everywhere. She picks up a book and tears out the pages and flings them.

"The mother comes out and puts her arm on Lindy's shoulder and hugs her and Lindy's crying, her shoulders are shaking so hard. The mother puts Lindy back into the backseat of the car and she slumps against the seat and the door and tucks her head down like she's going to sleep."

Tesh paused and Cal said, "And then I drove up and Tesh got in and told me to drive like the wind, before Lindy or her parents saw us."

"That's pretty messed up," Tucker said. She couldn't imagine Lindy tearing up books; her reverence for them was one of the aspects that had drawn Tucker to her in the first place.

"You never met her parents?" Cal asked.

"No, they live in like Kansas or something and she said they don't like to travel. I guess they're taking her home."

"I hope not," Alisa said. "She needs help."

"After what she did to you?" Cal asked.

"It's better knowing she's screwed up in the head somehow," Alisa told him. "At first, I thought it was my fault and then I just hated her and I was so afraid, and I still thought maybe it was something about me."

Tucker put her arm around Alisa's shoulders. "It wasn't."

"I knew that rationally, but listening to you and hearing this, and just putting it all together—realizing she had to be messed up to do those things—that makes it totally real that it wasn't me, and it wasn't even her. She's just sick somehow."

"I can't let her off that easy," Tucker said. "Sick or not, she never should have…If I never see her again, that's fine by me."

"Same here," Alisa said. "But it's not like I want bad things to happen to her."

"You're a saint," Tesh told Alisa. "What do you think it is with her?"

Tucker shook her head. "I've talked about her enough, you all can speculate when I'm not around."

"Is the quiche good?" Cal asked in a doggedly upbeat tone.

"Fantastic. Go get some before it's all demolished."

Cal and Tesh went toward the food. Tucker and Alisa returned their attention to their plates and for a few minutes ate in heavy silence. As much as Tucker wanted to never think about Lindy again, that was all she could think about right now. Tesh's story burned in her mind and part of her reveled in the idea of Lindy suffering with her parents, while another part argued that even Lindy didn't deserve that.

The pro-suffering part was winning. She hoped it was a long and miserable drive back to Kansas and that Lindy got a crap job that gave her lots of time to think about what she'd done.

She looked around, trying to get her mind off the topic and saw Vivien step out from the living room into the sunroom doorway and then stop in her tracks. Her face froze and she glanced around quickly. Probably wondering if she could run for it, Tucker thought. Then she set her shoulders and came the rest of the way into the room.

"You must think I'm awful," she said quietly.

"Why?" Alisa asked.

"I believed everything Lindy said about both of you." The words came out haltingly and she couldn't look up at either of them.

Tucker felt a quick wave of vertigo and fear that she'd never be able to escape people trying to talk to her about Lindy. And she knew how easy it was to fall for Lindy's stories.

"It's over now," she said.

Vivien looked up at her, met her eyes for a half-second and looked away again. "She told me you guys were splitting up," she said. "Back in early October."

"Oh hell, that explains the 'take a break' bullshit," Tucker said. She waved a hand. "You know what, I don't care. Don't tell me. It's over and done and I don't want to think about it."

"But I—"

"Did all of this get you to change your fucked-up politics?" Tucker asked.

"What fucked-up politics?"

"The part where you think trans women are men, did that come from Lindy too?"

"Uh, no, that comes from seeing all the incredible violence women are subject to all over the world." Vivien straightened up and glared at Tucker. "Have you ever seen a twelve-year-old girl who was sold into sexual slavery? Take a look at that and tell me how important it is to fight about what transgender person gets to use the women's rooms at Freytag."

"What you're really saying is you don't care if the university puts Ella in danger by telling her she's supposed to use the men's room because some other women are in danger too?" Tucker asked.

"I just think we're wasting resources on those kinds of issues when there are women being brutalized all over the world."

"No you don't," Alisa said. "You're just squeaved out by it all and you think this justifies your discomfort. If Tucker's inspired to help her trans sisters, you don't get to tell her how to do feminism."

"Who's telling whom how to do feminism?" The question came from Professor Callander who'd come up behind Vivien in the wide doorway. They all turned to look at her. Her face seemed rounder than when Tucker saw her last semester, but maybe that was because of the smile on it.

"I just think transsexuals distract attention from the real priorities of feminism," Vivien said. "Women are dying…" Her voice trailed off and Tucker saw the thin film of tears collected on her lower eyelids.

Callander put her hand on Vivien's shoulder. "Not everyone has seen the world you've seen," she said. "And not everyone sees the world the way you do."

"But there's so much to do," Vivien protested.

"That's why we need everyone," Alisa told her. "And to not fight each other."

Vivien shook her head, but she said, "I'm sorry" again and walked away through the living room. Tucker couldn't decide if she was repeating her earlier apology for emphasis or if she was saying it dismissively as in: I'm sorry but I don't agree.

"I read the new version of your paper for the Women's & Gender Studies course very closely," Callander said. "Your grade will be updated. And I saw you're not in any of our courses this semester."

"I'm getting some requirements out of the way," Tucker told her, but the excuse sounded lame as she said it.

"Your experience coming out as transsexual when you aren't, could you write that up into a presentation given, let's say, in six weeks?"

"Um, yeah."

"Good, come present it to me in mid-March and we'll talk about any edits and then I want you to present to my Intro to Gender Studies course in April. Does that work for you?"

"Sure."

"Do you have any teaching experience?"

"Not really. I mean, I have a younger sister."

Callander laughed. "I'll find a TA who can give you tips."

"Not Vivien?" Alisa asked.

"I don't think so. I hope that someday she'll see your point of view, but I'm not going to force it. She has a good mind; she'll work it through."

"You don't believe what she does?" Tucker asked. "You didn't say that in the meeting."

"I want you to learn to stand up to an opposing viewpoint on your own," Callander said. "But for the record, I've walked out of feminist events that didn't welcome trans women."

"Sweet," Tucker said.

Callander gave her another smile and headed back into the living room. Cal and Tesh had been waiting at a safe distance, watching the interaction, and now they rushed back to Tucker and Alisa.

"What did she say? Did she tell Vivien off?" Tesh asked.

"No, but she's cool. She's on our side," Tucker told them. "She asked me to come guest lecture about my experiences."

Alisa cleared her throat. "You're downplaying it. She's offering to mentor you and train you in presenting and teaching."

"She is?"

"She did the same for me last year. It kept me in school."

"She had you present to her class?"

"She matched me up with a TA who helped me with my essays and then she critiqued the later drafts. I'd hate presenting, but you'll probably like it."

Tucker thought about herself up in front of the class getting to talk about what she'd learned this last year by coming out in Ella's place and then getting to know Ella and having to fight for what she knew was right—she imagined being able to shape how other students thought about trans issues and misogyny and feminism, and she wanted to get started right away.

"I *would* like it," she said.

"Professor Tucker, in the house," Tesh said.

"You'd look good in tweed," Cal added with a wink.

CHAPTER TWENTY-THREE

Ella

Cal did the house in an insane amount of pink for Valentine's Day. He even hosted dressed in a pink T-shirt and the color looked good on him. I reprised my over-the-top eye makeup for the event and Nico showed up in a neon orange and pink shirt over tight gray pants. It hurt to look at yo for any length of time.

It surprised me when Nico said that Tucker had invited yo up for the party before I even got a chance to, and I wasn't sure whether to feel really happy about it or sort of weird, so I went with both.

"You're really testing everyone's resolve, aren't you?" I asked Nico as we walked into Cal's living room.

"What? I look fantastic."

"As in 'the fantastic legends of the fey folk'?"

"Precisely."

Nico's hair had grown out just far enough to hint at small curls tight against yos scalp and yo compensated by cutting back on the makeup and jewelry. Yo looked either like a classic butch woman from the fifties or a somewhat masculine disco queen.

The party was in full swing and the living room was jammed with people. We shoved through into the dining room where Nico grabbed a few carrot sticks and offered me one. I took it and nibbled as we kept going into the kitchen and through to the back porch.

Nico found soda in one of the coolers and handed me a bottle. Cal swept over with a hearty greeting for both of us, and then looped an arm around Nico's shoulders and steered yo back into the living room to meet Alisa. Apparently I'd gone from being the exciting newcomer last semester to the even more exciting trans girl to old news. I didn't mind.

I leaned against the back porch railing and pulled out my phone. *Text me when you're done*, I sent to Shen.

You miss me already, he sent back.

He had a project due in the morning and said he needed to skip the party to finish it, but he'd meet me back at my room afterward. I did miss him, but thinking about seeing him later also got me jittery again. It was Valentine's Day—we should do something special for it and yet most of the "special" things I could think of scared me.

On the bright side, I didn't have to worry about birth control. Ha, yeah, but that was the only thing I didn't have to worry about.

"You're scowling," Tucker said from next to my elbow.

"I'm fretting."

"About me inviting Nico up?"

"No, that's cool. About me and Shen."

"Did something happen?" Tucker asked.

"No, nothing happened, that's the problem. We just make out and it's been like almost five months."

"He doesn't seem upset about it," Tucker said.

"But I kind of want…more…you know?"

"So jump him."

"But what if it doesn't work?"

She raised an eyebrow at me. "How can it not work?"

I stared back at her and spread my hands apart. "I was built in a lab, remember? Miracle of science and all that. What if we don't fit together? Or what if I don't feel right to him?"

"Didn't I teach you anything?" she asked with a smile. "He's crazy about you. It'll only not work if you stop trying. Just mess around until things feel right—and I promise you, they will. Don't be so freakin' heteronormative."

"What?"

"Stop acting like a straight girl and go jump your man whatever way works for you two."

I grinned at her. "I have no idea how that made sense, but it did."

"You'd better tell me all about it too, but not in a creepy way."

"Perv."

"Whatever. Get out of here," she said.

I kissed her on the cheek and started shoving my way back through the party. Nico was in the living room chatting with Alisa and I pulled yo aside.

"Hey, I'm going to bail and go jump Shen, per Tucker's instructions."

"Kinky," Nico said.

"Yeah, right. Are you okay here?"

"Baby girl, I'm more than okay."

I stopped and looked hard at yo. Was Nico's look slightly more feminine than last semester? Was there a reason for that?

"Are you and Tucker...?" I asked.

"We're just friends," Nico said. "You know she needs a lot of friends right now."

"Yeah, but what if she did ask you out?"

"She knows she'd have to be cool with me not being a girl."

"You think it might be enough for her that you're not a boy either?"

"If it gets that far, we can only hope," Nico said with a grin. "But unlike you, I don't have to jump every pretty face I see."

"Oh shut up, you totally got more action than me in high school, I'm just trying to play catch-up."

Nico gave me a tight hug and I said a quick goodbye to everyone else in the living room. Outside the air was chilly. I held my phone in my hand while I zipped my jacket all the way up and then texted Shen: *leaving the party, miss you too much.*

Wonderful, he texted back. *Meet me at your room.*

How was he in *my* room? It wasn't like I had an extra key and I didn't know how to get one, so I figured he meant that he was going to head over and meet me there.

I walked the few blocks back to my dorm but when I got into the third-floor hall I saw there was light coming from under my door. I didn't remember leaving the light on. Must be getting spacey with all the Valentine's fretting I was doing. I unlocked the door and pushed it open.

The room was filled with flowers. And there were candles. And a box of chocolates held in the lap of the cutest boy I'd ever seen.

"Happy Valentine's Day," Shen said and held the heart-shaped box out to me.

"You didn't have a project?" The words sounded stupid to me, but I was still taking it all in.

"Not for class. Tucker left her door unlocked for me so I could sneak in. She's quite smart about these things."

"Totally. This is amazing!"

There were flowers in vases on my desk, and the dresser, and the nightstand, and a little teddy bear in a red T-shirt that said "Be Mine" and pink candles. I shucked off my jacket, climbed onto the bed and kissed Shen.

"Tucker gave me some advice about a surprise too," I said.

"Oh?"

I got up to turn off the overhead light. In the soft golden light of the candles, he opened his arms to me.

Praise for Rachel Gold and *Being Emily*

Winner 2013 Golden Crown Literary Award in Dramatic/ General Fiction.

Winner 2013 Moonbeam Children's Book Award in Young Adult Fiction—Mature Issues.

Finalist 2013 Lambda Literary Award

"Powerful and empowering, with an optimistic message that we all need more of in our lives. I'm thrilled to see this book is out in the world."

-Kate Bornstein, author of *Gender Outlaw* and *A Queer and Pleasant Danger*

"It's rare to read a novel that's involving, tender, thought-provoking and informative. Rachel Gold does all this in 'Being Emily.'"

-Twin Cities Pioneer Press

"*Being Emily* is a wonderful, valuable and very contemporary book that I believe will change minds and save lives. I was very much affected by the story, which feels piercingly real in all its details."

-Katherine V. Forrest, author, editor-at-large for Bella Books and supervising editor at Spinsters Ink

"…it's a wonderful read for any teen (or anyone else) dealing with gender issues or the question of non-conformity … [Gold] does a fabulous job of explaining what it means to know in your heart that something's not right, that the body you were born with doesn't match the true person inside."

-Ellen Krug, *Lavender Magazine*

"I think *Being Emily* should be assigned in classrooms. It's a great teen book club selection, as well. I'm glad this book is on our shelves and I can't wait to see more like it."

-The Magpie Librarian

"Rachel Gold has crafted an extraordinarily poignant novel in *Being Emily*."

-Lambda Literary Review

Bella Books, Inc.

Women. Books. Even Better Together.

P.O. Box 10543
Tallahassee, FL 32302

Phone: 800-729-4992
www.bellabooks.com